IT WAS ALWAYS THIS WAY

LEIGH DONNELLY

To my patient, loving, supportive husband.

CONTENTS

1

JULIA, JULY 2009

Julia's short brown hair clung to her sweaty brow as she plunged her dull garden spade into the thin layer of soil around her mailbox. Hidden beneath the soil was a dense and never-ending mixture of clay and rocks. It was bad around the mailbox, but it was worse in some of the side beds around the front and back yards where boulders hid a few inches beneath the surface. She'd have to do her best to hide the state of the garden beds from her husband, James. He was already on edge about the numerous flaws and imperfections they'd found throughout the house and property since they'd moved in a few weeks prior.

Julia had taken inventory of her neighbors' yards and flower beds on her walks around the neighborhood. She found the majority of houses had lush lawns and thriving floral arrangements. They'd either paid to have some of the rock and clay replaced with fertile soil, or most plants were able to adapt and thrive regardless of the rough terrain. She hoped it was the latter though she knew many homeowners in her new neighborhood could easily find the funds to transplant their half acre of yard.

Julia had been skeptical the first time James had driven her through Scarlet Oaks Knoll to look at the house. She'd never been able to afford anything outside of a townhouse in what her mother referred to as the "somewhat dodgy part of town." And there was James taking her through what appeared to be the set of *The Stepford Wives* minus the docile wives with perfectly coifed hair - at least from what she could see at that moment.

Her skepticism eased when they pulled into the faded driveway of the largest house in the development. The gleaming white for-sale sign was the only redeeming aspect of the foreclosed and forgotten relic in front of them.

The first time she took the kids on a walk around their new neighborhood she came upon three women adorned in matching Under Armor yoga pants and sports bras who were getting impressively deep with their quad stretches in the front yard of a house on Larkely Lane. The tall brunette in the middle caught Julia's eye as Julia walked by the woman's driveway. The Amazonian woman asserted her dominance by maintaining eye-contact while loudly discussing Julia's family without any regard to who may hear her. She nodded her head towards the Herrick family and said, "The new family that moved into Monica's house. Not much of an upgrade there. Let's hope *they* can keep up with the mortgage so we won't have another embarrassing foreclosure in the development."

The slightly smaller blonde lowered her voice and cautioned, "We're on the board now, Laura; we're supposed to be welcoming the new neighbors." She plastered on her best smile and waved to Julia and the kids. Alexis paused her balancing act on the curb and proudly waved back while

Julia ignored the petit blonde in order to continue her stare-down with Laura.

The third woman, almost identical to the second in appearance, added, "I can't believe we were ever friends with Monica. Did you all sign up for the wine-tasting fundraiser at the library yet? I want to make sure we all end up at the same table." Like that the two blondes had written off the Herrick family as they continued to drone on about their upcoming social calendar full of PTO events and fundraisers.

Julia, the product of a local uppity private high school thanks to a full merit scholarship, made a mental note to steer clear of Larkley Lane on future walks. She'd survived high school by laying low and keeping a tight social group of just two other girls. Though more than a decade had passed since her school-girl years, avoidance still appeared to be her best option. Those types of girls, women now, played dirty and she didn't have it in her to fight back. She looked away from Laura first, her head turned to the other side of the street in an effort to hide the scar-let-hued shame spreading across her lightly freckled cheeks.

So there she was, weeks later, still haunted by their comments and busting her ass to bring the house up to neighborhood standards. Julia threw a few more pulled weeds into a nearby bucket before wiping the sweat from her brow again and making her way to the porch for her wine – a Moscato, her favorite. Her youngest, Brice, was eleven months old and he had mercifully stopped breastfeeding on his own. She could drink and eat whatever she wanted without worrying about passing toxins on to one of the kids. Including her other child, Alexis, she'd been pregnant or breastfeeding for the past five years. The guilt-free indul-gence of a sweet wine while the kids entertained themselves in the little pen she'd set up in the shade from the willow was like heaven on Earth.

As she sat on the front steps and sipped her lukewarm wine, Julia noticed a white minivan parked on the other side of the road. A man and a woman sat in the front seat talking. The couple, she assumed they were a couple based on their body language, would frequently pause mid-conversation and then glance towards her. *Crap. They're probably going to fine us for not painting our shutters to match our door,* Julia fretted. She was about to call for James to come out when the driver and passenger emerged revealing two small kids of their own strapped into the backseat: a girl about the same age as Alexis and another little girl that looked just a tad bit smaller than Brice. But then Brice was giant for his age, so it was hard to compare other babies or toddlers to him to gauge age.

"Hi," the woman called out as she checked for cars before making her way over to Julia. The woman was wearing cut-off jean shorts and a light pink tank top. If she was the mother of the baby, she had already lost every ounce of her baby weight. She had long blonde hair pulled back into a stylish ponytail with some of her hair twisted and wrapped around the hair tie to hide it. Julia searched her memory for who this woman was. They had just moved into the area and had met different neighbors almost daily. She panicked as she tried to come up with a name for this woman she couldn't remember meeting. That happened a lot with Julia, she was terrible at placing names and faces.

"Hi," Julia responded with a bit of caution.

"Am I interrupting?" the woman asked as she motioned towards Julia's dirty gloved hands and sweaty outfit.

Julia's cheeks reddened as she took in the stark contrast of her disheveled self against the well-groomed family that was materializing, seemingly from nowhere. "No. We haven't gotten around to hiring a gardener yet, so I'm pulling a few weeds myself while the kids get some fresh air," Julia answered as she pointed to the bucket of pulled weeds sitting off to the side. "For every five weeds I pull out I get a pull of wine. Should probably be drinking water on a hot day like today, but it's not nearly as rewarding."

She and James had no intentions of hiring a gardener. But that's the effect the neighborhood was having on her. She felt on guard at all times to say the right thing and not draw too much attention to herself or her family. To not look too poor.

"No judgment here. I have a bottle waiting for me at home." The woman's husband had been tasked with wrangling the kids from their car seats. After a slight issue with a tangled strap, he approached the women with the toddler on his right and the littlest one in his arms. "I'm Lindsay, this is my husband Denny, and our daughters Liv and Hailey." Denny, a tall, lean man in his late twenties, maybe early thirties, with a full head of dark brown hair, and Liv, a small girl with pink bows in her curly blonde hair, waved as Lindsay introduced them. Hailey absently smacked Denny's face with her chubby little hands while blowing raspberries towards no one in particular. "We did a walk-through yesterday at 725," Lindsay pointed to Julia's neighbor's house which had been on the market for a few days, "and we stopped by again today to get one more look at the house from the outside. We saw you here and couldn't help but get out and hopefully ask you a few questions. Do you have time to chat?"

Julia was positively giddy at the idea of the picture-perfect family standing before her moving in next door. Her current neighbor had three teenage boys who smoked cigarettes (and sometimes weed) on the side of the house and played loud music as they sped out of the driveway. This young family would be a welcome and much-needed change.

"Sure. Do you want to come in for a drink? We have some toys and things for the kids to play with while we talk. Don't worry, everything is already baby-proofed."

"That would be amazing. It's so hot outside and the kids are sick of driving around and looking at houses. They'd love to have a little playdate with other kids. Well, Liv would. Hailey's too young to care one way or the other."

"I'm Julia Herrick. My husband, James, is inside somewhere and my two littles here are Alexis and Brice." Julia walked over to the pen to let Alexis out and pick up Brice to head inside. "How old are your kids?" Julia asked as she held the door open for everyone to enter the house. "They look about the same age as mine."

"They do," Denny agreed, grinning ear to ear. "Liv will be four in November and Hailey will be one next month."

"Get out! Alexis just turned four and Brice turns one next month, too. His birthday's August fifteenth. When's Hailey's?"

"August twelfth," Lindsay said. "How cute. Just a few days apart. Denny, we have to buy that house." Lindsay was holding Denny's one free hand in both of hers as she pleaded with both her words and her stunning blue eyes. "Look at our kids playing." Alexis had taken Liv's hand and walked her over to the living room to show Liv her stuffed animal collection.

Julia put a hand over her heart and said, "That's the sweetest thing ever. Yes, please move in next door." As if they'd been friends for years, Julia and Denny both set the babies in the playpen set up in the living room. As she returned to the kitchen to get a wine glass she continued, "Our kids will be best friends; our youngest kids could get married," Julia gushed. Denny and Lindsay each took a seat at the island.

Hearing muffled, unfamiliar voices, James entered the

kitchen from the garage with a slight look of apprehension, and said, "Who is our not-even-one-year-old going to marry?" He had a stockier build than Denny though it was all muscle. His dirty-blonde hair was cut in a neat crew cut and he wore a white T-shirt with jeans and a tool belt around his waist.

Julia began introductions: "This is Lindsay and Denny…"

"Moore," Denny added.

"Moore. They're interested in buying the Smiths' house. Look how cute our kids are; they already play so well together." James looked over at the kids in the living room. The two youngest were merely co-existing in the pen while the older ones each had a doll and had their backs turned away from each other to play independently.

"Mmmm," James gave in a noncommittal agreement. "Cute." He turned back to the Moores. "I'm James, nice to meet you. Please excuse my appearance. I'm trying to fix all of the colossal mistakes the previous owners here made."

Julia cut in before James could tear down their house again, something he was apt to do ever since they moved in. "Denny, do you want a glass of wine? We also have beer."

"No, thanks. I'm good."

Assuming she wanted some, Julia poured Lindsay a glass of wine. Since it was clear their company was staying a while, James went to the sink to wash carpenter's glue off his hands before taking a seat at the island next to Denny. Julia could tell he wasn't pleased to have unexpected company in the house while they were in the middle of so many home improvement projects, but he also believed in good manners. Despite the show he was putting on for their company, she needed to brace herself for the argument they would have as soon as the Moores left.

"Thank you," Lindsay said as she received her glass of

wine from Julia. "So, tell me all about the neighborhood. Where is Alexis going for Pre-K?"

An hour later the women had exchanged numbers and Julia walked the Moores back out to their car. She'd been so excited at the idea of new neighbors she'd forgotten about James's foul mood earlier. James had not forgotten. When she opened the door to go back inside, he was standing in the kitchen with his arms across his chest.

"You have got to be kidding me, Jules," James said as soon as the front door was closed. His voice dripped with exhaustion, as if he'd been slowly losing energy the past hour trying to keep his annoyance in check. "Bringing complete strangers into the house for drinks and practically planning out our kids' future with them? What were you thinking? Who knows if they're even interested in buying the Smiths' house? They may have been scoping out *our* house and *our* family. They could be leaders of a human trafficking ring and you had wine with them and exchanged numbers, birthdays, preschool information. Did you slip them our social security numbers, too, just for good measure?"

"Human trafficking? James, please. Not tonight. I need to start making dinner. I didn't realize how late it is." Julia put on an episode of *Dora the Explorer* for Alexis and Brice before washing her hands and pulling out various pans and ingredients.

"You don't know what kind of people they are. I'm not trying to hurt your feelings, but you're not good at reading people. In all honesty, you're the worst I've ever seen." Julia pointed to her chest and gave a mock look of surprise to James as if she hadn't heard a version of his you-need-to-be-more-careful speech a dozen times already.

"I'm serious, Julia. You're too trusting. Always believing

the best in everyone. I know it helps you feel good to think the world isn't a shitty and scary place, but it is. Regardless of whether or not you accept it."

"Fine," Julia conceded. "If this all goes to shit, feel free to shove it back in my face how you tried to warn me how hopelessly trusting and naïve I am. But don't hold your breath. That was my new best friend who just left. And, contrary to your opinion, I'm an excellent judge of character. I married you, right?" She gave him a quick kiss on the cheek and then turned to make her way back to the oven.

She stopped short when he grabbed her arm, turned her back to face him, and pulled her in for an embrace. He kept his arms around her waist and gave her a long look of concern. "I'm not trying to be a dick, and I'm sure they're fine people who may or may not actually put an offer in on the house." He paused to find the right words. "I'm worried about you. Remember how you latched onto Carla when we first moved into the townhouse? You were up all night dreaming up potential vacations and trips for our families. And then you were devastated when she moved away a few months later." He tilted her chin up so she was looking at him. "I don't want to see you get hurt again."

Carla had lived across the street from their old house. Coincidentally, Julia first met Carla when Carla was out weeding with a glass of wine. They weren't immediate best friends, but Julia was relieved to have a strong friendship in the neighborhood. It was lonely having no company outside of a husband and one or two small children. Having an adult nearby to talk and laugh with had saved her sanity on more than one occasion. While she may not have been devastated, per se, when Carla moved away, she did have some serious concerns about her mental health once her friend left.

"This isn't like that," Julia replied. "Lindsay is different; I can tell."

2
JULIA, OCTOBER 2019

Lindsay and Julia huddled together by the firepit which sat dead center on the property line separating their two yards. Just as Julia had predicted, the Moores had put an offer in on the house next door and they closed two months later in late September. By mid-October the women had convinced the men to build a patio and fire pit right in the middle of their two yards. It hadn't been an intentional symbolic bond between the two families, though intentional or not that's certainly what it was. The layout of their individual yards prevented each family from creating the seating area and fire pit that they both so desperately wanted. The only way to achieve the perfect setup was to combine yards. And why not? They had already started spending all their free time together and both families were committed to staying in their houses and school districts until the kids graduated.

The women had been right. There they were years later and nothing had changed. The women were in their usual spots at the fire pit lost in conversation again, this time talking about the annual Halloween party to be held at the

Herrick's. Always a crowd-pleasing event, the fall festivities included costume contests, games for the kids, and tons of fall-themed treats and drinks. The party began as a way to avoid trick-or-treating with small children. It was woefully painful waiting for them to toddle up each long walkway, the parents wincing as their kids took out a flower bed or two along the way. House after house they waited as their kids' chubby toddler hands hovered over the candy bowls, their eyes locked in a trance as they gazed into the mass of brightly colored wrappers. Finally, no matter how many times they reminded the kids to say, "thank you" and, "please," the kids forgot and needed additional prompting at every single house.

Not to mention the influx of crowds from other neighborhoods and developments who flocked to Scarlet Oaks Knoll for the ultimate trick-or-treat experience. There was Harlow Street with decorations and displays that gave professional haunted houses a run for their money. A few dozen houses, mostly on Larkely Lane, were renowned for giving away the coveted king-sized candy bars. And to top it off, there were half a dozen or so neighbors who always set up at the ends of their driveways with freshly made s'mores (over a make-shift fire pit right on the asphalt driveway) and fall-themed adult beverages in shiny red plastic cups.

After their first Halloween together, Lindsay suggested they host a party for the kids rather than deal with the hassle of trick-or-treating. They could set out bowls of candy in the basement for the kids, and the adults would be free to actually enjoy their night as well without worrying about which kids were wandering off or running into traffic.

This Halloween was Julia and Lindsay's tenth year hosting, so the ladies had big plans for the event. As per Moore and Herrick tradition, they'd arranged to have matching couple outfits per their preselected theme: famous couples.

Lindsay and Denny would be decked out in all denim, à la Britney Spears and Justin Timberlake circa 2001, while Julia and James would be dressed in medieval garments as Macbeth and Lady Macbeth.

The two women had decided on famous couples in history months prior, but they clashed when it came to identifying which couples they classified as famous and relevant. Lindsay was annoyed Julia's couple costume was of a fictional couple, while Julia couldn't fathom why Lindsay would go as a couple who never even got married and ended in disaster. Not that Lady Macbeth's suicide and Macbeth's untimely death soon after was a happy ending for her couple either, but the Macbeths as a couple stood the test of time. People will still be reading and analyzing Macbeth and Lady Macbeth's relationship for centuries to come. Surely everyone will have moved on and forgotten about Britney and Justin once a few more decades have passed.

Julia and Lindsay's party planning was put on pause for a few minutes when Lindsay went into the basement to get them drinks of water. They had already had two glasses of wine and they didn't want to get too tipsy the night before the party. Julia looked over at the husbands. They were up on the deck; both of them leaning on the railing and looking out into the smattering of backyards in the development.

She couldn't hear what they were saying above the soft music Lindsay was playing on the speakers, but she could still see their faces in the little bit of light left in the sky. James was talking and looking off into the distance somewhere while Denny was staring right at her. She had expected him to turn away when she caught him - something he frequently did. But he didn't. And because he didn't turn away, she didn't either. At first she was curious about why he'd suddenly allowed himself to stare her down so publicly - while standing next to her husband, no less. But her curiosity was replaced with sympathy when she noticed the hint of morose that touched every part of his face. It was subtle, but now that she could really get a good look at him, she saw how utterly depressed he looked.

Had it been different circumstances she would have said something to Lindsay about it, or James, or even Denny himself. But she knew Lindsay would dismiss it as his typical writer's brooding, and James would have said she was over-thinking it and it wasn't her business anyway. Approaching Denny about it was out of the question, too. They didn't have that sort of relationship. For years she'd tried to be friendly with him only to find his answers short and dismissive. She was Lindsay's friend, not his.

Lindsay returned with two ice waters for them and turned to shout up at the men, "Guys, come down for a minute so we can go over a few things before tomorrow." She took her seat again next to Julia and they sat in comfortable silence while the men made their way down the deck steps and out to the fire pit.

Denny spoke as they walked, "You've been planning this party for almost a decade. What's left to discuss?" It was a fair question. Julia herself wasn't sure what Lindsay was talking about. She too thought they would simply repeat everything from the year before. The women had been discussing plans for a slightly more elaborate version of previous parties to make it distinct as the tenth annual, but all the basics of what they would do was already covered.

When they reached the fire pit, each husband dutifully took the empty seat next to his wife. The women shared a seat resembling a wooden love seat. They'd found it at a flea market and split the cost fifty-fifty like the modern couple they were. They also worked together to sand and refinish the piece of furniture to its present glory. For years it had been their seat with chairs set up on each side for their husbands. Denny leaned back into his Adirondack chair while James was at full attention in his seat with his elbows on his knees and his eyes set on Lindsay. Julia let her eyes settle on Denny again, but he wouldn't return her gaze this time. She looked away, sure that she had imagined their previous connection. Had imagined seeing the sadness in his expression.

"Complacency is the work of the devil," Lindsay chastised. She took a long drink of her water before continuing. "I'd like to do a surprise party for Liv's fourteenth birthday, and I think the Halloween party is the perfect opportunity." Julia's eyes darted over to Denny who was shaking his head with what appeared to be disbelief or annoyance. "It's the only way to surprise her. Her birthday is too close to Halloween to have a separate, early party, and if we try to do it after her official birthday it will look like we forgot. She'd be devastated."

Julia gave her response with a bit more enthusiasm than necessary in a pathetic effort to help quell the tension she felt rising between Denny and Lindsay. "A surprise party! How fun! I've never been a part of planning one that worked. It's fine with us. Right, James?"

James did not share her excitement. "It's the night before the party. You couldn't have decided this any sooner?"

Julia's eyes narrowed at him. "It's fine. What did you have in mind, Linds?"

"I'm not sure, yet. I started toying with the idea this morning. I don't want it to look last-minute."

Denny eyed up Lindsay as he spoke, "Is that even possible since it is a last-minute birthday party? This is us, in the eleventh hour, trying to coordinate a surprise party that will coincide with an already planned annual party. It will be an obvious, last-minute failure." Denny rubbed the stubble scattered across his chin and stared into the fire as if looking for answers, or in an attempt to avoid meeting eyes with anyone else.

James was a big proponent of not airing dirty laundry in front of the neighbors or even in front of his own family. What happened in the house, stayed in the house. Public disagreements or arguments like Lindsay and Denny's tiff at the fire pit was, according to James, inappropriate and it made everyone else uncomfortable. Julia didn't disagree with the latter. She wasn't sure if she should comment anymore on the subject or if doing so would automatically put her on one of the sides of the escalating disagreement. She didn't want to take anyone's side. She only wanted to help Liv, who often felt like a second daughter to her, celebrate her fourteenth birthday.

Lindsay took a deep breath to push down any argument with Denny that had been about to come out. "I already contacted some of Liv's school friends and invited them to the party as well. I figured you all wouldn't mind, and I needed to move on this quickly since the party is tomorrow night."

"Right, good idea." Julia agreed. The party was usually for selected houses in the development, but they had a decent-sized house and there was plenty of room and food for more people.

"And we don't usually have cake," Lindsay added, "but I thought this year we could. I ordered a special birthday Halloween cake from Sugar, Sugar, the new bakery off of Elm."

Julia nodded, "I've been wanting to try their desserts." She thought for a minute then added, "We can set up a birthday photo booth station in the basement or even out here by the fire pit for the kids to do selfies. Also, Liv's been begging to take control of the music, so we can let her be the DJ this year - with some guidelines, of course."

"Perfect! See, I knew you guys would come up with some stuff!" Life sailed back into Lindsay and she was once again her confident and unbeatable self while Denny stayed lounged back in his chair and lost in his thoughts. James accepted his defeat from the women and stayed silent. It was hard to tell if he cared one way or the other.

"Wait, I haven't gotten a gift yet," Julia admitted. "I usually have it by now and am just waiting for her birthday, but she's getting older and it's harder to shop for her. I hadn't gotten around to getting anything yet."

"That's okay," Lindsay said. "We can both go to the stores tomorrow while picking up our other party supplies. I'll help you find something; she gave me a few ideas of what she wants."

"Just tell them," Denny said in a low voice to Lindsay.

"I think we're good here," Lindsay announced. "Jules, let's meet out front tomorrow at ten. I can drive. Guys, you have the kids and most of the decorations tomorrow, right? Be careful not to mention anything to Liv or the other kids. It's a surprise party and I really want to surprise her. I've never had a successful one either; someone always gives it away."

"Wait," James said before Lindsay could get to her feet. "We're literally doing everything the same as last year: balloons, dance floor and karaoke in the basement, creepy decorations, and so on? Denny and I don't need to do anything to help with the birthday part? That's all you and Julia tomorrow, right?"

"Exactly. This was my last-minute idea, so I'll take care of everything birthday-related tomorrow."

Now it was Julia's turn to stop Lindsay before she could get away. "But we'll still do a birthday dinner or something for Liv on her actual birthday, right? We always have in the past and I don't want her real birthday to pass without any presents or fanfare."

Lindsay started to appear slightly annoyed at what a fuss everyone was making over her child's birthday and how she wanted to celebrate it. "It's fine, everyone. We will seamlessly combine the birthday and Halloween parties tomorrow, and we'll make sure we do something extra special on the tenth, too. The girl will feel so loved and freaking special she won't know what to do with herself. Okay?" She flicked off the gas to the fire pit and started to gather up cups and small bits of trash that had accumulated over the past few hours they'd been out there.

Denny glared at Lindsay while Lindsay refused to look his way or acknowledge him in the slightest. Whatever was happening between the two of them, Julia hoped they would get over it before the party. Add a bit more booze (which flowed notoriously plentiful at the Halloween party) to whatever tension was rising between them and there would surely be a very public blowout.

Lindsay walked in front of Denny's chair on her way back to the house and he thrust his arm in front of her waist blocking her path. She must have been half expecting it because she didn't flinch or even turn to look at him. "Don't," she hissed. "We'll talk when we're inside."

Julia didn't mean to gawk, but she'd never seen the two behave like that before and she couldn't tear her eyes away from it. James, immune as always, began walking back to the house. It was none of his business whatever was happening between the neighbors and he did not want to get caught in the middle of it.

Denny withdrew his arm and Lindsay again began to make her way from the fire pit to the house. Denny caught eyes with Julia. Before, she could have sworn they were full of sadness. At that moment, she could see they were full of animosity and anger. For a split-second, Julia tried to imagine what *she* may have done to cause his anger. Then

Denny casually announced, "There won't be any birthday dinner on the tenth because we're moving to South Carolina next week."

Denny's announcement stopped Lindsay in her tracks. She whipped her head around to Denny with such fury Julia half expected Denny's head to explode from some sort of Jedi mindpowers. Unaffected by her glare, Denny continued to stare at the now extinguished fire pit.

Unable to escape, Lindsay turned to Julia with a softened expression. "I was going to tell you right after the Halloween party. I didn't want to spoil anyone's fun," Lindsay said to Julia.

"You're leaving?" Julia's tone was incredulous, so it came out more as an accusation than an actual question.

"I got an offer to be the store manager in Bluffton, South Carolina. It's right outside of Hilton Head. I couldn't turn it down."

"You're already a store manager. It's a lateral move. You hate the south. Why *wouldn't* you turn it down?" Julia demanded.

"That's what I've been saying," Denny added.

James had probably heard the beginning of the conversation, but he never stopped walking. He had already been heading for the house when Denny said they were moving, and James continued walking until he was back in the house. Julia suspected he knew it was going to be a long, difficult night sorting through everything whether he heard the fight first-person or whether he heard it second-hand from his wife as soon as she went inside. He probably preferred the latter because at least that way he could have a beer or two before he had to pick up all the pieces that would inevitably be scattered that night.

Julia's eyes widened and she raised her hands out to her

sides, "How are you going to leave all of this as if it means nothing? And in one week? I just...I don't understand."

"It's a great opportunity and it's time," Lindsay coolly responded.

Julia looked from Lindsay to Denny, and then back to Lindsay. There really wasn't anything else to say. She shoved past Lindsay on her way to her house and didn't look back. Like a hurt and angry girlfriend, she paused briefly at the door to allow Lindsay a chance to call out to her and to explain how it was all a misunderstanding. A chance to see Julia slipping away from her and to realize what a mistake she was making to leave her.

Julia's heart ached when all she heard was Lindsay and Denny quietly making their way towards their own house.

Much to James's surprise and relief, Julia didn't want to discuss anything that night. He had already made sure the kids were in bed by the time she walked into the house, ready to listen to all her complaints about Lindsay and how everything would be ruined. But there was none of that. Even more surprising was how she jumped him when he finally made his way to bed that night even though she hadn't initiated sex in weeks, if not months.

3

DENNY, SEPTEMBER 2009

Denny couldn't believe his luck. He was certain it was all some sort of mistake and the powers that be would realize Denny's fortunes were too numerous. They'd swoop in and reign down on him with tragedy and destruction in order to even out the playing field; to push him back into miserable obscurity with the rest of the moderately satisfied crowds of people.

And yet, as he waited for the bottom to fall out on him, his luck continued to increase. Or maybe it wasn't luck. He sometimes believed referring to success and positive outcomes as luck was too simplistic of an explanation given how many variables are involved with any given consequence in a person's life. This was true with his writing success as well. He'd worked his ass off as an assistant manager at P & L's Grocery while staying up nights drafting out a science fiction novel he couldn't get out of his head.

So many nights he'd considered scrapping the whole thing and forgetting he'd ever dared to dream of writing for a living. Months went by where he wasn't able to write at all because he had been stuck on a plot hole or he'd convinced himself the whole thing was crap and unworthy of anyone's precious time. Lindsay wouldn't hear it, though. She had been Denny's first and only beta reader back then. She'd helped him navigate plot discrepancies and pointed out characters she'd classified as too unlikable. Whenever Lindsay read a new chapter or section of his work, she would first gush over all the parts she loved before carefully providing targeted feedback with the help of her hand-written notes which covered the four margins of each page.

Maybe he had been lucky to have Lindsay for his wife, or maybe it was his decision to pick her as his wife that was to blame for all of his good fortune. He'd struggled in high school to write an essay about whether fate or free will had led Oedipus to his demise. As an adult, he'd made little progress in picking one over the other when assigning blame for his own various failures and successes.

Over a year after he'd started writing his manuscript, he'd finally finished and was ready to send out queries in order to land a literary agent. Most never responded. The one who did finally respond had nothing but caustic criticism for his "poorly conceptualized worlds and limited grasp of the sci-fi genre as a whole." He'd been devastated. Ready to trash the whole thing and apologize to Lindsay for having wasted so many nights on an unattainable dream. His lovely, endlessly supportive wife wouldn't hear of it. Lindsay had insisted on lifting his spirits with the most mind-blowing blow job of his life.

While her benevolent gesture couldn't undo the blow to Denny's ego, it did help to build him back up from the fall. He reworked the query letter he had sent out and researched new agents to send it to. The rejections continued to trickle in while Lindsay did her best to help him bounce back each time.

After a year of reaching out to literary agents and

publishers, he gave up on the traditional route of publishing and settled for what was commonly referred to as vanity publishing. Ideal circumstances in the literary world would have Denny getting a paycheck for his work. Vanity publishing required Denny to put up all the upfront costs associated with publishing and offered no help in the area of promoting or advertising his book. It felt shameful to publish his own work and he refused to tell family or friends about it.

Regardless, he overcame his pride and they had celebrated with a bottle of cheap wine and takeout from his favorite Chinese restaurant the night his book arrived in the mail. When the bottle was kicked and the inevitable leftovers from dinner were packed away in their tiny, somewhat fickle refrigerator, they stayed up talking for hours speaking hypothetically about what they'd do with all the money once Denny became an international best-selling author.

Weeks went by and no one ordered Denny's book. He'd made it available online through Amazon and convinced a local bookstore to carry it since he'd sold them a dozen units at just two dollars per book. Each morning he'd check his email hoping to see an order from Amazon; every few days he would call the bookstore to see if they had moved any of his books off of their Local Authors shelf.

And then one day there was a sale from Amazon. He and Lindsay did a little dance in the post office parking lot after they'd shipped it out to someone in Lexington, Nebraska. Remarkably, a few days later he found another order in his inbox.

People were finding Denny's book, miraculously, amid the thousands of other sci-fi books and best-sellers. With that little bit of encouragement, the two decided to spend Lindsay's entire annual bonus, a little over a thousand dollars, on digital advertising for Denny's book. They agreed to give one good push for an entire month just to see what would happen.

Sales increased exponentially. They quickly went through the case of books they'd ordered from the publishing company and had to order a second round of copies. Large brown boxes of Denny's books filled their tiny living room and evenings were spent fulfilling orders and creating expense and profit spreadsheets in Excel.

Within a few months Denny's book had a cult following complete with fan mail to the apartment he and Lindsay were renting. But his biggest victory came when one of the agents who had previously rejected him reached out with a series offer and a generous advancement.

Denny was able to quit his job and focus full-time on writing out the rest of the series. He had his dream job. They were able to afford night classes so Lindsay could work towards getting her MBA and start climbing the corporate ladder at her job. They had babies and started saving up for a house. His writing profits helped them begin to build up a down-payment, though at the time they still couldn't afford the predicted mortgage that would come with the home they'd envisioned and built up in their minds over the years.

And then luck, or ambition combined with skill and ability, or maybe a combination of all of it, struck again when Lindsay was promoted at work. She had been the department manager of the paint department at Moyer's, and she'd been told in order to move up to the next position of assistant store manager she would first need to get her degree in Master of Business Administration. Fate intervened when one of the district big-wigs had noticed Lindsay reading a textbook for an MBA class on her lunch break. When he heard she was taking classes towards her degree, he encouraged her to apply to the current opening and suggested a woman of her ability who was already on track to graduate would surely have a strong chance of getting the position.

The two found a sitter for Liv, and Denny took a very pregnant Lindsay out to a celebratory dinner at her favorite restaurant, The Gin Mill. It gave them anxiety to spend such an enormous amount of money on dinner, but Denny insisted they forget about their finances for the evening. Their date night often popped into Denny's head when he was feeling nostalgic. It was as if everything in their life had fallen into place that night. Their journey, though years in the making already, was officially getting into the good stuff.

For their first night in their new house, the plan had been to get takeout and to eat at the island. They'd spend the night on the blowup mattresses, a makeshift camping trip for Liv, and then get an early start on painting in the morning. They didn't want to move any furniture in until they'd painted, and they still had three weeks left on their apartment lease anyway.

That had been the tentative plan. But their neighbors, Julia and James Herrick, wouldn't hear of it. They were outside enjoying the brisk fall weather with their kids when the Moores had pulled up to their new house. Julia and Lindsay started talking like old friends who hadn't seen each other in ages, while Denny and James engaged in a little bit of small talk about the structure of the houses and the Scarlet Oaks Knoll Homeowners' Association. Denny was taken aback when Julia insisted they all eat dinner together on the Herrick's deck that evening. She said James was grilling up burgers and he could easily throw a few more on for them.

It was supposed to be their first night, as a family, in their new home. Denny imagined playing hide and seek with the kids and walking around making final decisions about paint colors with Lindsay. He'd assumed they would toast cheap champagne to their new house and new beginning. Lindsay must not have had those same visions. She enthusiastically accepted the invitation without consulting Denny. He'd gone along with it, of course, because Lindsay was excited. He would always do anything he could to make his sweet wife happy. She'd deserved it.

The annoyed vibe from James was not lost on him, though he wasn't exactly sure where it was coming from. Denny couldn't tell if James had already decided he was disinterested in anything to do with Denny, or if he just resented them invading their family time. Denny could understand that; he felt the same way. Regardless, James was able put it behind him and eventually seemed to enjoy the company and dinner overall.

After everyone was finished eating, the kids were let loose in the safety of the closed-off living room while the adults got to know each other a bit better on the porch.

The table was big enough for eight when seats were added to each end. Lindsay and Denny had sat on one side with Hailey between them and Liv on the end next to Lindsay. Similarly, Julia and James sat on the other side with Brice in a highchair between them and Alexis on the end next to Julia. Once the kids were gone, the women each moved over a seat to sit next to her husband; they shared a quick laugh at how they had done it naturally and at the same time. Already perfectly in sync with one another.

James got two beers for himself and Denny, and the rest of the bottle of wine for Julia and Lindsay. James handed Denny his third beer and asked him about his work.

"I'm a writer," Denny replied with as much confidence as he could muster. For some reason he still felt like an imposter in the writing world. As if someone could and would arbitrarily decide all his work was, in fact, utter crap, and his sales would dry up instantly. He forced himself to elaborate since he knew what questions were coming next. "I'm three books into my five-book series, *Time and Again*. It's science fiction about a man who discovers time travel and different universes."

"His first book sold thousands of copies without a publisher. He did it all on his own," Lindsay gushed as she squeezed his knee under the table.

"I have a publisher now," Denny knew this probably meant little to anyone outside of the industry, but to him he was never a legit author until he was officially published by one of the big five publishing groups.

"I've never heard of it," James commented casually. Even though his tone lacked any malice, Denny noticed Julia gave him a scolding look. But James hadn't turned to see her and so the look faded without achieving its intended effect.

Denny brushed off the comment. Lindsay was his biggest fan and she would rave about his books all night if the present company allowed it. He didn't know Julia and James very well yet, but he bet Julia would have politely listened all night, too, while James would have either steered the conversation in another direction or flat-out left the table with some excuse about checking on the kids.

"What about you?" Denny directed towards James in an effort to turn the conversation before James had the chance.

"I'm an attorney."

Lindsay's eyes widened so dramatically Denny noticed her reaction in his periphery even though he was focused on James.

"What kind of law do you practice?" Lindsay asked. Apparently, she was not only Denny's biggest fan, but potentially James's biggest fan as well.

"Family law," James said without any hint at elaborating. Lindsay's eyes shrunk down to their normal size and Denny was once again, in her eyes, likely the most successful of the group depending on how you looked at it.

"Family law," Denny repeated. "That must be difficult. Emotionally. I bet you've heard some crazy stories." He was always interested in hearing the sordid details of such cases. Not that he enjoyed hearing them; he was more interested in trying to capture the essence of the people involved and predicting how it may impact their lives later. He would sometimes use the basic details of news stories as background for characters to explain their motivations, fears, or goals in his novels.

"I don't hear stories," James clarified. "I listen to factual accounts of what are sometimes horrific, home-life situations."

The whole table grew quiet with a sudden awkward pause in conversation. Denny considered apologizing for insulting James and or his profession, but he was starting to get the feeling it wouldn't matter either way. James was the type to lay everything out like he sees it without regard to how it was taken by the person with whom he was speaking to. In the current situation, James felt the word "stories" was inappropriate, and so he let Denny know. It was nothing James would dwell on so Denny let it go, too.

Julia, the one Denny dubbed the peacekeeper of the house, said, "I was a dental assistant up until Alexis was born. I know, everyone makes that face when I tell them what I do." Denny, though probably not Lindsay, immediately felt guilty for making a face at the thought of working with other people's mouths all day long. "But I love it. My brother, Kaleb, is autistic and dentist visits were a nightmare when we were kids. Getting him to brush was difficult with the sensory aspects of brushing, so he frequently had issues with his teeth and needed to see the dentist a lot. One day we went in and there was a new assistant who had a daughter similar to Kaleb. She brought out a weighted blanket, which was a new theory at the time, along with special headphones to drown out the drill noises. It was still an absolute nightmare, but no longer to the point where it was unbearable. It always stuck with me how much of a difference she made and that maybe I could do the same. That and the light music in the background and chill atmosphere. I know it sounds crazy, but I fell in love with dental offices."

Denny was fascinated by Julia's career backstory and began to wonder if maybe a character loosely based on Julia would ever work in his sci-fi series. Lindsay looked for the corporate ladder climb. "Will you ever go to school to become a dentist?"

"I don't think so. I don't have a desire to be a dentist. I like assisting."

"Really? I'm an assistant manager at Moyer's now, but I'm on my way to district manager and beyond. It's one of the reasons I love working there; so many different paths and possibilities to work my way up. Especially once I finish my MBA - just three more courses to go," Lindsay said with zero fear of coming off as too arrogant or ambitious. Denny always admired that about Lindsay: her ability to fight to the death for what she wanted without worrying too much about how other people may interpret her actions.

If Julia felt slighted, she didn't show it. She listened intently as Lindsay regaled them with stories from her work. And they were good stories, especially when Lindsay told them. That was another thing that had drawn Denny to Lindsay in the first place - her ability to captivate a crowd with her wit and personality.

That night Lindsay dazzled with a cluster of stories about appalling interactions she'd experienced while demonstrating their latest vacuum cleaner at the front of the store. She pre-empted it with a quick summary about how a bad egg salad at their recent Memorial Day potluck left the store short-handed during one of the busiest days of the year which was why she had been filling in in the flooring department.

"It's fine; I'm not too good to do a few vacuum demonstrations – even though it was a sexist assignment only given to me because I work with a bunch of chauvinistic jerks and have a vagina which apparently makes me a professional when it comes to housework.

"Anyway...speaking of vagina, I'll go into my first story. I know when I start with that it sounds dirty, but it actually involves a man with pure and good intentions. He was an older man looking for a new vacuum for his wife as a surprise birthday gift. Cute, right? But what wasn't cute was his pronunciation of the vacuum manufacturer. The name is pronounced ruh-jee-nuh, with a hard e sound. And it's spelled r-e-g-i-n-a. Like the name Gina. But he pronounced it ruh-jy-nuh with the hard i sound instead. When you say it quickly enough, which the customer did, it sounded like he was saying, 'I really like your vagina model. It picks up everything!'"

The table erupted into laughter picturing a sweet old man commenting on Lindsay's vagina in front of both customers and coworkers in the crowded hardware store. Denny still laughed even though it had happened months ago and he'd heard the stories a few times since.

Lindsay didn't wait for them to stop laughing before she continued, "And he wasn't quiet about it either. He yelled to be heard over the vacuum, and he yelled because he's an older man and he probably didn't even know he was yelling that loudly. But everyone around him heard it, so guess who has another nickname?"

She pointed to herself and drank another sip of wine before continuing with the not-so-sweet and innocent

comments she received from the contractors. Creativity was
not their strong suit, so each comment contained either the
word "suck" or "blow" in reference to both the vacuum and
Lindsay's mouth.

It wasn't funny to hear about Lindsay's experiences being
sexually harassed at work; Denny cringed to think of the
terrible experiences Lindsay had at work as a female in a
predominately male industry. He knew he only heard a few,
select stories from her myriad experiences. If he was honest
with himself, he knew he should ask her about it to make
sure she was okay. Because he wasn't sure how Lindsay actually felt about what occasionally happened at work. Based on
her stories she always turned the joke back on them and
walked away unscathed, but was anyone really *that* immune
to harsh and unrelenting commentary?

For the time being they all laughed along with her as she
expertly transformed her voice into that of a male contractor
while periodically standing to act out their exact expressions
and reactions to her comebacks. He'd ask her about it eventually, but not that night. There was too much good to focus
on instead.

Later that night Denny and Lindsay turned on the gas
fireplace and set up the air mattresses in the center of their
empty living room. The adults laid on the outside acting as a
barrier to keep the girls in the middle from rolling off and
onto the floor in the middle of the night. As their beautiful
little girls slept, they recounted the night with the neighbors
and tried to figure out the intricacies and dynamics of their
new friends.

"James is a bit of a downer, isn't he?" Lindsay whispered
to Denny. They both had their heads propped up on their

elbows and their faces were aglow with the light coming from the fireplace.

Denny's eyes narrowed as he tried to politely express his opinion on James. Were it a romantic comedy, James would be the aggressive, stubborn husband who was eventually abandoned by his sweet wife because his cold, negative heart was just too much for her warm, optimistic personality to take anymore. "Yeah, I'm not really sure how he and Julia fit together. She seems so perky and jovial, while he's brooding and pessimistic."

Lindsay nodded her agreement to Denny's assessment. "Maybe his work makes him brooding and pessimistic."

"Maybe. Do you think you and Julia will hit it off long term? So far you're just drinking buddies given how much wine you've had each time you've hung out."

He hadn't meant to hurt Lindsay's feelings with the question, but he could tell he did by her dropped head and serious consideration. "I don't know. I hope so. I could use a few good female friends."

"I know. You'll find them here." Denny oh so carefully leaned over Liv to meet Lindsay for a chaste kiss as she cautiously navigated over Hailey to meet him halfway. "Everything is going to change with us moving here. I can feel it," he said.

Denny and Lindsay got little to no sleep that night. Sleeping on an air mattress on the floor with small children may have worked in their late teens or early twenties, but they were officially getting old in their early thirties. They ached in the morning and were exhausted, but it was still a glorious feeling to wake up in their cavernous new house.

4

JULIA, OCTOBER 2019

S aturday morning, the morning of the party, Julia and
Lindsay were supposed to meet out front at ten to get
supplies and a gift for Liv. A gift for Liv's last-minute
surprise party. She wondered if the kids had been told their
whole world was about to be rocked and how they would
soon be pulled from everything they knew. Julia's heart
ached. Liv and Hailey were like daughters to her and like
sisters to her own kids. She had no interest in going shopping with Lindsay and pretending as if everything was
status quo.

At nine thirty she pulled out of her garage. In the corner
of her eye, she could see Lindsay walking out to get the paper
that had been tossed haphazardly onto the Moore's driveway. Julia acted as if she didn't see her and turned to drive
down the road in the opposite direction of Lindsay's house.
It would mean she'd need to drive a little out of her way
through the development to get out to the main roads, but
she didn't want to see or be anywhere near Lindsay. She'd
considered canceling the Halloween party altogether since
she wasn't in a good place to host dozens of people at her

house. But canceling the Halloween party would mean canceling Liv's birthday party. Doing so would leave Liv celebrating her fourteenth birthday in a brand-new city away from her closest friends. Imagining Alexis in the same situation literally made her heart hurt. She couldn't do that to Liv.

That was all wishful thinking anyway. She knew the party would happen regardless, and that she would, in a few short hours, need to see and be cordial to Lindsay again. In the meantime, what she really needed was a little bit of time to herself to understand what was happening and how she felt about it. Anger and sadness were closely intertwined she couldn't distinguish between the two anymore. On top of that, she wasn't even sure she had a right to those feelings. Julia wasn't married to Lindsay. They hadn't promised their lives to each other in a ceremony complete with rings and witnesses. When it came down to it, all Lindsay had done was buy the house next door to hers.

Julia's stomach began growling as she arbitrarily navigated down the back roads of her community. She hadn't eaten since dinner the night before and her metabolism worked quickly. She turned up her radio to drown out the buzz of her vibrating cell phone in the passenger seat. Lindsay would have to wait until after she got some food in her stomach.

Minutes later, Julia eased into the parking lot of Go Burger and queued up behind four other cars in the drive thru. As she was waiting, another car pulled up perpendicular to hers and started to nudge forward as if they wanted to cut in front of her. *What the hell?* Julia thought. She glanced in her rearview mirror and was surprised to see three more cars right behind her. Who knew half the town hit up the local Go Burger just before ten on Saturday mornings?

Regardless, she was not about to let this person cut in. The cars in front of her hadn't moved yet, but she started to inch her way forward to show the other car she would not be yielding to them. Why did everyone think they could push her around? That she would just roll over and take whatever other people gave her? No more.

Oddly enough she felt empowered with each inch she crept forward. There was little space between her and the car in front of her and little space between her and the interloper; but still, she eased forward again. Julia raised her foot off the break slightly and let her car drift forward another smidge. Unfortunately, the other driver was a worthy opponent who met her smidge with one of their own.

She refused to look over at the other driver. It didn't matter who the driver was: an eighty-year-old with dementia or some teenager with something to prove. She didn't care. It was probably best she didn't know. Whenever she heard any sort of backstory or knew too much about other people, she let her feelings get involved. If she saw some sweet looking elderly person behind the wheel she would relent and let them in. And then she'd hate herself for being such a pushover yet again. For putting everyone else before herself. *Not today*, she thought as she gripped the steering wheel a little tighter.

She drifted forward again the tiniest bit, shocked she hadn't hit the other car yet. Remarkably, the other car eased forward, too. From her point of view, it looked like she was on top of the other vehicle. How was it possible that they weren't touching yet? For the dozenth time she went to turn the already silenced radio down so she could concentrate on the task at hand. Just as she gripped the volume knob, she heard the sound of screeching metal and the tiniest jerk as her vehicle collided with the other. The slowest, most anticlimactic game of chicken ever played had ended with the paltry, almost imperceptible collision of a Toyota Corolla and a Dodge Status in the drive thru of Go Burger.

Julia swore as she threw the car in park. She got out and started towards the other driver who turned out to be a woman about the same age as she was. Julia pitied this woman who was so desperate and lost that she ended up in such a pathetic situation. And then she realized *she* was that woman, too. *No, no, no, no, I'm not that woman*, Julia thought as she conveniently slipped into a state of denial.

As if to help prove the other woman wasn't a version of her, Julia went into attack mode. "You can't just drive into the middle of a line at the drive thru! Look!" She shouted as she pointed down at the drive-through traffic lines painted on the street at the drive-thru. "These lines show you where to go," Julia was laying on the sarcasm thick as if she were speaking to an imbecile. "You have to stay *inside* the lines and follow the arrows."

The woman had a crooked smile on her face as she accepted Julia's abuse and remained silent. To the people behind her, Julia probably looked like the lunatic with the way she was ranting and raving at this woman who was showing no signs of aggression or retaliation. When Julia finished her exaggerated pantomime of what it looked like to correctly navigate the drive thru lane, the woman finally spoke up. "I always come through this way. The Go Burger guys will tell you that at 9:55, every day for I don't even know how many years, I come through the side here and order the breakfast sliders with hash browns and a coffee."

Julia's confusion was blatant when she answered, "So you're telling me because you break traffic laws daily it means you're now immune to them?" Julia realized a little too late she was still screaming.

The customers behind them had been patient and possibly even enjoyed the show. Their patience ran out, they were in a fast-food drive-thru after all and everyone there was in a hurry. The beeping horns from the other cars pulled

Julia back to reality. She was having a verbal altercation with a stranger and she was complicit in an intentional car accident in a drive-thru lane. What had her life come to?

In an outer body experience, she briefly saw herself from the perspective of one of the cars behind her and she was mortified. She quickly exchanged insurance information with the woman and then left without getting anything to eat. She wasn't able to face the workers at the restaurant who undoubtedly saw the whole thing on their cameras and likely took bets as to who would be the first to pull a shiv or pepper spray from their purse.

Julia's original plan had been to drive around and cool off a bit before she faced Lindsay. Julia would clear her head and get all of her thoughts and emotions in order so she could enjoy - was that even the right word? - her last week with the Moores as her neighbors. Just seven days more with friends who were like family to her. It was all still too much to take in, and on top of that she had to worry about how she would tell James what had happened at Go Burger. She shuddered at the thought of her impending conversation with her husband.

It was a no-win situation, of course. James was frequently confrontational with just about anyone, but never to the extent that Julia had just taken it. He would never understand why she kept creeping forward and he would give her absolute hell about the whole scenario until the day she died. Nothing major, but certainly little digs here and there about how her emotions can get the best of her.

It was also ammunition for the argument that would inevitably come up once again: She was too close to the neighbors. He'd warned her before they had even moved in how it would end badly. It had taken years to come to fruition, but he had been right.

There was no way to hide the accident. Even with the

slowest and briefest impact of her life, both vehicles sustained paint damage and it looked like her whole front bumper had been knocked out of alignment. The average person wouldn't notice, or at the very least wouldn't notice right away. She would not have noticed, herself. But James? She was sure he got a slight chill when it happened, a sixth-sense sort of premonition which fueled a strong desire to check the car as soon as she pulled up though he wouldn't be able put his finger on where exactly that urge had come from.

Sure enough, there was James when she pulled into the driveway. He was in the garage taking perfectly labeled totes from a shelf high up on the garage walls. He effortlessly pulled a tote from the top shelf and eased back down the ladder as Julia stepped out of the car.

"Are you okay? Did someone hit you?" James asked with his eyes wide and going back and forth from Julia and the front bumper of the car. He quickly walked over to her and gave her a hug before pulling away to search her face and body for any signs of physical harm.

"I'm fine," Julia snapped at him with a bit more sass than she had meant. But really, the damage on the car was beyond minimal. How injured could she have possibly been when the car itself looked almost immaculate?

James's facial expression and tone changed from concern to annoyance. "What happened to the car, Julia?" James asked again with more insistence in his voice.

"I got into a small accident. Everyone is fine."

"This is about last night, isn't it? About the neighbors moving away? You shouldn't be driving when you're that upset." After a pause he added, "And you shouldn't be that upset about the Moores. People move in and out of here all the time. Families don't stay in the same house the way they used to."

"Don't tell me how to feel." Julia wasn't looking at James. Her eyes were on the garage floor behind him where all the Halloween decorations lay scattered on the floor like some gruesome massacre.

James ignored her comment. "Will you please tell me what happened so I know everything is okay?"

"Someone cut in front of me at Go Burger and we had a slight fender bender."

"Did they cut in front of you on the road or while you were in line?"

"In line."

"Why would they do that? Did they not see you?"

Julia shrugged her shoulder and said, "I don't know. The woman said she does it all the time. She always cuts the line in the mornings and people let her in."

James narrowed his eyes as he realized what she'd done. It wasn't at all what James would ever expect from his responsible wife who was known to back down in most confrontational situations. To make sure he was understanding the situation clearly he asked, "You hit her? On purpose?"

Julia shrugged her shoulders again and continued to look at the floor instead of her husband.

He gave a disgusted half laugh and sarcastically asked, "You don't know if you hit her?"

He'd never believe her, but Julia did not know if she hit the woman or not. She was moving so slowly sometimes it was hard to tell if she was moving at all. Maybe she hit the woman; maybe the woman hit her; maybe they both hit each other.

"Jesus, Julia! Will you answer a damn question?" James shouted.

"No, because I know you're going to turn this into something it's not," Julia spit back at him.

"You have no idea how dangerous that was. You don't

know how mentally unstable some people are. People have killed for less. They purposefully hit your car over a spot in the Go Burger drive thru. Who does that?"

I do, Julia thought but didn't dare say. She didn't dare say anything. James was in a full rage and he needed time to cool down before they could discuss what had happened. Although it made him angrier in the moment, Julia locked eyes with him but remained quiet. His eyes searched hers as if trying to find anything familiar in his wife. After what seemed like minutes, James turned and walked through the garage and back into the house. He stepped on one of the ceramic pumpkins on his way in. The pumpkin shattered under his weight and shot in different directions around the garage. She knew she would find those tiny orange pieces of plastic for years to come and would sadly be reminded of this moment.

5

DENNY, SEPTEMBER 2010

D enny and Lindsay were late to breakfast the last full day of their vacation in the Outer Banks. Taking advantage of hearing Julia and James already up and feeding their own children, Denny and Lindsay enjoyed uninterrupted morning sex and it was everything they remembered it to be. They knew the kids would follow the scents of pancakes and bacon down to the kitchen and that James and Julia would get them fed. Just as Denny and Lindsay would do the same for them.

When the two emerged from their room and made their way down to the main floor, Julia teased, "About time you two woke up"

"We weren't sleeping," Lindsay said as she winked at Julia and used her hands to make a quick obscene gesture (out of view of the children) to drive home the fact that they were having sex. Then with a coy smile Lindsay smacked Denny's butt on her way to get her morning coffee.

Julia blushed. She and James were openly affectionate but did not openly discuss sex, ever. Denny didn't like Lindsay flaunting their sex life either, but he knew it was useless to ever try to change his wife. As Lindsay often reminded him, he knew what he was getting into when he married her.

Lindsay and Julia had organized every aspect of the vacation; the men were merely along for the ride and were there to provide additional support with the kids. They took their vacation in September because that was the slowest time at Lindsay's work, and she was determined to make store manager within the next few years. To appease James they found a house with a heated pool and a pool table.

Overall, Denny thought it had been the perfect vacation. The older kids had a friend to play with, and the adults each had extra eyes helping to watch and care for the smallest kids who were into everything. He could put up with James's occasional snide remarks and general dismissive attitude towards him since it meant being able to rent one of the stilted mansions on Hatteras Island.

Denny had hoped he and James would bond over fishing with the kids and taking their families out on the boat that came with the house. Nope. One night, Denny and James were in the basement playing pool while the women were putting the kids to bed. Everyone had been in the game room taking advantage of having a pool table and foosball table at their disposal, but when bedtime hit Denny and James were left alone in the giant basement. They made a little bit of small talk about weather, fishing, and plans for the rest of the vacation, but mostly all they heard was the clacking of the balls or the soft swooshing sound when they dropped in the old-school netted holes. They would remain friendly for the sake of their wives, but they would never be what Lindsay and Julia had become.

Part of what had created the women's strong bond was their bi-weekly pinochle games with other women from around the development. Twice a week Lindsay and Julia met up in Lindsay's kitchen to create whatever dip or dessert they were going to take to the game while consuming a bit of wine and a bit of whatever they were making. Music blared from the speakers while the ladies let go of any stress and anxiety that had built up all week. As they prepared their dishes they danced and laughed with the anticipation of their much-needed break from their kids and husbands.

The morning after Lindsay's first game, he'd woken up to find both women passed out and spooning in their guest bedroom. They had smeared mascara under their eyes and disheveled hair. The whole room smelled a lot like his old frat house. Julia was clutching a piece of pizza crust she must have taken for the walk home from the house of the neighbor who had been hosting that night.

In the kitchen of their OBX rental the memory of Lindsay's first pinochle night randomly popped into his head. Along with it came the fleeting fantasy that they had both drunkenly stumbled into his room rather than the guest bedroom that night.

It wasn't as if he was unhappy with Lindsay. As far as he was concerned, he'd never been happier with her. Their marriage had had its ups and downs, but they were currently as high as they'd ever been – and that was including their wedding night. But there was still something about Julia he couldn't ignore. In some ways, she was the exact opposite of Lindsay with how soft-spoken and laid back she was. If he had to come up one word to describe what drew him to Julia it would be "natural." Her natural hair color, unpolished nails, and barely-there makeup only made her more attractive to him. And while he'd heard her complain to Lindsay about her curves, he loved that she didn't diet or obsess about workouts. Guiltily, Denny sometimes wondered what it would be like to be married to her. He imagined it would be easy to be with a woman like that.

"Denny?" Lindsay, along with the rest of the adults at the table, was staring at him.

Damn. He'd spaced out again. "What?"

Lindsay smiled back at him. She was amused by his tendency to space out every now and then. "We're doing a beach day today."

"Yeah. Sounds good," he said. He put his head back down and finished his breakfast hoping no one noticed the slight color running over his face. Hoping that no one could guess he had been imagining himself with someone else's wife at the breakfast table while on a family vacation.

James started to clear off the table while Lindsay and Denny, the late arrivals to breakfast, finished the last bites of their eggs and bacon. Julia and Lindsay took on the daunting task of getting the kids into their suits and covering every inch of their skin with sunscreen, while the men were instructed to set up tents, chairs, and toys on the portion of beach directly behind their rental.

Since it was their last day on the beach, they set up for the long run. The women wanted to stay out in the sun all day, an end-of-summer attempt to hold onto the bronze glow they'd built up over the summer months through pool days and sunning in the backyards while the kids played. Denny and James set up a large tent for the kids to lay under when they got tired. Mercifully, after a week of running around, all four kids easily went down for naps on the beach under their tent. Each one was overcome with exhaustion and happy for the break.

James disapproved of Julia's sunning and made multiple mentions throughout their vacation of how skin cancer ran in her family. He set himself up under an umbrella with a

Steve Martin biography. A little surprising given that Denny saw James as having a stick up his ass most days. Denny was an avid reader himself, and yet he and James never seemed to have any books or interests in common. He thought James looked disappointed and maybe a little annoyed as he sat under his umbrella with another umbrella and chair, for Julia, empty beside him.

Denny took the opportunity to get some last-minute fishing in. He used to visit OBX and other spots along the coast with his parents. He and his sister learned everything they knew about fishing from their vacations over the years. They were a catch-and-release family unless it was for dinner. That's what he was hoping for that day on the beach. To wow the kids and the women by catching and filleting fresh fish for dinner. He didn't bother considering how James would feel about it.

Denny set up a few rods along the water's edge and then sat next to Lindsay who was laying out on a towel and talking quietly to Julia.

"Are you lovely ladies enjoying your last beach day?" he asked them. He moved carefully so sand didn't get kicked onto either of their towels.

They both laid on their stomachs with the top straps of their bikinis undone. With effort, Denny kept his gaze on his wife and away from Julia. He'd already had his fill the first day they went swimming in the pool. It had taken a few hours for Julia to get comfortable enough to strip down to just her suit at their pool. Once she did, Denny found it hard to look anywhere else. He'd even excused himself to get a drink to help take the edge off of seeing half-naked Julia frolicking around the pool a few feet or even a few inches away from him. He kept his sunglasses on longer than necessary that day to help prevent anyone noticing what, or rather whom, he was really looking at. He'd hoped James hadn't noticed. Though he wouldn't be able to tell either way since James's attitude towards Denny was already somewhat short and hostile to begin with.

When Denny sat down on the beach, Lindsay slid down on her towel a little so that she wasn't directly between Denny and Julia and wouldn't have to turn her head back and forth to talk to both of them.

"Absolutely," Julia said. "I can't believe we're leaving tomorrow. This has been, hands down, the best vacation we've ever had."

"Agreed," Lindsay said.

"It's been a good week," Denny agreed. "We're lucky it didn't rain the whole time we were here." After a bit of what Denny considered to be comfortable silence, he asked, "Julia, is everything okay?" He hadn't meant to be nosey, but he was genuinely concerned something bad had happened. He noticed her brow was furrowed as she furiously tapped at her old-school cell phone which required four hits on the seven button just to type an "s."

"Kari's husband left her," Lindsay told Denny.

"Who's Kari?" he asked. Julia ignored them both and continued to text.

"She's across the street from Maureen, who is right behind both our houses. Maureen's married to Josh…" Denny still couldn't place her. "She was at our Halloween party last year as a bloody Lady Gaga from that awards show."

"Oh, right." Denny and James had had one of their longest conversations that night as they'd discussed how disturbing Kari had looked covered in fake blood and dressed in some scantily clad outfit. A bit much for a family Halloween party. "Is she part of your pinochle group?"

"Yeah. She just hosted the weekend before we left for vacation. Stan was there for a bit and everything seemed fine.

They were laughing and joking with each other. Stan was talking about Halloween costumes and he said he'd see us all at the party next month."

"There must be another woman," Julia said. She flipped her phone shut and set it on her towel. "Right, Denny?" Julia's polarized sunglasses showed only his face when he looked at them, but he still squirmed under the gaze he knew was behind the lenses.

"I guess." Denny had no idea; he didn't know any of the other neighbors that well. "Do they have any kids?"

"No. They were going to wait a few more years before they started having kids."

Lindsay's head perked up. "Do you think that was it? Or maybe they disagreed about kids in general. One desperately wanted them and the other didn't. Jules, what did her text message say again?"

"Hold on; let me pull it up again." Julia gave a few taps on her phone and then maneuvered the screen to be in her shadow so she could read it.

Ladies, you've undoubtedly seen the moving truck in our driveway these past two days so I'm sending out this text to get ahead of the rumors and gossip. Stan is moving out. It's a mutual decision and we both agree it's for the best. Please respect our privacy as we navigate the unknowns.

"She sent that in a text message?" Denny was beyond shocked at the divorce announcement casually shared via a group text message.

"To all the people in the pinochle group. We're all friends. How else do you get in touch with that many people in a short amount of time?" Julia said. The women were quiet as they once again took in the details of the message and tried to make sense of it. Denny lost interest and looked back at his three poles which were all standing rigid and upright.

"It's another woman," Julia repeated.

"But Kari's always going on about what an amazing sex life they have and how they have this whole section of their closet devoted to toys and outfits," Lindsay countered.

"Maybe she's lying," Julia said.

"I guess. That seems weird though. Most of the women openly talk about their nonexistent sex life during our pinochle games. Why lie and risk making other women feel bad about their own sex lives in comparison to her fake one?"

"I don't know. We don't actually know her, or him, that well. We only see her twice a month for our game."

"True. And even then there are over a dozen of us," Lindsay conceded. "What do you think?" She nudged Denny who was still staring at his poles and willing them to bend and jerk towards the ocean.

Off handedly, Denny offered the only comment he could think of that would take into account both of their theories. "Maybe there is someone else, but it's not just about sex. Maybe the sex with his wife can be amazing but he's still looking for something more. Something outside of sex that he can't get from his wife. He might be cheating even though he loves his wife."

Both women silently stared at him. Even with their glasses on, Denny could tell from their facial expressions that they were assessing him with narrowed, accusing eyes.

He leaned back a little and said, "I don't feel that way. I've *never* felt that way." Denny's hands raised instinctively in surrender though clearly neither woman was going to raise a hand or attack him physically for what he'd thought was an innocuous comment.

"Then why would you say a loving marriage with healthy sex life could still result in an affair? You must feel that way or at least feel it's possible for you, too." Lindsay said.

"I've never cheated. Even in high school I've never cheated, so I have no idea as to why anyone would. I'm going off of what I limited experience I have as an innocent bystander. My theory on adultery stems from what happened to a guy I used to work with at P & L Grocery."

He hadn't planned on going into specifics, but reluctantly he continued when he realized Lindsay and Julia were not about to let his comment slide without a thorough explanation. Denny sighed. "Remember Dan? Worked in the deli with me? He and Laura went out to dinner with us a few times?"

Lindsay nodded. Denny shifted more of his attention towards Julia since she wasn't at all familiar with Dan's sordid marriage details. "I worked with Dan in the deli department for a few years. When I first started working there, he was happily married: texting back and forth all day, she'd stop by and see him on breaks, and so on. As the years go by that all slows down a bit, but it still appears to be a happy marriage based on conversations with Dan at work. There were a few kids by that time, too. Then out of the blue he says he and Laura are splitting up and he starts up with an older woman in the bakery department. Looking back now they probably had something going on prior to the divorce. I'm assuming he was cheating and Laura kicked him to the curb when she found out."

"Then he must not have been as happy with Laura as you thought he was," Lindsay said.

"I don't know. I'm not Dan. This is all from my perspective on the outside looking in. Just like you all are looking at Kari's marriage. Maybe Laura and Kari are both raging bitches to their husbands when no one else is around to see it. Or maybe they're both the best wives a man could ever hope for. I've seen seemingly happy spouses cheat and I've seen miserable couples remain hopelessly devoted to each other till death did they part."

"What happened to Dan and the older woman?" Julia asked.

"I'm not sure. They both eventually left the store for other jobs. I guess they're still together. He seemed as happy with her as he'd been with Laura."

Both women silently considered what Denny had said. Lindsay did so as she picked the last of her nail polish off. Julia turned to look at James as if she could read on her spouse's forehead whether or not he would ever do the same to her. Denny noticed Julia's hands were once again at a small pendant hanging from her necklace. She always wore it and occasionally, and seemingly unconsciously, would rub her finger over a small engraving on the back. He wondered if the necklace had religious significance or if the act of touching the engraving was merely a nervous habit. Satisfied with whatever information she'd gleaned from the sight of James in his chair reading, Julia turned back towards the ocean.

"You've got a bite," she said.

Denny scrambled to his feet. He was relieved to have finally gotten a bite, but he was more relieved to leave the conversation with the women.

"James would never..." Julia began to say as he walked towards his straining fishing line and pole and out of range of their discussion. He found it interesting she hadn't started with "We would never," or "James and I would never," instead of mentioning only James.

. . .

That evening, Denny was out on the back patio at the fish-cleaning station prepping the five bluefish he'd caught for their dinner that night. James had gone out for a run while the women and children enjoyed one last night in the house's impressive game room.

He'd just started to run the recently sharpened fillet knife through the first fish when Lindsay screeched from inside causing him to jump. It all happened so quickly he didn't even realize what he'd done until he noticed the fleshy pad of this thumb flop away from his hand when he went to make another cut. The weight of the chunk of flesh strained against the small amount of skin struggling to keep it attached to his thumb.

Denny grabbed a clean towel hanging nearby and wrapped his thumb to contain the gushing blood while he assessed the situation. The nearest hospital was almost an hour away and he didn't want to spend what little time they had left of their vacation in a packed ER waiting for someone to give him a few stitches.

With his uninjured hand he walked up the deck steps and slid open the glass doors to pop his head in the house. "Is everything okay?" he asked, noting the irony that he was likely the only one who was not okay.

"Denny!" Lindsay called from the billiard room. "Jason was just arrested on drug charges. They're posting his position now and the DM wants me to apply. I'm going to be a store manager!" As she was yelling Denny could hear her bounding through the rooms and hallways towards him.

Her eyes widened even more when she saw the bloody towel wrapped around Denny's hand. "Oh my god. Are you okay? That's a lot of blood."

"What?" Julia called. Her steps sounded closer as curiosity led her partially through the maze of halls and rooms towards the sliding patio door.

Lindsay called back to Julia, "Denny cut his hand. He's fine but I need to take him to the ER. Can you watch the kids and make sure they eat? Maybe order a pizza or something." Lindsay added after she spied the blood-soaked fish out on the prep station below them.

Lindsay was inspecting Denny's wrapped thumb when he cupped her cheek and chin with his good hand and raised her head up to meet his gaze. "Store manager. I'm so proud of you."

She blushed slightly then turned the situation back to his injury. "Thanks, hon. But you know we need to go to the ER, right?"

He sighed. "Whatever you say, boss. Can I drive?"

She rolled her eyes at the "boss" comment and reached into the deep pockets of his cargo shorts to grab his keys.

"Absolutely not."

JULIA, OCTOBER 2019

Julia did not want to follow James into the house after he'd yelled at her and stormed off. Instead, she walked back to her car to retrieve the contact information from Shaina, the woman who hit her car just thirty minutes earlier. Was it fair to put all the blame on Shaina? Technically they'd hit each other. James would say she's as culpable as Shaina. Usually in this sort of situation she could always rely on Lindsay to have her back. She'd say something like, "That trailer-trash bitch had it coming. I'm proud of you Jules; you were a badass standing up to her like that. Fuck James." She missed her best friend already.

Julia opened the passenger door and grabbed the crumpled remains of an old Go Burger bag that had Shaina's information scrawled across the back. The handwriting and random capitalization reminded her of Alexis's first attempts at writing back in elementary school. As she slammed the door shut, she almost backed up into Denny. He was quite the two-hundred-pound ninja since she hadn't heard him approaching. Seeing him right behind her startled her; Julia quickly turned and stepped back towards the car slamming the base of her spine into the door handle in her rush to put distance between herself and Denny.

"Holy shit, Denny," she breathed, clutching the bag to her chest with one hand and reaching to soothe her newly bruised back with the other. "How long have you been out here?" She looked around down the street and to the neighboring yards to see if anyone else had seen or heard her and James's very public argument. It was too late in the morning for the three walking witches of Scarlet Oaks Knoll, but one could never be sure in a tight-knit community such as this one.

Denny took a step back and lowered his head a bit. "I'm sorry. I didn't mean to scare you."

Julia's adrenaline inched its way back down for the third time that morning. "I'm just a little jumpy. I was in a minor car accident this morning." Julia noticed Denny's eyes started to widen and so she quickly added, "I'm fine. Not a big deal. At all. But obviously James and I don't agree about that." As soon as she said it Julia wished she could take it back. James would kill her if he heard her discussing their argument with a neighbor. Even if it was Denny Moore. Especially if it was with Denny Moore, a male neighbor and somewhat friend to James. "Anyway. What's up?"

"Nothing. I was going to start to set up for the party; James was supposed to meet me out front. I'm guessing that's not happening any time soon now." Denny looked back to the garage and then to Julia again. "Are you okay?"

Denny's sudden concern for her was out of character with their usual interactions. An obvious physical injury, like a tumble during one of their annual ski trips was one thing. Denny would be there in a heartbeat. But they didn't do emotional concern for each other. Lindsay and James were the same way. Denny took another step back. He seemed embarrassed that he had initiated what could be a very personal conversation.

"Really. I'm fine." She almost left it at that but something about his face and eyes made her want him to stay. She wanted to talk to him, mainly because he was the only person around, about what had happened with James, and what was currently happening with Lindsay. "I was just about to go get some coffee and run an errand or two for the party. Want to keep me company?"

When Denny didn't immediately respond Julia added, "Never mind. I know you have a million things to do with a sudden surprise party tonight and moving your entire life this week - "

"Coffee's good," Denny said before Julia could finish her babbling stream of consciousness. "I can drive. The extra space in the back of the SUV is good for errands." Denny nodded towards the black 4Runner in his open garage.

"Perfect. Thanks," Julia said. She shoved the nasty, crumpled bag to the bottom of her purse. The call to the insurance company could wait until Sunday, or maybe even Monday depending on how the weekend went.

The two climbed in and started to get settled with seat belts and the radio. As if reading her mind, Denny brought up Lindsay, "Lindsay left a little after you did."

Julia nodded. She had assumed as much since very little stood in the way of whatever goals and plans Lindsay made for the day. Julia's defiant and childish behavior was merely a blip on Lindsay's radar, if that.

"I know she puts on a tough front, but she was hurt when you left without her."

"Nope," Julia said as she undid her seatbelt. She had wanted to eventually broach the subject of why she'd driven off and how she was feeling about the move, but she'd wanted to do it on her terms. She'd also been hoping for empathy rather than accusations - especially from someone like Denny who was the most empathetic person she knew.

"Now hold on…" Denny gently coaxed as he reached out to her. Julia had expected him to grab her arm as James sometimes did, and as she saw him do with Lindsay once before. But instead, he touched the back of his hand to her forearm as if intentionally not grabbing her while still offering her some sort of non-threatening physical contact. Had he grabbed her, Julia would have yanked her arm away and slammed the car door behind her. This light, familiar touch, from Denny of all people, caught her off guard and she remained seated.

"I'm sorry. We don't have to talk about it. We can talk about whatever you want, or we can silently coexist the whole time. Whatever you prefer," he offered. Julia turned her head and they caught eyes again. His eyes looked hopeless, and she was sure he could see her expression move from anger to sadness as well. She nodded her head and put her seatbelt back on. If things got too weird or if he started verbally attacking her again, she could always call James for a ride. Maybe not James. She could Uber home if she needed to.

He didn't ask her where she wanted to go for coffee, and she didn't speak up when he passed the only Starbucks in their little town. The radio softly played the greatest hits of the nineties, two thousands, and today, while Denny watched the road and Julia stared out the window at the passing houses and businesses. In the next town over Denny pulled into an indie coffee shop with only a few patrons scattered throughout the quaint dining area. It was an ideal place for them to talk, though she wondered about the quality of the coffee when there weren't many customers.

Julia ordered her coffee and then turned to see Denny

was already seated at a table. "Is their coffee lethal? Is that why you're not getting one?" Julia questioned as she sat in the seat across from him.

"I already had a cup this morning and lately that's my limit."

Julia gave a meek nod. There was an awkward silence while they waited for her order to come up. Denny had already said something that caused her to bolt. He likely saw her as a flight risk and remained silent in an effort to mitigate that risk.

Julia imagined a movie-cliche car scene where she stormed down the street yelling, "Just leave me alone," over her shoulder. Meanwhile, Denny slowly drove behind her and begged her to get back into the car before he gave up and peeled off leaving her, the miffed female protagonist, on the side of the road with her morals and pride intact but with no way home. She didn't expect it to come to that; the whole scenario didn't fit their personalities or their relationship.

Business was slow so it didn't take long for them to call her name. She hoped she didn't look too awkward when she shot up out of her seat and tripped on the leg of her chair in her haste to get her drink and to escape the silence. Julia returned with her coffee, a large French vanilla with extra sugar and cream, and she took a large sip of the scalding hot goodness. Despite its lethal temperature, the effect of the coffee on her body was immediate and orgasmic as it flowed through her veins.

"I don't know where to start," Julia said after taking a few more sips.

"Me either," said Denny as he fiddled with a sugar packet from the holder on the table.

"Well…," Julia ventured, "you can start by telling me when all of this happened. I helped Lindsay organize the community yard sale in August. The neighborhood had gone a few years without it, and she'd insisted we resurrect the annual tradition. I clearly remember it was her idea to do it. At the time she'd said she was desperate to clean out the garage and basement, but now I'm thinking she was just getting rid of all the junk she didn't want to move."

"No," Denny said. "Well, I don't think so." He seemed to be searching for the right words to finish his thoughts. "Lindsay and I haven't discussed moving. Ever. All our talk about the future has been here. In this town, and specifically, in our current house. We just renovated our master bath this past spring. And we only thought of ourselves when we did it. Not resale values or potential buyer preferences."

Julia nodded slightly as if conceding to the idea that verbal future plans to remain in their house and a bathroom remodel proved Lindsay was likely being impulsive and hadn't been hiding secret plans for the past year or so.

Denny continued, "Lindsay mentioned a few weeks ago some big things were happening at her work. Changes in management above her meaning her new district and regional managers may want to make some changes as well. But when we talked about it, she said she was ready to walk if they tried to force her to relocate. She'd promised me work wasn't going to consume her the way it has in the past."

"How's that promise working out?" Denny ignored the rhetorical question and Julia allowed herself to get lost in her own thoughts for a bit as she sipped her coffee. "Can they force store managers to relocate? Why would they even want to do that?"

Denny shrugged. Although he clearly knew the basics about his wife's career, Julia was aware Lindsay didn't talk about it much with him and rarely went into specifics about what she did. According to Lindsay, neither spouse talked too much about work. There were other more interesting things to discuss and both of them preferred to leave whatever work issues they were having at work, at work. Their places of work being Lindsay's store and Denny's home office since he worked from home. Once they left those areas, they left work problems there as well.

Denny cleared his throat. "Yes, they can make managers change stores. They do it sometimes, according to Lindsay, to find a better match for the store managers and the stores they're running." He looked around and lowered his voice slightly. "You can't tell Lindsay I told you this. She would kill me. I know last night she made it seem like the move was her idea and would benefit her, but it's not. Whatever is going on with her at work, it's not her choice. But you know how Lindsay is. She doesn't want anyone to know she's struggling. It's hard enough being a female manager at a hardware store. Most people already assume she can't hack it before they even see her in action."

Julia sat back in her seat and took in the new information Denny provided.

"I was mad last night, too." Denny looked embarrassed remembering his public argument with Lindsay. "She said she would walk if they tried to make her move. But I was wrong to try to force her to leave a job she loves. I can write anywhere. She won't necessarily find another store management position like the one she already has." Denny's eyes met Julia's again. "Lindsay defines herself with her work. She would be lost without it, so she'll do whatever it takes to hold on to the position she's achieved."

Julia's hatred towards Lindsay was decreasing by the second. Her friend was struggling with this just as much as they all were; Lindsay just refused to let anyone see that side of her. Julia felt a little guilty remembering how she'd left Lindsay in the driveway that morning and sped off to her impending doom at Go Burger. She ran her hand through her short hair and twisted the small jade pendant hanging from her necklace. It was something she did as a slight stall tactic before doing whatever it was she didn't want to do, or whenever she was feeling guilty about something. James had pointed the poker tell out to her years ago and she's been acutely aware of it ever since. "I should have known Linds wouldn't just up and leave like that. I shouldn't have driven off this morning. Is she okay?"

"I have no idea." Julia's heart hurt for Denny as his eyes, devoid of any certainty and hope, gazed into hers. "She won't let me in anymore. I don't know what I've done to make her feel she has to hide from me as well. Or maybe it's narcissistic to think I have anything to do with it. But for whatever reason, she has a wall up around me, too. I know she hurts, gets embarrassed, feels anxious, and so on. But she never lets me see it anymore. I haven't seen her cry in years."

Lindsay had built the same wall with Julia, so she wasn't surprised to hear about it from Denny. Though she was surprised to hear there was a permanent wall around Lindsay that no one was able to penetrate. How was that even possible? To stay guarded at all times and keep up the pretense that everything was perfect even when it was all falling apart.

"I haven't told anyone this. Ever. Please keep this between us."

"It's okay, Denny. I'm not going to say anything to Lindsay. I get it." She wanted to hear more but she didn't want to push him. His one leg was already bouncing up and down at an impressive pace. Julia could feel the vibrations through the floor and her own chair.

"I can't handle another coffee of my own," Denny said. He stopped shaking his leg and looked a little embarrassed at his public display of anxiety. "Do you mind if I get a sip of yours?

I just need a little something to take the edge off, but a full cup will send me over the edge, and I don't have time or the mental capacity to indulge right now."

Had Lindsay and James not shared dozens of drinks in the past, Julia may have hesitated with the implied intimacy of the request. But as soon as Denny asked, a vision of Lindsay tasting each of James's fall beers last Halloween flashed across her mind. Lindsay's bright red lips closed around the mouth of the bottle before she handed it back to James who then placed his lips in the exact spot where hers had just been. Besides, she and Denny weren't strangers. Even though the coffee house conversation was the most they'd ever talked without spousal chaperones or kids running around, he was still like family. Like a brother.

"Sure," Julia said as she slid her cup across the table to Denny.

Denny took off the lid and helped himself to a generous gulp of coffee before replacing the lid and sliding the cup back to Julia. He looked like he was ready to head out, so Julia tried to make small talk to keep him at the table. To see if eventually he would circle back to Lindsay and the move. He'd already discussed it, but Julia was sure there was more to it.

"How'd you know about this place?" Julia asked.

Denny looked around as if to confirm they were still in the coffee house. "I come here to write sometimes. More so when the kids were younger and needed more attention. I came here to get away from it all. But lately it's been relatively quiet at the house. I haven't needed to come here much."

"The stereotypical writer tapping out his next best-seller in an indie coffee house. Sounds about right. So, how is your writing going lately? I feel like the last time we celebrated a publication was back when the kids were tiny little things."

"It's been a while since I've published under my real name. After I finished the *Time and Again* series I wanted to get away from sci-fi; try my hand at another genre." He shook his leg a bit again and looked around the coffee house before settling his eyes back on hers.

Julia slowly nodded her head as if to say, "And...please continue..."

Somewhat reluctantly Denny added, "So I did, but I didn't want any connection to my old work. I created a pen name and even used someone else's image in my author bio."

"Really? How many books have you published as your alter ego?"

"Six."

"Shall I beg for more details or, as an author and lover of words, can you be a little more verbose when describing your work?"

"Nope. I don't even discuss it with Lindsay."

"I'm not Lindsay."

"You'd laugh."

"It's a comedy? Are you writing rom coms now? I love to read rom coms. Now you really have to tell me. I tried to read *Time and Again* but sci-fi is not my thing. To be honest, I felt pretty dumb trying to keep up with all the technical details and had to put it down before I even hit the halfway mark."

"Still a hard no. You ready to go? I know you said you wanted Lindsay to help you get something for Liv. We can go do that if you'd like." Denny was already out of his seat and ready to move on. Julia couldn't tell if it was discomfort from making small talk with her, talking about his book, or just sitting still in general. The man did shake his leg a lot and seemed hard pressed to sit in one place for a long time. How on earth did he ever decide to become a writer and sit and type at a desk all day?

"Really? You have a few ideas of what Liv wants? Because I gotta tell you, James is the last person I would ever trust when picking out gifts for Alexis. At least that's how it's been since she stopped asking for toys." Julia gathered her drink and the few bits of trash they'd accumulated, and they started to make their way back to the car.

This time the overall mood in the car was lighter. Denny turned up the music and they chatted as he navigated effortlessly through the back roads of the neighboring town. A few miles later, Denny pulled up to a used bookstore.

"Liv doesn't think it's cool and hides it from everyone, like mother like daughter, but she loves to read and write. She's on a banned book binge right now tearing through *Catcher in the Rye* and *The Color Purple* in the last week alone." Denny continued to talk as they walked up the sidewalk and entered the small building with a ding of the bell. "A few weeks back she asked me about *Nathan's Run*. Some book she overheard her teachers discussing that was being re-released with toned down language. She and I got into this whole debate about censorship and appropriate language and topics for different ages."

"You were debating censorship with her? Do you think books should be banned?" Julia was intrigued and wanted to hear an author's perspective on it. They wove through the crowded stacks with Denny leading the way.

"More like playing devil's advocate. It doesn't seem right to have a concrete, black and white, yes or no stance on book banning - something that deals with controlling what other people do or do not experience and learn about. I wanted her to make up her own mind." Denny led Julia to a back corner with five shelves on each wall. Above the shelves was a handwritten, but still professional-looking, sign with the words, *Banned Books*. "Here it is," Denny said with a slight flourish of his arms.

"*Nathan's Run*," Julia repeated. "I've never heard of it." There were five tattered copies on the shelf, so she grabbed the one that looked the least used and flipped through the pages.

"Hold up; not that one," Denny said. He grabbed a different *Nathan's Run* and flipped open the cover, then repeated the process again and again until he got to the last book. "Here, this is the one." He proffered the book with the front cover open. Inside she saw it was an old schoolbook from Liv's private school.

"Property of Sacred Heart Academy," she read. "How did it end up here?" Julia took the book from Denny and ran her fingers over the old stamp as she read the different names of the various students who'd had the book throughout the decades. The last name, Larry Henderson, had 1997 written next to it and the word *good* scrawled under the column labeled condition.

"Hard to say. I'm guessing this kid, Larry, never turned it back in. When I looked it up online it said the book was banned the next year. They probably didn't bother harassing poor Larry here to return it and he decided to sell it when he graduated and moved out of his parents' house. Or maybe his parents sold it. Though I don't think it's very ethical of the store to buy it when it clearly wasn't Larry's to begin with."

"That's really cool, Denny. A book that was banned from her school. Why don't you give it to her?" Julia held the book back out to him.

Denny took only a small step away from her before his back hit another shelf. "Nope. It's all yours. Lindsay insists she take care of all of the kids' birthday gifts each year and she doesn't like doing individual gifts from the parents. The whole united front thing, I guess." Denny was still eyeing up the book. He was too nice of a guy for Lindsay. He refused to rock the marriage boat over a present, but he was too excited about the present to not get it to Liv some other way.

Denny sighed. "Anyway. I had planned to sneak it under the Christmas tree this year. Now I'm not so sure it will matter as much when she's not attending the same school district as the stamp on the cover. Best to give it to her today while it still has a strong connection to her current school."

Julia was surprised to feel that sharp pain in her heart again. It was just as punctuated and severe as the first time she'd heard about the move the night before. When was time going to start to ease the pain of losing her friends? They hadn't even left yet. What she was feeling wasn't even the worst of what was to come once their car drove away for good in a few days. Even Denny. Now that she'd had such a good morning with him, she wasn't ready to let him go either. It was impossible to imagine someone new, someone not Denny in the same situation with her and helping her to pick out a birthday gift.

"Okay. I'll get it for her. Thanks." Julia turned to make her way back to the front of the store but stopped short when she noticed the dark blue velvet curtains hanging in a doorway next to the banned books section. In equally lovely print was a sign above the doorway that said, *All Things Dirty.* With a devilish grin she turned to look back at Denny who looked back at her with trepidation.

"No," he said shaking his head at her. But she was already pulling back the curtain with one hand, and casually pulling him in with her with the other hand. Even though he had verbally protested, his body made no effort to resist the gentle tug of her hand in his.

Once inside, she realized what a mistake she had made. For one thing, she was still holding Denny's hand which was weird enough as it was. They had rarely touched prior to that morning, and suddenly they were sharing drinks and holding hands as they ducked into the naughty book section of the store. It was too much too soon. She stood frozen in the middle of the tiny room, likely a former closet, with half-naked men and women on the covers overflowing each shelf. And she was there with Denny.

If sex sells, the tiny section of real estate must have been the money-maker of the store. The rest of the store, and every other bookstore or library she'd ever been in, had books lined up on shelves with their spines pointed out. Here and there, when room allowed, popular books were front faced with the cover, rather than the spine, showing from the shelf. All Things Dirty had nothing but front facing books, similar to how Blockbuster and old-school video stores back in the day would shelve their movies to show as many full covers as they could. No wonder there was a velvet curtain and a warning sign; some of the covers would have made *Playboy* spreads look conservative and amateurish in comparison.

In her periphery she saw Denny snicker as he took in her immediate discomfort. His hand, still warm and casually holding hers, gave a gentle squeeze as if asking her if she were okay. She could feel a tiny raised line along his thumb and wondered if it was from the infamous OBX fillet incident of 2010.

"First time in the adult section of a bookstore?" Denny teased. "Just give it a minute and you'll get used to the onslaught of skin and cleavage assaulting your eyes."

She cocked one eyebrow at him and asked, "Come here often?" He was right. Once she had time to take it in, she felt much better. She reluctantly (*why was she reluctant?* she wondered) let go of Denny's hand and stepped up to one of the shelves that specialized in what she could only assume was erotic historical romance. Brush up on your history and anatomy all at once; two birds with one book.

"I've been in a few times," Denny admitted as he casually perused the shelf next to her. They were at different shelves, but their arms still brushed against one another in the small closet-like section. He picked up a novel with a shirtless man on the cover. The half-naked man held a golf club over his muscular shoulder and was embracing what appeared to be a topless female golfer. Her nipples strategically covered by his arm and her skirt so short it revealed the bottom of her tan, toned ass. "Mostly sex but with a little golf thrown in as a bonus," he said.

Julia's eyes widened and she whispered, "You've read it?" The whole trip with Denny had turned into an eye-opening experience for her.

"This one? No, I hate golf. But a few..." Denny put the book back down. When he saw Julia open her mouth to speak, he quickly added, "I will never say which ones. I'm a writer. Sci-fi is my favorite, but I read a little bit of everything."

"Oh my god," Julia said. "You started writing smutty sci-fi romance. Didn't you?"

Denny turned bright red. "We should head back to help set up for the party." He was out of the room and up at the register in record time. Julia grabbed a random book from the shelf. It had a scantily clad woman kneeling on the cover and three shirtless, muscular guys standing behind her. Then she scurried to catch up to Denny as she fished through her disorganized purse for her wallet.

"You're really not going to tell me?" she asked Denny as the clerk rang her up.

"No."

Julia turned to the clerk and asked, "Do you own this store?"

The clerk, a middle-aged woman with curly red hair with streaks of silver throughout brushed a ringlet of silver curls from her face as if in an effort to get a better look at Julia. The woman's green eyes studied Julia through thick black glasses with a chain around her neck to keep her from losing them. A few seconds passed before she responded with little interest. "Yes, I'm the owner."

"Great. Is this one of your All Things Dirty authors?" This got the attention of the two other customers in the tiny store. They stopped what they were doing and looked at Denny and then at the owner, curious to see her response.

"Are you asking me if I can recognize every author in the All Things Dirty section of the store?"

"Well, when you say it like that it sounds a bit unrealistic. But if you *could* recognize every author that would be pretty impressive."

The owner looked at Denny who was wearing slightly ill-fitting jeans, a 2004 concert tee, and well-worn sneakers. She sneered a little. "No, I don't recognize him. I also very much doubt this man writes anything filthy enough to land back there."

Denny mocked a look of offense with a hand to his chest to emphasize his disbelief. Julia then looked him up and down as well before she said, "I guess you're right. Thanks for the books. You have a lovely store."

As they walked to the car Denny said, "I see you got *Manly Defenders*. Are you really going to read that?"

"Absolutely. I'm intrigued. In fact, I think I'll read a few passages on the car ride home."

Julia needed only to flip to the second chapter before she got to the main action of the book. The protagonist was a sexy CIA agent on a secret mission with three bodyguards to keep her safe. A few chaotic events in chapter one had one of the manly defenders narrowly escape death. This logically led to chapter two where all four characters were having passionate sex in some secret underground bunker. Julia wasn't sure what kind of plot she'd expected, but that wasn't it.

For some reason she couldn't quite put her finger on, Julia felt compelled to read the juicy details out loud to see if she could make Denny blush again. Why not? They were friends and happily married. It's not like anything was going to happen between them. In some ways they felt like brother and sister. Not that Julia could imagine reading smut to her actual brother. But still, it was all harmless fun. Right?

"Oh, yes. This is it. I've found the good stuff a mere twenty pages in. Listen to this," she said as she fought back giggles. "It was my fault Smith took that bullet to his bulging bicep. I hadn't heeded their warnings, and now Smith was seriously injured. I was the only culpable member of our party of four. Johnson and Cooperman were deep in conversation about the forbidden map we'd found, so I made my way over to Smith to see if there was anything I could do to make him feel better."

"Uh, oh," Denny said with a huge grin. "I bet I know what's going to make him feel better."

"You're absolutely right, Denny. She's about to get real creative with her apology. Go the long way home so I have enough time to get through this scene." Denny obliged with a left turn and bought them another ten minutes of drive time.

Julia began again in a high-pitched and breathy voice as she tried to get into character, "I hadn't meant to kiss his shoulder. It just happened. He had his shirt off to take care of his wound, and instinctively I wanted to kiss him to make everything okay again. I tried to pull away once I realized how inappropriate I was being, but he firmly grabbed my chin and turned my face back towards him. Our eyes met and then he was crushing my mouth with his. His tongue searching every part of my mouth.

"It was a hot, sensual kiss that left me desperate for more.

When we finally parted I became distinctly aware of the fact that Johnson and Cooperman were still in the room with us. I looked over expecting to see disapproval and disgust on their faces. I was sure they'd be shocked to see such unprofessional behavior between Smith and me. But instead, they both looked turned on, maybe even jealous that I was making out with Smith instead of them.

"I physically distanced myself a bit more from Smith and was about to tell him it all had been a mistake and that this was all completely out of line given our mission and our positions. Smith must have read my mind. Before I had a chance to say anything, he grabbed my hand and held it tight. His eyes pierced mine when he said, 'Let them watch if they want to.' I glanced back over at Johnson and Cooperman and they both did look very interested in watching what was about to go down in the bunker. Interested in watching me go down on Smith."

Julia continued to read the seedy details of the foursome after just barely escaping death and having only met the day before.

"Whew," Denny said when Julia had finished. "That escalated quickly."

Julia suppressed her giggles and put on her most serious face. "Are you writing smut, Denny?"

"No. You think I can come up with that? How many different words did the author use for penis during the blow job scene? Some I'd never even heard before." Julia thought he would leave it at that. They were almost home, anyway. She was pleasantly surprised when he said, "I will admit that since my sci-fi series concluded, I've been pressured to include more explicit sex scenes in my books. Sex sells, which you proved today with your purchase of *Manly Defenders*, but I have no interest in writing pure erotica. I guess you could say I'm writing something between what you read there and what I wrote in *Time and Again*." He turned into their development and Julia put the book back into her bag so James and the kids wouldn't see it.

It took a decade, but Julia and Denny had finally become actual friends. Not just people who made polite conversation because they shared a properly line and a mutual interest in Lindsay. It was exactly what Julia had needed after the rough night before, and the disastrous morning which followed.

They were friends to the point where Julia was disappointed her outing with Denny was over. She had to pull up her big-girl pants to go back into her house and deal with the insurance company and James. She needed to finish setting up the house for the very last Herrick and Moore Halloween extravaganza. Changing back to a serious tone, Denny turned and looked at Julia after he pulled the key from the ignition. "Are you going to be okay?"

"Yeah. I'm fine. Thanks for this morning and for the gift idea."

"My pleasure." Before Julia could get out of the car, Denny added, "Do you think you could do me a favor? Please?"

Julia kept a smile on her face, but her mind wrestled with the idea that maybe Denny intentions weren't as altruistic as she'd thought, and their adventure that morning had actually been some sort of ploy. "Maybe. Depends on what it is," Julia said.

"Be nice to Lindsay. I know you're hurt. We all are. But Lindsay is, too. I know it. Despite whatever show she puts on tonight, and from her actions last night and this morning I guarantee it will be the biggest Lindsay show we've ever experienced, remember this isn't her choice. She's trying to put on a good face. I also know she's probably scared as hell to tell the kids they're changing schools and need to make all new friends."

Julia nodded. "Sure," she said as she opened the door and climbed out of the vehicle. She called back to him as she crossed the yard back to her house, "Thanks, Denny." She saw him wave just before he was out of sight and moving towards his own house.

7

DENNY, JULY 2012

The fearless leaders of the HOA all stood on the curb in front of Laura's house on Larkley Lane. Laura likely wanted some distance from herself and the ground the peons around her stood on, but also didn't want too much heigh since she already towered over most everyone there.

Her lackeys, Mandy and Mary Jane, were perfect mini clones of Laura with their matching bright red fake smiles and Lilly Pulitzer dresses. In his defense, Denny only knew the brand because Lindsay had already scoffed and commented to Denny at the sight of Laura and her cronies' attire.

Despite Laura's passive aggressive digs at multiple members of the development, most of the neighborhood wore fake smiles back as they crowded in the street for the annual Scarlet Oaks Knoll Chili Cook-Off Block Party. Each year on the third Saturday of July, homeowners throughout Scarlet Oaks Knoll brought their favorite chili recipes (or sides and beverages) to compete against their fellow neighbors for the title of Chili Master.

Denny felt sweat trickling down his neck and back from

having Hailey sitting on his shoulders to get a better view. He hoped it was sweat. Hailey had had a few accidents recently though mostly at night while in a deep sleep.

Liv was off with Alexis, Brice, and a few others running around a bubble-making machine set up a couple houses down from Laura's. Laura didn't want children running around her yard and trampling on her prized zebra plants. She was known to conduct a small ceremony each summer when it was warm enough to transplant the flower back into her flower beds, and then again each fall when it was too cool and she needed to rescue and relocate the plant back to the safety of her living room.

Lindsay was with Julia and a small group of women, pinochle members, he assumed, sorting out dishes and cutlery on the tables set out. Laura and Co. ran all the events in Scarlet Oaks Knoll, so one of the three should have been at the tables helping to arrange and coordinate. He couldn't tell if Laura and Co. felt above the responsibility, or if they were intimidated by Lindsay's leadership. When he looked over at the tables, he saw Lindsay at the helm pointing here and there with curt instructions as she walked up and down the tables, taking it all in.

He had to look away before he got too excited at the image of his confident and capable wife. He'd have to be careful not to eat too much or to eat chili that was too spicey if he wanted a shot at having his way with her later that night. The year before he'd had terrible gas all night and she's made him sleep in the guest bedroom. There were a few notably good chefs in the neighborhood, the Herrick's being amongst the best of the best, but no chili was worth passing up a night with Lindsay.

Denny caved and looked back again at Lindsay. She was wearing tight white pants (a daring choice for a chili cook-off) flip-flops, and a silky dark blue top. When he looked over, she happened to be bent over to inspect the contents of a cooler on the ground. And that was all it took. Even with Laura's screeching voice nagging about the importance of a stable and supportive community, Denny's dick still jumped at the sight of his wife in such a compromising position. He kept one hand on Hailey's ankle to hold her in place and used the other to adjust his pants. He couldn't imagine the shaming he'd get from Laura if she caught him with a hard-on during the family-friendly chili cook-off.

When the speeches were finished, five in total, the then famished audience bee-lined for the food tables. In what looked from a scene from the *Lord of the Flies*, it was survival of the fittest at its finest. Older siblings tripped younger siblings even though it was a hard fall on the asphalt. Some spouses divvied up responsibilities, one would tend to the hurt child in the street and the other made plates for the family, while others merely called over their shoulder, "You're okay. Brush it off," to their wounded offspring while they hustled for a better position in line.

No one officially handed out serving roles so Lindsay unofficially took the position to keep everything running smoothly and with some sense of organization. Lindsay and the pinochle crew set up and then remained at the food tables to help the smaller children get what they needed, kept cutlery and stacks of plates available, and manned dishing out some of the food.

Denny went through the line with Hailey still on his shoulders. They played a game where he would point to different items and she would tug his right ear if she wanted some or his left ear if she didn't want any. Every now and then Denny tried to scare her by turning his head quickly and nipping at her hands. She squealed in delight each time and he could feel her hesitation in her light grip of his ears and hear it in her nervous giggles.

When he got to Lindsay, he asked her if she'd eaten yet and if she needed anything.

"No, we all made up plates while Mandy went on and on about nothing at all." Lindsay put a smile back on as she helped a little boy open up his bag of chips. Then she looked back at Denny and Hailey and said, "I gave our plates to James to take to the table. We'll be over in a few minutes. The line is just about finished."

Not long after, they were all eating at one of the many folding tables which had been brought out to the middle of the street for the party. James had already surrounded himself with the kids since he had most of their food plates while Denny found himself sandwiched between Julia and Lindsay.

"Trina's offered to house the kids in her yard for the rest of the evening so the adults can relax a bit," Lindsay said. Trina and Het had a large, fenced in yard with a state-of-the-art play set and a handful of trees that were perfect for climbing.

"Trina, Het," Denny called out to table next to them, "Thank you for letting our heathen children run amuck in your backyard. I'm sure the eye-in-the-sky is aware and she's proud of what supportive neighbors you are." The only reason he'd made the dig against Laura so loudly was because he noticed she ducked into her house a few minutes prior and wouldn't hear him directly. She'd certainly hear it from someone else, though he doubted she didn't already know the neighbors all jokingly called her that due to her keen observation skills when it came to anything happening in the neighborhood.

A few chuckles rose up from some of the neighbors, including James and Julia, while Lindsay suppressed her own grin and gave him a playful swat on the arm. "Can we not piss Laura off? Please? The last thing I need is one of them in our yard measuring our grass height or clocking when we put out and take in our trash."

The kids were still eating but they'd started to get restless once they heard about the giant playdate about to commence in one of the backyards. Hailey, in particular, was giving them a hard time. She'd barely eaten anything and was already a peanut compared to her counterpart, Brice. In all fairness Brice was at the other end of the spectrum and was in the 99th percentile in weight and height for his age while Hailey hung out in the low twenties.

Brice asked, "Why doesn't Hailey eat?" He really wanted to play but he didn't want to go without Hailey.

Before Denny could answer James scolded Brice for his rude behavior.

"It's okay," Denny said. "She's just a slow eater, Brice. She likes to eat a bit then wonder off and play for a while before settling down to eat some more."

Brice considered Denny's answer then asked, "Like a dog?"

Julia held back her smirk and Lindsay let out a belly laugh before she removed herself from the table. James was not amused; he chastised Brice again about his manners. He drilled Brice until he was certain Brice knew to never, ever compare a woman to a dog again, no matter how innocently he meant it. Hailey took a few more nibbles of her burger, brushed the crumbs from her hands, and announced, "I'm done. Let's go, Brice."

Denny caught Julia's eye for a moment and shared in her smirk before turning his attention back to his own food. He worked hard to keep Julia at a distance while still remaining polite and friendly. It was a gray area, and he was sure he was messing it up royally. Denny saw the hurt in her eyes when he ended conversations abruptly or distanced himself in general when it was just their two families. It hurt him, too, but it was a small price to pay to safeguard his marriage and family.

James asked Julia to dance to with him. Johnny D, a urologist by day and a dee-jay by night, had started to kick the party up a notch with some country songs Denny had never heard before.

"No one's dancing, James," Julia said.

"They will once we start. Besides, what do we care what everyone else is doing? I want to dance with my lovely wife. Are you really going to deny me?"

Denny busied himself with the small amount of food on his plate while the love birds went back and forth as to whether or not they would dance. The debate ended with the first chords of Garth Brooks singing "To Make You Feel My Love." Julia glanced over at Johnny D who looked back at them and gave James a wink.

"Did you bribe JD?" Julia asked James. She was already out of her seat and taking James's proffered hand.

James confirmed that he did indeed slip the dee-jay five big ones to play their wedding song and that he'd have paid one hundred if he'd needed to.

Lindsay returned and sat back down with Denny. "That's sweet. How come you didn't bribe Johnny to play our song and ask me to dance?"

"You want to dance?" Denny offered.

"Not when you ask like that, no." Lindsay said. She looked around to see if anyone from the HOA board was in sight before slipping a mini bottle of rum from her bag. She raised an eyebrow to Denny and he nodded his confirmation back.

She added a little to each of their cokes before slipping the bottle back into her bag.

"What happened to all your pinochle friends?" Denny asked her.

"Laura and Mary Jane busted most of them for sneaking booze into the party. They left to have their own shindig back at Maureen's. Josh is still here somewhere. I think he's playing cornhole. Want to join him?"

"No, I want to stay here with you."

"This is exactly where I want to be, too," Lindsay said with a tap of their red plastic cups.

They finished their drinks as they caught up. It was a rare and wonderful time when the kids were in eyesight but not interrupting them every few minutes.

Lindsay made them each another drink and their conversation melted into a comfortable silence amid the music and dull roar of voices and laughter from the party. Denny was looking out into the party when he broke the silence. "Are you ever disappointed that I'm not as romantic as James?" They both looked over at James who was expertly guiding Julia through different dances in the low light from the streetlamps.

Lindsay thought for a minute. "It gets to me sometimes. I wish you were, yes. But I'm very happy you're not a dick like James is. I'm pretty sure by comparison you and I are the winners when it comes to marital bliss."

He should have seen that coming. Lindsay could turn anything into a competition. Half the time she wasn't even competing against anyone else, just herself. And she was as vicious with herself as she was with any competitor.

Lindsay rested her head against Denny's shoulder as they listened to the music. Her free hand laid comfortably on his leg and she gently rubbed his inner thigh with her thumb. It was heaven.

Their moment was interrupted by Laura who was doing rounds as night started to fall. She was on the lookout for booze, drugs, and anything else she deemed inappropriate for a Scarlet Oaks block party. Lindsay double checked the bag to be certain nothing was sticking out then she fell back onto Denny's shoulder again. This time she gently bit his shoulder and kissed his cheek before laying her head down again.

They watched Laura walk away and assumed they were in the clear. Lindsay practically jumped into Denny's lap when Mandy called from behind them, "Save room for Jesus! Don't want couples to get too comfy when there are small, impressionable children around." She wagged her finger at them then went off to find and scold whoever just loudly swore during a heated cornhole match on the other side of the party.

"Save room for Jesus? What was that about?" Denny asked.

"I don't know. Some days I think we live in Eden with this neighborhood and with Julia and the kids next door. Then other days I want to pack our bags in the middle of the night and flee this crazy development with its rules and traditions."

"It's not *that* bad, is it?"

Lindsay ignored his question. "Let's dance," she said as she pushed back her chair and stood with a hand outstretched to Denny. He took it and then guided her with his hand on the small of her back onto the make-shift dance floor in the middle of the road. She did not leave any room for Jesus as they danced, and he was certain Jesus would not have approved of all the dirty things she said; nor would he have approved of the way she licked his neck when she thought no one was looking.

8
JULIA, OCTOBER 2019

Julia contemplated doing some outside decorating rather than going inside and seeing James. Whatever light feeling she'd achieved with Denny, it was officially gone once she was back in the real world at her house. She passed her dented car in the driveway, another subtle reminder of the disaster she fled that morning, and made her way through the garage into her house. Only salespeople used the front door. Everyone else knew to come in through the garage which was open 99% of the time.

"James?" she called as she made her way to the kitchen. The coffee hadn't done much to fill her up and she was suddenly starving. "James?" Still nothing. "Alexis? Brice?" Julia stood absolutely still as she listened for any responses or even footsteps in the house. James's truck was out front and there was a ton of stuff to do at the house, so she doubted they were out anywhere.

She turned to look out the window above the sink which overlooked the backyard. It was one of the things that made her fall in love with the house when they first saw it. She had pictured herself making dinner and occasionally checking out the window to see how the kids were getting along. And there they were. Over a decade after she'd first imagined it, she was looking out her favorite window and watching James and the kids stringing up lights around the deck and fire pit. Her perfect family.

Julia wondered how everything was going to go down with James. He was a hothead at times and she couldn't tell if he'd simply lost his temper earlier and would be over it, or if their argument was going to be drawn out all day and potentially even all weekend. It was impossible to tell because regardless of how angry he was with her, he was able to turn it off when he was around the kids. So even though he'd yelled at her a few hours earlier, he was nothing but smiles and jokes with the kids out back.

With more than a sliver of reluctance, she opened the window and called, "Hey, guys. I'm home." Three smiles looked back at her and she let out a sigh of relief.

James turned to the kids and said, "Alright, Lex and Brice. Don't let me down. I'm passing on the lights to you this year. You can do it. I need to talk to your mom for a bit. You have one hour to finish up here. Think you can handle it?" James had been speaking while walking backwards towards the house, so by the time he finished talking he already had his hand on the basement door.

"An hour? More like thirty minutes, Dad. And it's lights; even dummy Brice here can't mess it up too bad." Alexis teased. Julia heard a door slam and assumed James was in the basement and making his way up to see her.

Brice mumbled something to Alexis. He must have struck a nerve because her face tensed and she spat back something equally venomous, Julia was sure of it. "Hey! Not today, you two!" Julia called out as a warning. She then slammed the window shut before the kids could get themselves into any more trouble. They were good kids. They'd work out whatever tiff they were having on their own.

Before Julia could brace herself for James, he was already in the kitchen giving her a hug while saying how sorry he was about what had happened before. And before Julia could adjust to what was happening, the scene changed again to where James was kissing her neck and sliding his hand down her back and cupping her ass through her jeans.

"I just confirmed we have thirty uninterrupted minutes," James said in a husky voice.

Julia's body responded to James's and she struggled to push him away enough to see his face and look into his eyes. "What about earlier?"

"We'll talk about it later," James practically growled in more of a brutish way rather than a violent way. He was on her again kissing down her neck and starting to tug at the button of her jeans.

Julia's eyes closed and she let her head drop back a bit giving James even more access to her neck. She was vaguely aware that this was not acceptable to her. That she wanted to discuss it more and wanted to argue with him about how he'd left her earlier in the garage. But having sex and just forgetting any of that had happened was too tempting to her. She also hated to admit even secretly to herself that reading *Manly Defenders* earlier in the car had turned her on. She could use a release before the party.

"Mmmm, later," Julia agreed. She wriggled out of his arms and turned to make her way back to the bedroom.

She squealed with anticipation when James followed and slapped her ass saying, "Strip down, sexy."

James pulled on his jeans and grabbed a new sweatshirt from the closet. Julia took a little longer to recover as she laid in bed and enjoyed the residual effects of her intense orgasm. She looked up to see James taking her in. After almost two decades of marriage, she felt no need to cover up. He could stare at her naked body all he wanted. In fact, she frequently gave a quick 'thank you' to God that her husband still couldn't keep his hands off of her. James walked back over to the bed to give her a quick kiss. "We're good?" he asked.

Was that what the sex was? Make-up sex? A way to avoid the conversation that really should have happened? She already knew the answer because it wasn't the first time they'd had a quick, heated argument which was never resolved. Many arguments were covered up with sex and then classified as irrelevant though Julia didn't truthfully believe they could successfully continue to function that way. Simply brushing all the negative aspects of their marriage under a giant sex rug which would inevitably continue to grow from a bump, to a mound, to a mountain.

"We're good." Julia heard herself say. It was not a good day to hash out years and years of old arguments that were never settled. She had to deal with the Moores first. She and James could figure out their issues after the neighbors moved away. They're be plenty of time for that once her best friend was in another state.

"Good," James said with another kiss. He stood back up again and started to put his shoes back on. "Where did you and Denny go?"

"To get coffee and a gift for Liv," Julia said. She started to stir, too. No time to lay around in bed, and she knew she was pushing her luck with the kids. They had impeccable timing and she was certain one, or both, would be knocking on the door at any moment for whatever non-emergency they felt justified interrupting Mom and Dad's quiet time.

James nodded and said. "That was nice of him. You've never hung out just the two of you, have you?"

"No. It was a little odd at first just the two of us without Lindsay's conversation filling the void. But it was fine. He helped me pick out a thoughtful gift for Liv." She searched her wardrobe for something comfortable to wear while she was decorating and cleaning for the next four hours. She settled on sneakers with yoga pants and an Under Armor sweatshirt. "He's not too bad. He talks a lot more when Lindsay isn't around. Did you know he's published six books since he finished the *Time and Again* series?"

James smirked at her. "Yes. We've shared a dinner table with the Moores at least once a week. How did you *not* know that about Denny?"

Julia's shoulders slunk a little in acknowledgement that while Denny wasn't exactly screaming at the top of his lungs about his latest books, she hadn't asked him either. "Lindsay is always commandeering conversations. And before today, Denny's avoided me. You know that. I used to complain to you about it all the time. The only reason I stopped is that I finally accepted that Denny didn't like me and that was fine."

James shrugged. "I always thought that was a bit in your mind." He took note of Julia's quick dissension from blissful and glowing after sex to thoroughly annoyed by her husband and added, "You do that. A lot. Misread what's actually happening between you and someone else. Assume the worst like they don't like you or that you must have somehow offended them even though you didn't. It's hard to tell what's real and what's not."

A very loud voice in Julia's head said, *I don't do that* with all the attitude of a teenager. A much softer voice conceded immediately after with, *Maybe I do a little*. Regardless, it was not a good time for so much honesty. She debated going after one of his character flaws: anger issues, inability to work through arguments...she couldn't come up with any more at the moment, but she was sure there were more.

"Hey," he said, bringing her back out the black depths of her mind. He cupped her chin and raised it to him so he could kiss her again. One of the things she truly loved about James was his open adoration for her. Public affection, sweet comments regardless of the company, and undying commitment to her no matter what. "I love you," he reminded her. "We're good. We're going to get through this party tonight, we'll say goodbye to the neighbors next week, and then life will continue as it always has. You know that, right? This is not the tragedy you're making it out to be?"

Julia was almost placated, but James's last line was like a jab to the gut. She pulled back her face from his hand. "Can you acknowledge that my best friend is moving to another state and that I may be sad for more than a few hours? That's not me having exaggerated feelings. I'd say my reactions so far have been on point for what anyone else in a similar situation would feel." Before James could even mention the Go Burgers incident she beat him to it. "Aside from me purposefully hitting some stranger in a drive through who tried to cut me off." She said it quickly like a radio disclaimer as if that would somehow make it better or at the very least less damning.

Right on cue, one of the kids knocked on the door and broke the tension between them. "Dad, we need to put together the photobooth station out back. Can you help us? Brice is being annoying, and he won't do it right," Alexis's whiney voice drove nails into Julia's brain.

"Knock it off, Alexis. I'm sure you're part of the problem, too. Dad will be out in a minute," Julia called back through the closed door. She knew her response to Alexis was too harsh and she promised herself she would apologize later.

James gave an annoyed look at Julia before calling, "I'm coming now." No more kisses. He turned and walked out; he even closed the door behind him as if to tell her not to follow him.

"Hey," Lindsay called from the driveway, just outside the door of the garage.

Julia stood up and shook out her clothing a bit. She'd been on her hands and knees trying to clean out one of James's massive bison coolers. He used it for packing meat to bring home when he hunted, and it could get a little gross if he didn't thoroughly clean it out the last time he used it. It was probably fine given how careful and neat James was about his hunting equipment, but Julia didn't like the idea of filling it with drinks until she knew for sure that it was thoroughly cleaned of any deer carcass as well as any lingering odors.

Julia assessed Lindsay as if she were just meeting her. She had on tight fitting jeans and a corporate sweatshirt for Moyer's. Her long blonde hair was pulled back in a sloppy bun, but her make-up was on point. It always was on her days off since she didn't wear much make-up to work and she missed it. Denny was right. Lindsay was hurting, too. She always had good posture in general, but today especially Lindsay seemed to be holding herself a little higher than usual. As if standing up even taller could somehow get her above the unavoidable circumstances that were surrounding her. Somehow help her over whatever anger and sadness she was feeling.

"I'm sorry I drove off this morning," Julia offered. She hated herself as soon as the words left her mouth. For the first time in their friendship Lindsay actually looked like she may have something to be sorry about. Like maybe she wasn't always right; maybe Lindsay rather than Julia had something to be uncertain about when it came to their friendship. But instead of hearing out whatever Lindsay had rehearsed prior to making her way over, Julia immediately caved and took all the responsibility and blame.

As if Julia's admission of guilt gave Lindsay permission to enter the garage, Lindsay confidently stepped in and said, "It's okay. I mean, it was a bitchy move, but I get it. You guys are upset that we're leaving." Julia waited a beat for Lindsay to add that she and her family were upset as well and that it was actually their family who was leaving and causing the change and hurt.

So many comebacks and accusations flooded Julia's mind, but she couldn't bear to say any of them. Was it because she didn't want to ruin what little time she had left with Lindsay, or was it because old habits died so hard? Another factor was that she couldn't bring herself to confront people even if she'd felt slighted or wronged. She had tried once that morning and it ended horrifically. Julia had nothing but regrets and she didn't feel like she'd won anything. The whole point of the crash earlier had been that she didn't want people to walk all over her anymore. To feel like they could treat her badly and she would just accept it. Standing up for herself had yielded nothing positive, and so there she was rolling over again.

At a loss for any other options, she went with what she knew: Ignoring the bad behavior and acting as if everything was fine in order to keep an even keel. Julia even wondered if she had had any reason to drive off like the way she did earlier in the morning. Maybe Lindsay was being the bigger person brushing off Julia's bad behavior. Julia really could not tell anymore, and she didn't trust herself to even guess.

"How's everything going for tonight? Need any help in the kitchen?" she asked Lindsay. The Herrick's house was better equipped for entertaining large groups of people while the Moores had the giant luxury kitchen. Each year they worked together with the Moores bringing all the food while the Herricks provided the house.

"No, we're good. I wanted to come by really quick to see how things were with you. It's really important for Liv that tonight be perfect. I wanted to make sure we were good and you guys are still hosting," Lindsay said as if it's what she had done for the last ten years - wander over to the Herrick house the day of the party just to make sure it was still happening.

"Why wouldn't we be?" Julia challenged.

Lindsay continued into the garage but did not acknowledge the question. "Where did you and Denny go?" she asked.

"He didn't tell you?" There was something about Lindsay's smug strut into her garage as if Julia had been the irrational bitch and Lindsay was kind enough to still grace her with her presence that was too much for Julia. And then, for the first time in their relationship, she felt like she was the one making the decisions; she was the one in control of how things would go. Well, maybe not the one in control, but at the very least they were equals.

"He said you got coffee and a gift for Liv. What did you get her?" Julia could tell Lindsay was fishing for details. She likely did not want to be outdone in the present department which is the only reason she cared and bothered to ask. It may even be the only reason she stopped over to see Julia: to make sure her party for Liv was still on and to make sure the Herricks didn't outdo her when it came time to open presents. Julia almost laughed at how predictable it all was.

"Yup. Coffee and a quick trip to the bookstore."

Lindsay scoffed without any attempt to hide her contempt. "You didn't buy that stupid inappropriate book for Liv, did you? I should have known Denny would find a way to sneak the damn thing in one way or another."

"Denny said she was interested in the book and had

talked about it before. He said she's been tearing through banned books for the past few weeks." Julia couldn't let her win this one. She couldn't believe she had somehow gotten in the middle of a fight between Lindsay and Denny. She was also dismayed to find she may be on the losing side of their argument.

"That's what Denny does. He tries to mold everyone, including his daughters, into what he thinks they should be. He's been on me for years to read more books and get involved in local book clubs. I don't have time and it's not my thing, but he doesn't care. He just signed me up for some sort of book of the month club that sends out books each month and then orchestrates virtual book clubs through whatever your preferred social media outlet is. It doesn't matter that I'm working sixty plus hours a week and don't have the luxury to sit around reading all day like he does."

She examined some light-up pumpkin decorations as she spit each caustic sentence out. Julia wasn't surprised to hear Lindsay speak that way about Denny. She frequently vented to Julia about everything she didn't like about her husband. But this was the first time Julia had to resist the urge to defend him. Once Julia spent the morning with him and heard him defend Lindsay, she couldn't bear to hear Lindsay so casually cut him down.

"It's a thoughtful present that perfectly aligns with her interests and it has nothing to do with monetary value."

Lindsay's eyes widened and she nodded her head. "Well, it didn't take long for him to get you to drink the Kool Aid. Anyway, I have a few things cooking right now and I can't start the other stuff until it gets closer to the party. Do you want any help setting up?"

Julia did not want any help. She wanted to get lost in her thoughts so she could try to sort everything out. She wasn't ready to be ambushed by Lindsay's quick tongue; Julia was much slower in that department. Sometimes it took days for Julia to dissect a conversation with someone and to realize she did, in fact, feel slighted by their comments. But then she'd still have to let it go since so much time had passed since the offending conversation occurred. To confront the person felt like bringing up old arguments with nothing to gain from it.

"Jules," Lindsay snapped. "Are we good, or what?"

Julia realized she'd dazed out again lost in her thoughts. And she was so tired, and there was so much to do to prepare for the party. "Yeah, we're good," she said with a bit of conviction. "Stay. Help me out. I'll put on some music."

9

DENNY, OCTOBER 2013

"Third time's a charm, right?" Denny asked Lindsay. She was getting ready to interview for the store manager position.

"Stop talking, please," Lindsay shot back. Her gaze remained in the mirror as she applied what she described as just enough makeup to look like she was making an attempt without looking like a hooker.

Denny turned back to his dresser and pretended to look through shirts. When she bombed the first interview a few years back she had come home and told him everything. She replayed the questions asked, her answers, the interviewers' reactions and follow-up questions. They'd analyzed every detail together, as a team. He'd catered to her every desire in bed that night similar to the way she'd supported him through his failed efforts at being published.

The person they'd hired instead of Lindsay, an external candidate from another big box store, lasted just over a year before leaving the company for their biggest competitor. The position opened yet again, and Lindsay got another subtle message from the higher ups that she should once again put her name in the hat.

She'd come home from her second attempt at store manager excited. She'd nailed the interview; she was sure of it. Denny and Lindsay didn't go over every detail the way they had last time. There was no reason to. Because of her initial confidence, it had been an even bigger blow to her ego the second time she was passed up for the position. What else could she do? She gave a perfect interview and her recent performance at work had been practically flawless.

At the time, Lindsay had somewhat accepted her climb up the corporate ladder would likely halt for at least five to ten years before another position opened up. She couldn't believe her luck when her store manager, the one who had been promoted instead of her, announced his early retirement to care for his ailing wife. A shame about the wife, but what luck the position would come up again at her store in such a short amount of time. It was a sign. It was her turn this time.

As small children are apt to exist oblivious to the tension of their parents, Liv made her way into the bedroom and started to bounce on the bed while recounting the latest episode of *Victorious*.

"Bounce on over here, knucklehead," Denny teased. He caught her in a hug then set her back on the bed. "Mom's about to go on a really important interview for work. Can you tell her, 'Good luck,' and, 'We know she's going to kick butt'?

Liv repeated the message with one punctuated word each time she bounced on the bed.

"Thanks, honey. Now go downstairs and get some breakfast while I talk to Daddy."

He stole one more hug from Liv before she hopped off the bed and clambered down the steps. After she left, his shoulders slumped and he prepared himself for whatever anger and annoyance Lindsay was about to throw his way. He couldn't do anything right with her lately. Sometimes he could guess his misstep and try to right it before Lindsay got mad; sometimes he didn't care enough to bother and simply accepted her wrath with indifference.

Lindsay stood and turned to face him. "Can we *not* tell everyone this time?"

"Not even our daughter?"

"She's a child, Denny. She'll probably announce it at school, in the carpool, and anywhere else she goes today. Remember the time she told the mailman about your vasectomy?"

"Okay. I'm sorry."

"Not to mention she'll tell Alexis and then Julia will know before I even have the damn interview."

"You didn't even tell Julia?"

"Don't talk about my work life with people. Why is that so difficult for you to understand?"

Denny rubbed his chin and started to make his way towards the door. Lindsay side-stepped to land in the middle of his path and placed her palms on his chest. She was about to speak, but first she lowered her chin and touched the crown on her head to his chest, between her two hands.

"I'm sorry."

Denny gently rubbed her back, careful not to wrinkle her outfit.

"I don't want to tell everyone I didn't get the position, again. Three times Denny. I can't."

"You won't," he whispered.

Lindsay shook her head and pulled away. "You don't know that," she said as she walked out of the room.

. . .

Three days later Lindsay ran into the house after work and jumped into Denny's arms. Almost. They tumbled backwards onto the couch and the kids came running to join in on the random antics occurring in the living room.

"You got it?"

"I got it! I really got it! I'm the new store manager!"

The girls danced and jumped on the couch together as Denny and Lindsay shared a somewhat unbalanced embrace on the bouncing cushions.

"You girls want some iPad time?" Denny offered.

"Yes!" the girls screamed back in unison. They scurried off to the playroom to hunker down with their favorite mindless iPad games and videos while Denny carried Lindsay back to their bedroom for a proper celebration.

"The girls have been on their iPads for almost an hour."

Lindsay's head was on Denny's chest and he was stroking her hair and back. "Yeah, we should probably transition them into something else. Guess we should feed them dinner, too," he said.

Lindsay put up a hand to high five Denny. "Parents of the year," she said. "Right here."

Denny started to get up when Lindsay said, "Wait. I have a request." Lindsay sat up and turned to face Denny. "Can we wait till the party to tell everyone about the job?"

"Of course. Whatever you want. It's your big news," Denny said with a smile and kiss.

That year the two families went as characters from *The Incredibles.* The specific details of their Halloween costumes had been finalized, as always, weeks in advance around the fire pit in the backyards. The women made most of the decisions while Denny and James engaged in small talk about football or politics.

Denny had half-listened to the women's conversation while James droned on about who was to blame for the recent government shutdown. He knew his wife; he could tell she was dead set on being the main character, Elastigirl, even though she was spouting off nonsense about wanting to cast everyone with the characters which best fit their personalities since it would be a critical part of winning the costume contest they always hosted at their Halloween soirees.

As he knew she would, Julia sparred a few times with Lindsay before relenting and offering herself up as the less glamorous, but much more interesting character, Edna. At that point James asked for Denny's opinion on the government shutdown and he missed whatever tactics Lindsay had used to get her perfect Mr. Incredible, James.

So, there they were in the Herrick's living room before the start of the party posing for their annual Halloween picture with Denny dressed in his Syndrome onesie complete with a tall red wig, and Lindsay in her tight-fitting Elastigirl outfit. Liv and Alexis both dressed up as Violet, while Brice and Hailey both dressed up as Dash.

They did one regular picture where the adults lined up in the back next to their spouses and the kids found a random spot in front of their parents. Then Lindsay requested a themed picture where they all took on their characters. She directed everyone's poses and facial expressions to achieve the most accurate portrayal of the characters.

"Denny, you're the bad guy. Stand a few steps that way," she commanded as she pointed off to the left side.

"Julia, you're kind of off to the side, too, since you're only there as a support for the family." Julia walked a few paces to the right side of the group. Denny noticed her eye roll and gave a smile in solidarity, but she didn't see him.

"Kids and James, get in tight with me and give your best superhero about-to-attack poses. Oh, wait. James, pick me up like you're about to throw me. Just like they do in the movie."

James balked at the command. He'd been working out in the yard landscaping after work and likely did not want to be lifting anything for the rest of the night. But Lindsay always knew the right things to say to get what she wanted.

"James, you're Mr. Incredible for a reason. You didn't even need a muscle suit." Her one hand stroked his bicep while her words stroked his ego. She got two more action shots from him before the other guests started to arrive and the party began.

Halloween was on a Thursday that year, so they started at six with an end time around nine. Sometime between the guests arriving and the start of karaoke in the basement, Lindsay made her big announcement, and everyone took a celebratory shot in the kitchen. Even though he hated shots, Denny took one in support of his wife, and then he gave her a hug and kiss while repeating how proud he was of her.

As the party continued, people spread out around the house. The basement had the music and most of the kids, while the main level had a smattering of adults in various groups engaged in various conversations.

One conversation in particular caught Denny's attention when he heard Lindsay's name.

"What's going on between you and Lindsay?" It was Julia's hushed voice coming from the office area a little way off from the kitchen.

"Unbelievable, Jules." James's voice. Denny hated gossip and he didn't like getting involved in other people's marriages, but he stayed still and eavesdropped this one time. He wanted to know what was going on with his wife, too.

"Yes, it is unbelievable the way you're letting her hang all over you tonight and *sample* all of your beers. She doesn't even like beer."

"You've been hounding me for years to be nice to Lindsay. I'm being nice."

"You're being more than nice you're - "

"We're done here," James interrupted. Denny took his cue and slowly made his way to anywhere but right outside the office. The last thing he heard on his way to the basement was, "You have a problem with what's happening? Confront Lindsay. But we both know you won't."

Me neither, Denny thought as he made his way down into the basement and out the back doors. They hadn't lit the fire pit that year because none of the adults were willing to stay outside all night and tend to it. Denny sat alone on one of the retaining walls just outside of the basement and thought about what the hell he was doing with his life. His wife was climbing the ranks at Moyer's while his Amazon book rankings, along with his sales and profits, were plummeting. *Time and Again* was still doing okay, but his agent was asking for more best-sellers, and he couldn't deliver. He was out of ideas and practically incapacitated lately as overwhelming feelings of imposter syndrome struck every time he sat down to write.

Lindsay started to hint at leaving his writing career behind claiming it wasn't making him happy anymore. He even found a job posting print-out once on his pillow. A not-so-subtle clue she wanted him to get a proper job now that his writing career was fizzling out. Things between them were best when they were both taking three steps forward with just an occasional step back. But lately he was taking more steps backwards than forwards, and she was moving steadily ahead without him.

Denny smelled the faint odor of cigarette smoke coming from somewhere nearby. He walked to the side of the house and found Kari. Her eyes were closed, and she was leaning against the side of the house. She was dressed as a flapper and held a long cigarette holder as a working part of her costume.

"Hey," Denny said.

Kari opened her eyes and turned to the backyard and the sound of his voice. "Hey," she returned.

She didn't turn back away from him so Denny walked over to join her. Lindsay hated the smell of smoke which may have been the driving force in Denny asking to bum a cigarette off of Kari.

"Did you bring Michael?" Denny asked after the rush of nicotine went through him. It had been years since he'd quit smoking. It tasted old and stale but the feeling of the nicotine hitting him was even better than he remembered.

Kari went on a bit about how she dumped Michael because he lost another job and wanted to slum around the house all day instead of doing something with his life.

Denny nodded at all the right times and wondered if he was getting a glimpse of what really happened at pinochle. A bunch of women sitting around drinking and complaining about their husbands or boyfriends. He wondered what Lindsay said about him.

"I miss Stan," Kari whispered. "It's been years and I still miss him as much as the first day he moved out." Tears were streaming down her face. Denny had long since finished his cigarette and wished he had exited sooner. He cared she was upset, but he was sure he would say the wrong thing or make a wrong move. Luckily, she didn't want him to say anything at all. He continued to nod, easy enough, and she continued to let out a stream of consciousness about her marriage to Stan and her failed relationships since Stan.

Even though it was hard to understand Kari since she'd had a few too many shots and was crying while she was talking, Denny was able to glean the basics about what happened. Stan admitted to an affair then begged for forgiveness. She kicked him out. A few months later she'd realized she'd made a mistake ending their marriage and begged for him to come back. Ironically, he was too hurt by her refusal to work it out, and he couldn't forgive her. He'd moved on by then.

Denny found himself moving slightly towards Kari to offer some sort of comforting physical contact, maybe a hand on her shoulder, but Kari misread his gesture and collapsed into his arms. Denny wasn't up for comforting Kari; he had his own marriage problems to deal with. He wondered how long he had to stay there with her before he could politely pull away and seek shelter back in the house.

"You guys coming in for the costume contest?" Lindsay asked.

They didn't immediately break away from each other at the sound of his wife's voice. Why would they? She was crying on his shoulder about how much she missed her ex-husband. There was nothing remotely sexy or inappropriate about the interaction.

And yet, when they did turn to look at Lindsay, there was nothing but accusation and fire in her eyes. Lindsay didn't wait for an answer; she was back in the house once she knew they had seen her disapproving expression.

"Shit. I'm sorry. She looks pissed."

Denny shook his head. "It's fine. She'll be fine. You coming in?"

"Yes. I am." Kari's hand found his and gave it two quick squeezes before releasing it again.

Denny had expected Lindsay to be cold and distant towards him the rest of the night. As a punishment of sorts for his physical interaction with another woman at the party. Maybe it was because they won the costume contest and she was still on a high with her big promotion reveal that night. Either way, she was over it before the end of the party, and all over him when they got home that night. He didn't want to rock the sturdy marriage footing they'd found again, so he didn't comment on how she tasted like James's beer.

10

JULIA, OCTOBER 2019

Halloween was on a Friday, so the party started at seven that year. The Moores, always the first ones to the party, brought over all the food at six, helped set up the tables and drink areas, and participated in the annual pre-party photo with the two families.

Julia had just slipped her medieval gown on when she heard the front door open. Lindsay called out, "It's Britney, bitches!" with a high-pitched laughter.

"Oh, god. Please don't, Mom. You're so embarrassing," Liv pleaded. Julia could hear Liv making her way up the steps and over to Alexis's room.

"'I'm coming," Julia called out. She left James to finish getting ready on his own so she could help set up the kitchen and dining area with all the food. The last thing she needed to do to prepare for the night was to dye her hands red with some washable markers which she would do as soon as the food was all set out and ready to go. She loved Lady Macbeth's ambition; she hoped wearing the costume would help her channel her own inner Lady Macbeth. Not the murderess part, of course. She wanted the part of Lady

Macbeth who did what she needed to do without looking back and without apologies. The one who stood up to anyone, including her husband, who stood in her way.

As she bounded down the stairs she almost plowed into Denny - or rather Justin Timberlake. Denny's brown hair had frosted tips which could barely be seen beneath his denim cowboy hat. He wore large rose-tinted sunglasses, a denim jacket over a denim-colored T-shirt, and of course, denim pants. Julia put her hand over her mouth to keep herself from literally laughing in Denny's face.

"Don't even say it, Julia," Denny warned. There was no malice or threat in his voice though. It was more playful than that. "Besides, you have to admit I look pretty damn good." He set down his bags and did a few old school moves for her. Julia, despite herself, was mildly impressed by his dancing. Aside from a few slow dances, she couldn't remember seeing him dance in the past. He must have in all the years she'd known him, but she couldn't bring any memories to mind at that moment.

Lindsay came up behind Denny with two giant bags in each hand. "Denny, set the crock pot on the island. Hailey, put your bags on the counter, please, and then go see if Brice can help you figure out the zipper snafu on your costume." Everyone shuffled their way into the kitchen with their swinging bags and somewhat awkward gait from the costumes they were still getting used to.

Julia picked up the lid to a dish Liv must have set down before sprinting up the stairs. It was her absolute favorite crab artichoke dip which Lindsay only made for Halloween and Julia's birthday in April. Julia inhaled deeply and her mouth reflexively began to water in anticipation. It was heavy on the crab, onion, and butter - just the way she liked it. Julia replaced the lid and took it over to the section of the island where all of the food would eventually be spread out for guests to enjoy. *Would Lindsay really move without sharing the recipe?* Lindsay wondered. In the past, Lindsay had always sworn she would take the recipe to her grave. But that was just a joke, right?

"Okay, Denny. You are officially dismissed as well so you don't get in our way." Denny obeyed Lindsay's orders and dutifully made his way out to the garage to get himself a drink before pictures. "And you," Lindsay said with her eyes gleaming and one painted red nail pointed at Julia. "Are you ready for the best Halloween party this neighborhood has ever seen?"

Hours later the party was in full swing and it was a raging success. Lindsay and Denny circulated the party and had conversations with all of the neighbors as if nothing was amiss. As if they wouldn't be moving away within a few short days. Julia cringed hearing them discuss the yard sale coming up that spring and the tree lighting event downtown the weekend after Thanksgiving. What would all of the other neighbors think when all of this came out? Surely they would be mad at Julia and James, too, for going along with the ruse and lying right along with the Moores.

Julia reminded herself that it wasn't just about the adults. Liv deserved one last wonderful birthday with all of her neighborhood and school friends. That part of the party was successful as well.

Both kids deserved as many normal days as they could get before the rug was pulled out from under them. Lindsay and Denny weren't keeping mum so they could carry on as if everything were normal; they were playing along for the kids' sake, and the least the Herricks could do was go along with it.

Each year as the kids got older and more independent,

the natural divide between the parents and the kids grew as well. All of the kids, including the now teens, hung out in the basement while the parents held court upstairs. The Herrick basement was one large circle around the stairway leading down, and then there were large rooms jutting off of each side of the circle. One room contained a home gym for James, and the other housed a few couches, a movie screen, and a wet bar. The parents thoroughly cleaned out any booze and stocked it with kid-friendly drinks and food.

When the kids were younger there were sometimes concerns about if the kids were playing nicely together and if they were completely trashing the basement. Now, Julia was more concerned about random games of spin the bottle or seven minutes in heaven.

The parents, allowing the inner child in themselves to come out, drank heavily while listening to Alexa play the biggest hits of 2000 as they gossiped about what was going on around Scarlet Oaks Knoll, caught up with how school was going with everyone's kids, and enjoyed each other's company in general. There was always a good flow at the Herrick and Moore Halloween party. People moved about the kitchen, dining room, and living room throughout the night and everyone made their way around and chatted with everyone else there.

Sometimes throughout the night Julia was sad to think Denny and Lindsay were leaving such an amazing neighborhood. Sad to think they wouldn't find a similar group of neighbors and friends anywhere else. After all, what were the odds of finding a neighborhood like Scarlet Oaks Knoll twice in one lifetime? Other times she wished Lindsay would just go already so they could all move on without her. The limbo was starting to get to her. In her mind she knew this was the last Halloween party, the last holiday party even, but it still didn't feel that way. It was hard to accept the reality when the facade was still being played out so well.

As it got later the party became more intimate. Half of the neighbors with younger kids had to call it a night. Many left with their child screaming from under their arms as they wrestled them out the doors; many left with a child sleeping on their shoulder as they walked back to their houses. What was left was the Moores, the Herricks, the Fishers, and the Brineys.

The Fishers, Tim and Abigail with children Lillian and Laurel, lived over on Harlow Street for the past five years. They were one of the newer neighbors but they fit in immediately. The Brineys, Josh and Maureen, didn't have any children so they tended to be much more carefree at holiday parties and events in comparison to the adults with children who needed to be monitored at all times.

Tim, Denny, Josh, and James were in the living room with a football game going in the background, while the women all found themselves seated around the island and picking at the remaining food.

Julia, one of the more conservative parents of the group, said, "Should we be worried about the kids in the basement? They're not that little anymore. I remember kissing boys when I was younger than Liv and Alexis." It wasn't like she wanted to go down and check on them or attempt to enforce any rules. Julia was more than comfortable in front of the crab dip with the vodka drink Lindsay had made for her. She was just looking for confirmation from the others she was over-thinking things with the kids who were likely doing fine on their own.

Maureen, who didn't have any children, stayed quiet when it came to discussing child rearing. She'd mentioned before she felt it wasn't her place to tell anyone else how to raise their kids when she herself had zero experience with the subject. That left Abigail, who mostly opted to go with the flow. She would wait for someone else to chime in before giving her opinion about most things.

Lindsay cocked an eye towards Julia. "They're fine. Even if they *are* playing spin the bottle or something, it's harmless fun. They're not going to have sex or anything."

The women around the island, subdued by the boozy drinks at the party for the past few hours, all nodded in agreement. There was strength in numbers. If they all agreed the kids were fine, then they probably were.

"Speaking of sex," Lindsay went on. She often told bedroom stories once the booze hit her, so this turn in conversation was expected. "I just started using nipple clamps and they're freaking amazing." Lindsay wasn't shouting, but she also wasn't whispering. Julia sneaked a quick look at the guys, but they were all into the game and whatever manly conversations they were having in the living room.

"Clamps? Like S & M? Sounds painful." Abigail was gently rubbing her breast at the thought of a clamp on her nipple.

Similarly, Maureen crossed her arms, either consciously or unconsciously, at the thought of someone clamping her nipples. She said, "Ouch," and gave a look of apprehension.

Julia wasn't thinking of her own nipples at all. In her mind she was back in the All Things Dirty book section, and then in the car with Denny reading the sexy passages. It didn't surprise her to hear about Lindsay and Denny's rocking sex life which was full of toys and pushed boundaries. She'd heard Lindsay's stories for years and often wondered how much of what she heard had been true. After hearing Denny admit to reading erotica, she was convinced all the stories were true.

For a quick second she pictured Lindsay and Denny in the throes of some crazy sexual frenzy and she blushed. She blushed an even deeper shade of red, a shade closely resembling the bright marker on her hands, when she acknowledged the ache between her legs as she imagined her neighbors having sex.

The women all looked at Julia waiting for her response to Lindsay's big news. Julia knew Lindsay wanted the women to be in shock and awe over her recent sexcapade story. Lindsay expected them to insist she share all the gory details. The played-out interaction didn't end there. After the women asked for more details, Lindsay would pretend to be offended anyone else would dare ask such personal questions even though Lindsay herself had opened up her bedroom door to begin with. Julia was over the tired scene they'd played out for the past however many years. But since this was the last time, she went along with it and asked the leading questions to guide the rest of the conversation. "Do they hurt? Who suggested them, you or Denny?"

She was going to ask more but she suddenly felt uncomfortable and knew she was going to feel more uncomfortable as the conversation went on. She no longer wanted any part of leading the discussion. She no longer had any interest in hearing about Denny's sexual encounters with Lindsay.

"No, they don't hurt. I mean, they don't hurt me. But I really like it when Denny's rough with my nipples. The harder the better." More unwanted images flooded Julia's mind. Most had Denny's mouth expertly working Lindsay's nipples with alternating licks and gentle sucking. But every now and then it wasn't Lindsay's nipples. It was her own. Guilt washed over her as she reached for her necklace. Her fingers searched her bare chest briefly before she remembered she'd taken it off because it didn't go with her Lady Macbeth costume.

This time, Lindsay didn't need Julia as her go-to person. Maureen was happy to take that spot for her. "But who initiated? I mean, did one of you just whip them out one night or did you talk about it before?"

Julia again turned back to the men only to see them completely oblivious to anything the women folk were discussing. She was sure at least one of them would hear the word "nipple" or their name and their ears would perk up. But no. They were experts at tuning out their wives.

Lindsay's cocky attitude returned even stronger than before. "I initiated it, of course. I always have to initiate anything outside of the usual with Denny. Lately I've been the one to initiate all sex. It's like he's already an old man with no sex drive." Her tone was dripping with disgust as if she couldn't believe her husband hadn't already broached the subject of clamps. As if all the other husbands had already done so and Denny was behind the game, so to speak. It wasn't true. None of the other couples at the party were having the recommended amount of three to five romps in the sack each week. Julia couldn't fathom anyone sustaining those averages through decades of marriage. Even her lustful husband James went through stressful weeks at work which left him uninterested in sex for extended periods of time.

Poor Denny. He had warned Julia to be nice to Lindsay because Lindsay was hurting, too. And then there she was badmouthing Denny behind his back. Julia wondered if the husbands did it as well. The women tended to make mild complaints about dishes that weren't put away or insensitive comments from their husbands. But those comments were never to the extent Lindsay had just displayed where she practically cut off Denny's balls and served them up to the women along with the dips and appetizers which surrounded them.

"Anyway, I'm not the type to get into too many details, so I'll just leave it that I highly recommend you get some." Lindsay leaned her head back and took a swig of her drink.

She clearly enjoyed the surprised looks on the other women's faces. When Maureen opened up Amazon and placed an order with a few taps on her phone, Lindsay was downright giddy with pride at the effect she'd had.

Julia was done with all of it. It was her house though, and weekend parties never ended before ten. The best she could do was make a brief escape to another room. "I'm going to go check on the kids." Julia held up her hand to stop Lindsay who was just about to protest Julia's brief departure. "It's fine. I don't mind. I'm well aware they're probably in the theater room spread out on couches and watching some PG-13 horror movie."

Lindsay rolled her eyes as if to say, "It's completely unnecessary but if that's what you want to do, go ahead." Then she continued her conversation with the women. "So, tell me all about the crazy things you ladies have been up to since the last time we hung out."

It was difficult to say where the conversation was headed, and Julia didn't care anyway. She put it out of her mind as she went down into the basement to check on the kids. The youngest was nine and the oldest was Alexis who had already turned fourteen a few months prior to Liv. While she wasn't thrilled to see them watching *Halloween H2O*, she was a bit relieved that everyone had on clothes and didn't seem to be engaging in any indecent behavior. She also couldn't help but smile when she noticed Liv sprawled out on the sectional and engrossed in the book she'd gotten from Julia. Point for Denny. She wondered if Lindsay really felt Liv wouldn't like the gift, or if Lindsay wanted Liv to not like the book for the sake of winning the argument, or for whatever other random reason Lindsay may have had. It was hard to say what Lindsay's motives were.

Satisfied that all was right with the world in the basement, she turned the corner back to the main section of the basement and almost yelped as she ran right into Denny. Her face turned bright red as her eyes involuntarily flickered to Denny's lips and again pictured them roughly attacking her nipples. She also blushed as her entire body had slammed up against his and he had instinctively grabbed her shoulders and held onto her as he asked if she was okay.

"Yeah, I'm fine." She chuckled slightly for effect before saying, "The kids' horror movie must have made me jumpy. Sorry."

"Don't apologize. It's fine." He looked away from her and over her shoulders back towards the kids. "Are they okay? What are they watching?"

"They're watching *Halloween H2O*, the TV version. Everyone seems to be a nice distance apart with no blankets in sight. I didn't see any illicit substances, either."

Denny chuckled, "I should hope not."

From the back room one of the girls shouted, "We can hear you. Just go back upstairs. Please."

Denny mocked a hurt expression before touching Julia's forearm to guide her away from the theater room entrance. "Bunch of spoiled brats, huh? They used to beg us to come hang out with them down here." His voice was low so that the kids wouldn't yell at them again.

"Agreed. But this is nice, too. Having a conversation without one of them needing the bathroom or snacks or attention."

"Yes, this is nice," Denny agreed. They were still standing close to one another so they could speak softly.

"We should probably get back upstairs. It looked like you guys were really into the game and the after show."

"Yeah, but it's not nearly as interesting as your conversation about nipple clamps."

Julia's eyes widened. "I knew it. I knew you guys had to be able to hear us. Maureen gets so loud when she drinks."

"Yeah, sometimes we hear you. But we know if we go about our business, you assume we can't and then your conversations turn candid and interesting."

Julia put her head in her hands and searched her memory for anything mortifying she may have said over the past decade. "I can only imagine what you all have heard over the years," she said into her hands.

Denny gave a gentle tug at her wrists to pull her hands down from her face. He said, "You've never said anything worse than what Lindsay said about me tonight."

Julia knew he was right. She was always careful with what she said about James, regardless of if the men were around or not. She asked, "You're not mad Lindsay practically called you impotent in front of all her friends? And since you men have been listening on and off all along, in front of all of your friends, too?"

"We've been married a long time. I know that's just how she is. It's all for show. I'm pretty sure the other guys know it, too. Besides, what do I care when I'm leaving anyway?"

When Julia didn't respond, Denny added, "We should get back before people start talking."

"Is there something to talk about?" Julia's mouth hung open slightly for a second after she said it. She couldn't believe she said something flirty to Denny in a shadowy basement. It must have been the Justin Timberlake costume. She'd always had a thing for JT, even in his denim prime. Or maybe it was Lindsay's description of Denny working her nipples, or their adventure earlier in the day that had ended with Julia reading erotica to Denny in the car. Whatever it was, she wasn't feeling like a sister to him anymore.

The booze was doing dangerous things to her inhibitions, too. Because even if she had felt that way earlier in the day, or any other day in the past decade, she never would have said anything like that to Denny in the past. The possibility of Denny moving, her own husband's flaring temper earlier, and Lindsay's nasty attitude lately - everything was perfectly aligning for her uncharacteristic eyelash batting. All she had needed was a little liquid courage from the booze and she'd certainly had plenty of that thanks to Lindsay's infamously heavy pour.

"Lindsay always has something to talk about. Whether there's an actual cause for it or not." He sized her and the situation up for another few seconds before continuing. "Run over to my house with me really quick. I have something for you." Before Julia could decide if she should be offended or excited about whatever Denny was going to show her at his house, Denny put her at ease. "Get your mind out of the gutter. Not that."

"I wasn't thinking that," Julia protested with little conviction.

"Come on." Denny led the way out of the basement through the walk-out doors. It was a mild October night and Julia was wearing a long sleeved, flowing dress so she wasn't too cold. The moon shone brightly between two clouds as Justin Timberlake and Lady Macbeth made their way through the backyards and into Denny's house via the basement door.

"It's upstairs," Denny said as he looked back to make sure she was still following him.

Julia realized it was probably something silly like a crockpot or an old dish that they'd borrowed years ago and wanted to return before they moved. Her heart sank at the realization that this wasn't some sexy rendezvous. What she was feeling was not being reciprocated by Denny. He was a nice guy who took pity on her earlier. End of story. Which was probably for the best since doing anything with Denny that could be seen as emotionally or physically intimate would only end with catastrophic consequences for her and for Denny.

Just as Julia expected Denny to turn into the kitchen, he passed it and went into his office instead. Julia couldn't remember having ever been in Denny's office before. There had been no need, and it had always been closed off to the kids whenever they had been over for playdates. It was a stereotypical office with a desk in the middle which looked meticulously kept with everything in its place. The wall behind the desk was covered with a built-in bookcase that was filled with books, little knickknacks, and framed photos here and there. The other walls were painted a deep blue and had decorative white paneling that came one third of the way up the wall.

Julia took in Denny, in his JT costume, as he stood behind the desk looking through his bookshelf. He pulled one of the books from the top right corner. So high up he could barely reach it without using the rolling ladder they'd attached to the bookshelf. Then he turned and held out what looked to her like a romance novel. On the cover was a man with brown hair leaning over a fence and kissing a woman, who in her mind, looked a lot like her.

Denny blushed as he noticed her reaction. "It's not you, but I do pull a lot from people I know when I write. Every character seems to be some mashup of all the people I've encountered throughout my life."

"Oh, like when you're at the coffee shop watching and listening to everyone around you. Looking for inspiration for your next character or plot twist."

"Yeah. Kind of like that." He looked a bit sheepish as he explained his process to her. "I can't tell if that makes me a good writer who uses life to inspire him, or a hack who has no imagination and is incapable of actually creating something new and unheard of."

"Your whole first series was a fantasy made up of new worlds, dimensions, and even life forms," Julia said. She was surprised at how insecure he was about his writing since in her mind he'd achieved immense success as an author. Julia almost went to him in some sort of effort to provide comfort, but the desk was still between them and the moment passed. "You're not a hack. And I can't wait to read this."

"You don't have to read it right away. I know you love books, and you probably already have a to-be-read pile a mile high on your nightstand."

"Oh, no. This is going right to the top now. I just finished a book last night and I'll get started on this one right away."

"Perfect," Denny said. He walked around the desk and started to make his way to the door. "Now we should really get back. We've both been gone a while."

Denny guided her out of the office and out of the house, via the front door this time, with his hand on the small of her back. Both acted as if it was the most natural thing in the world for Denny, her best friend's husband, to do so though nothing remotely like that had happened before between them. They'd never been more intimate than small talk for the longest time. And when he removed his hand as they entered Julia's house, she felt a chill and she longed for him to return it, regardless of who was around to see it.

11

DENNY, APRIL 2014

"Do you think you'll ever write about me?" Kari asked. Her head was on Denny's chest and she was absently twirling a small patch of his chest hair between her finger and thumb. Every now and then he winced but she didn't stop.

Never, Denny thought. "Do you want me to write about you?"

"I don't know. Just seems like it would be cool to be in a book. You know?"

Denny looked at the digital clock bolted down to the nightstand. They'd been there for one hour and forty-three minutes. He'd give it seventeen more before he started to collect his things and head home to his empty house. He couldn't tell which place was more miserable, his vacant house or the motel room with Kari.

He'd started writing romance novels about the same time he and Lindsay hit a rough patch in their marriage. Looking back it was probably a way for him to cope. The idea for his first book came during a weekly dinner date with the Herricks. Lindsay and Julia had been joking about how close the families were, almost like the families in the show *Big Love* where three houses backed up to share a giant yard. The glaring difference between them and the television show being that Julia and Lindsay did not share a husband.

It wasn't much, but it triggered an idea about two neighbors, both free of spouses because people didn't like to read about cheaters, who fell in love and blended their families and houses. Denny always thought James was a bit too hot-headed and unlikeable for a character, but Julia was the opposite. Readers would relate to her; would find her plenty likeable just as he did.

He told himself he'd made minor changes so it wasn't an exact replica of Julia. Was careful to change up actual events with stark differences. But in the end, most of his changes were edited out. What was left, surprisingly, was a love story between him and Julia. One that he'd created from start to finish, complete with detailed, steamy sex scenes. It felt dirty and shameful throughout the entire writing process. But at the same time, it felt like the most realistic story he'd ever written.

He flipped the TV off and rolled on top of Kari again. She sometimes slipped and called out Stan's name while Denny was inside her. And that was okay with Denny, because in his mind he was always with Julia. It was her birthday that day and he imagined they were celebrating together, in bed, oblivious to the rest of the world.

"Here you go, beautiful. Happy thirty-ninth birthday." Lindsay presented Julia with her famous dip along with her actual present in a meticulously arranged gift bag. Denny had no idea what the gift was even though it was always presented as being from the entire Moore family.

The kids didn't bother with any formalities beyond greetings as they rushed through the kitchen and up the stairs to see Alexis and Brice.

"Thanks, guys," Julia said as she gave a big hug to Lindsay and then led them all into the kitchen. The original plan had been for them to have dinner outside on the deck. A last-minute change in the weather drove them inside.

"You could have had dinner at our house. You're not cooking or cleaning today, are you?" Lindsay asked.

"No, James is taking care of everything," Julia said.

James, donning one of Julia's flowery pink aprons, threw a few spices into a pot before turning his attention to the kitchen and guests. "Lindsay, Denny. Thank you for coming to help celebrate this amazing woman." He grabbed Julia from behind and nuzzled into her neck until she squirmed away. When she did untangle herself, his eyes went straight for her ass as she reached up for some wine glasses.

"Wouldn't miss it for the world," Lindsay said.

Unable to resist, Denny added, "No, can't miss Julia's birthday dinner. No problem missing mine last month, but not Julia's. Never."

"It was a work emergency. Let it go," Lindsay said.

"Who wants wine?" Julia interrupted before things could escalate.

Lindsay's demeanor changed back to pleasant and cele-bratory. "Please. We brought your favorite, Jules. I'll pop the cork."

Denny said, "None for me, thanks. But I will take a beer if you have any."

"In the garage," James said. "We have Tröegs and Yuengling. Grab me one, too, if you're heading out there."

"Any preference?"

"Whatever you get." James was less interested in beer

selections and more interested in Julia who was standing with him at the stove. James's thumb was caressing a small section of skin peeking out between her shirt and pants while his other hand stirred the pot. Julia whispered something suggestive which made him smile and cock an eyebrow at her.

Damn, Denny thought. *Married for over a decade and they have two kids. How are they still acting like love-struck teens?* And yet he was certain that if had married Julia, he would have never been able to get enough of her either. He returned from the garage with two Tröegs, since it was the strongest beer of the two, and handed one to James.

"Are those corn hole boards in the garage?" Denny asked.

Julia giggled and nodded. "Yes, they are. Can you guess who built them and who painted each board?"

"You got a corn hole game? I wanna see." Lindsay poked her head out to the garage before returning to her usual seat at the island. "That's easy. James made the boards," James confirmed by raising his beer and tilting his head, "probably with the help of the kids because he loves doing family projects like that."

"Also correct," James said. "Alexis is a beast with a hammer."

Lindsay continued, "I know Brice painted his all black, his favorite color, and Alexis painted the unicorn. It looks like she may have thrown a handful of glitter on as well before you sealed it."

James put a finger to his nose and said, "There was glitter everywhere. We're still finding it weeks later."

"You should have seen the kids lead me out to the garage to surprise me. They insisted on blindfolding me which in itself was an experience. Alexis took out a chunk of my hair when she ripped off the blindfold," Julia put her head down and showed the small patch of scalp where her hair used to be, "and Brice accidentally walked me straight into the kitchen table. I'm sure I'll have a giant purple welt on my thigh tomorrow. But it was also just the sweetest present and they were so proud of themselves for helping." Julia looked gorgeous; she was glowing with happiness as she told them about the gifts from her family. She stood at the island facing Lindsay and Denny, but she turned and playfully bit her husband on the shoulder who returned the favor with a quick pinch to her side.

"Looks like a friendly cornhole tournament is looming in the near future." Denny said.

"I'm on Jules's team and you men are on notice. I was the pitcher on my softball team. We made it to states back-to-back my junior and senior year."

Denny, who had been leaning against the island, took a seat next to his wife and put his hand on her thigh, his thumb moving in a circular motion against her jeans. "I'm pretty sure the custom is for spouses to team up with each other. It'll be like Game of Thrones and we'll play for the honor of our house, House Moore."

Lindsay turned to face him knocking his arm away as she did. "I'm in it for the victory, sweetie, and I don't think you have it in you."

"That hurts, Linds." Denny said before taking another swig from his beer. That would be his one attempt for the night. He'd been giving at least one attempt each night for the past month for Lindsay to embrace his touch or at the very least act apathetic to it. No. His attempts were always met with something between a casual brush-off to outright disgust.

"So, did James present you with his annual here's-every-thing-I-love-about-our-most-recent-year-together   list?" Lindsay asked.

Julia was still glowing from the wine and overall bliss of

being surrounded by loving friends and family. She took a bashful sip of wine and nodded.

James turned back to join them again. "Thirty-nine of my favorite things about the past year with my lovely wife. I also mixed in a few things I love about her in general. An annual tradition since we started dating."

Denny miserably finished his beer then went out to the garage to get another one. It was going to be a long evening of rejection from Lindsay and intense jealously from watching Julia with James.

When they returned home that night Lindsay offered to put the kids to bed so Denny took the opportunity to sneak in some writing. After staring blankly at his screen for a while, he gave up and grabbed a book from the shelves behind his desk.

A few chapters into the book he sensed Lindsay in the doorway of his office. "What do you want?" Denny asked without looking up from his book.

"Nice, Denny," Lindsay said.

At that he looked up to see Lindsay leaning against the door frame, one leg bent with her bare foot resting on the frame. Her back was arched so her scantily clad chest was pushed suggestively higher.

"Jesus, Linds. What if one of the kids sees you?"

"Then they'll be happy to see their parents are still in a loving marriage. Complete with passionate sex." Lindsay made her way over to Denny's desk.

She was wearing the outfit they'd bought back when they were on vacation - before they'd had kids or well-paying jobs. The two had splurged not only on a weekend getaway, but also on a little black teddy from the adults-only section of a touristy clothing store. The adult section was the entire upstairs and Denny had had to coax Lindsay into venturing up the winding staircase with him to check out all the naughty toys and outfits.

They had run into another couple nervously making their way up the stairs while Denny and Lindsay were on their way down with their black-bagged purchase. To break the tension and to ease Lindsay's obvious embarrassment, Denny joked, "There's no snack bar up there," as if they'd gone upstairs for hotdogs and not sexy lingerie.

The other couple had not been amused or perhaps they'd thought Denny had been serious. They shuffled by them and refused to respond or make eye-contact with Lindsay or Denny. Lindsay had cackled with laughter before grabbing onto Denny's arm as they strolled out of the store. She was still giggling when she said, "I love you, Denny. I'm going to show you how much I love you as soon as we get back to the room."

But in his office years later, he had no interest in Lindsay showing him anything. He couldn't remember the last time she'd thrown her head back and really laughed at something he'd said. He couldn't remember the last time they'd naturally initiated sex with a passionate kiss or a gentle caressing touch rather than the forced encounter Lindsay was attempting in the office.

Denny's cold attitude filled the room, but Lindsay ignored it and sat on the edge of his desk with her head turned over her shoulder so she could see him. One of her legs dangled off the side and the other was bent at a ninety-degree angle opening up the skirt of the teddy and revealing her toned thighs and the taut string which made up her string bikini panties.

"You didn't seem very interested in me touching you at the Herrick's tonight," Denny said. He was still seated at his desk, but he did put the book he'd been reading down.

Lindsay moved a few items on his desk to make more room and Denny swallowed his annoyance.

"I'm trying, Denny. It'd be a lot less painful if you could meet me halfway." Having cleared a path on the desk, she swung her legs around and awkwardly eased herself down onto Denny's lap with her arms around his neck. To his credit, he shifted a little in the chair to make room for her. He looked over her shoulder at nothing in particular until she cupped his jaw and turned his face towards hers. Her soft thumb rubbed his stubble as his gaze went around the different areas of her face before meeting her eyes with his.

It wasn't that he didn't want to look into her eyes. Things were difficult and tense between them, but he still loved her. Loved her tenacity, creativity, sense of humor, quick tongue, and intimidating intelligence. The problem was that he didn't think she loved him anymore based on her attitude and actions towards him in the past months. And the problem was him, too. He'd started an affair with Kari, and it was tearing him apart inside.

A few weeks after the Halloween party, Kari had texted Lindsay and asked if Denny could go over to help her with a few things around the house. He had no idea how exactly Kari spun it to Lindsay who had, at least initially, thought the worst of his hug with Kari at the party. Whatever she said, it worked. Lindsay asked Denny to go over as a favor to her and to Kari. Had even joked (had it been a joke?) before he'd left the house not to get into any funny business with the neighbor. "Save room for Jesus," she'd called out to him right before he walked out onto the deck to make his way to Kari's house.

While he walked through his and Josh's backyards to get to Kari's house, Denny had been annoyed by Lindsay's comment. As if he would risk his marriage and family for a neighbor he barely knew. Did Lindsay think that little of him?

He was mortified that she'd been right. Kari took him around the house asking for a few things here and there to be fixed or looked at. Her ex-boyfriend Michael, it seemed, was as lazy as Kari had claimed and what little work he had done around the house had often made things worse.

He'd told Kari she didn't have to hang around while he worked if she had other things she needed to get to. She insisted she didn't. She'd said the least she could do was keep him company since he was the one doing her a favor. Awkward, superficial conversations soon turned into genuine, interesting conversations. They'd laughed together and found they had a number of common interests to talk about.

At one point she'd offered him a glass of water. He'd turned to get it from her and they'd bumped into each other, pouring the water all over the both of them. Kari offered him one of Stan's old shirts he had left behind years ago, and she'd gone into her room to get it and to change her shirt as well.

Kari walked into her room, but she didn't shut the door behind her. She took off her shirt, and then looked over her shoulder at Denny through the wide open doorway. It wasn't love or even lust that he couldn't resist. It was the escape into a pretend life where Kari, his wife, needed his help and inter-acted with him as though he was the most interesting person she'd ever spoken to.

The look Kari gave him begged him to go to her. She needed him, and he couldn't resist the opportunity to fulfill that need. As he walked through the doorway, he knew it was shitty and it made him less of a man. It betrayed everything he loved about how independent and self-sufficient Lindsay was.

That's why it was so difficult for Denny to look into Lindsay's eyes in his office all those months later. She was looking at him the same way Kari had, as though she needed him. But if she knew the truth, she'd never look at him like that again. Even if she was capable of forgiving him, she'd never get over her wounded pride.

"Hey," she whispered.

Her plump pink lips were so close to his, and he couldn't deny how badly he wanted her regardless of how frequently he'd felt slighted by her over the past few months. He closed his eyes and gave her a soft kiss as if he were testing the waters. It had been weeks, maybe months since he and Lindsay had had sex. He couldn't risk turning her down and potentially increasing the chasm that had formed between them. He deepened his kiss and ran his hands over her firm body. He pushed Kari and Julia out of his mind as he and his wife rediscovered one another.

12

JULIA, OCTOBER 2019

The party broke up a little before midnight. As usual, the Moores were the last to leave. But that year felt different and more final when the door shut. That was the last Halloween party with the Moores. Maureen, Abigail, and the others would still be around, probably, but Lindsay wouldn't. They wouldn't have the designated first arrivals to help set up and do make-up together; they wouldn't have the crab artichoke dip; they wouldn't have their best friends as the last guests to leave after they'd helped to clean up.

Julia was certain Lindsay had purposefully loaded up her arms with bags so she couldn't do long hugs goodbye or anything like that. It was the last time for the party, but they couldn't acknowledge it yet because of the kids.

She couldn't sleep that night so she read Denny's book in bed while James snored away next to her. He saw the book, but he hadn't commented on how similar the woman on the cover looked in comparison to his wife. He also didn't comment, and therefore likely didn't know, it was Denny's book, so Julia kept that detail to herself. It was a lie by omission, yet it all seemed trivial and fleeting since everything would be changing in a week anyway.

Julia had planned to read a chapter or two out of curiosity before exhaustion would finally hit and she'd have to call it a night. She found it was different reading a book when she knew who the author was. Instead of a generic voice in her head reading the narrator's words and other random generic voices popping up for the other characters, she found herself using Denny's voice for both. Denny's voice was the narrator in her head, and Denny turned into the main character in the book, Michael Wright. She tried a hundred times to picture someone else as Michael, but as soon as she got too deep into the book again, he turned into Denny every time.

She saw herself, too. She was Lydia, the widow next door with two young children. Michael moved next door to Lydia after a nasty divorce from his wife, Cassie. And although they were both scared of the feelings they had for one another, they couldn't deny the chemistry between them. One winter night, Lydia's heater went out and it was too cold to just bundle up. She'd never learned to make a proper fire in the fireplace and the blizzard prevented her from running to the store to purchase a few space heaters.

It was Michael to the rescue as he walked over to check on them after dinner that night. When he heard their heat was out, he insisted they do a sleepover at his house. He had two small children as well and it was his weekend to have them over. It would be like a giant playdate, he'd told the kids. Michael carried their overnight bags to his house. The kids trudged ahead through the snow, eager to get their play-date started, while Lydia hiked through the snowy yards behind them, with Michael bringing up the rear.

The scene was early in the book, somewhere around chapter three or so, and it was the sole reason Julia kept reading. Denny had been writing about them. Julia was

Lydia, and Denny was Michael in some alternate universe where they were both single and their spouses had never been neighbors. The real story was that the Herrick's heat had gone out in the middle of the blizzard of 2013. It was not as dire as the situation in the book was. The Herricks would have been fine camping out in front of the blazing fire James had made, but the adults preferred the real beds at the Moore's house over the couches and inflatable beds in their living room. Similarly, the kids preferred a sleepover at their friend's house to hanging out with their parents all night.

In Denny's universe, Lydia and Michael found themselves falling asleep on his couch as the children watched a Disney movie in the living room. In the morning they both found their arms around one another and gazed deeply into each other's eyes. There had been mounting sexual tension throughout the morning as Lydia watched Michael make pancakes in the shape of Mickey Mouse and flip them high into the air to the delight of the children.

The kids begged to stay a bit longer and the parents obliged. But while Lydia was getting changed in the bathroom, one of the kids barged in and Michael got an eyeful of her perfectly shaped body that was usually hidden under her modest wardrobe. That was it. He couldn't stop thinking about her after that. He'd begged them to stay for dinner as well and he'd cooked his best meal for them all. The adults enjoyed wine with dinner and started to relax around one another in a way they never had before.

After dinner there was a dance party in the living room and the kids insisted the adults join in. A slow dance, in front of the fire, after a few glasses of wine was too much for either adult to handle. While the kids ran off to play games in the toy room, bored of the dance party after just a few songs, the adults continued to slow dance. Then Lydia pulled away and looked into Michael's eyes as they continued to sway.

Without thinking, she gently pressed her lips to his and tasted the sweet aftertaste of wine, and inhaled the dizzying scent of his musk.

It was extremely late or extremely early, depending on how one looked at the time, when Julia read this part of the story. At first, she had to put the book down. It sat on her nightstand with the cover slightly bent up from being held open for so long as she'd read. She'd closed the book and shown restraint from reading further, to witnessing, in her mind, what was sure to read out as an epic sexual fantasy from Denny's perspective of what could have happened between them under different circumstances.

But then her mind would wander back to it. She laid down and tried to fall asleep but Denny as himself and as Michael kept creeping back into her mind and showing up whenever she dared to close her eyes to get some much-needed rest. Julia sat back up in bed and flicked on her nightstand again. She didn't worry about James waking up. The man slept deep as if he hadn't a care in the world. Her eyes went back to the cover again and heard Denny say, "It's not you," over and over again in her mind. But it was her. It had to be her. The woman looked exactly like her and the scene with the busted heater and the blizzard had actually happened. There were liberties taken, of course. The most blatant being that he'd killed off James and turned Lindsay into an evil ex-wife.

Julia's hand ran through her hair and she grabbed at her necklace and twisted it between her still red fingers. If she was really honest with herself, she knew she would finish reading the book at some point in the near future. It would be naive to pretend her curiosity wouldn't eat at her nonstop until she relented and gave in. Rather than fight the temptation, she picked up the book and went back to her dog-eared page. It took just seconds for her to slip back into the world of Lydia and Michael.

She'd left off with Lydia and Michael sharing a passionate kiss in the living room with music playing softly in the background. Although the story was based on real life events, she had no idea what could actually happen between the two characters. In real life James and Julia spent the night in the Moores' spare bedroom while the kids all bunked in each other's rooms with sleeping bags and extra pillows. If she remembered correctly, James had even initiated a quickie that night. She and James, her husband, had had sex. The next morning they'd had breakfast together, frozen waffles and cereal, before heading back to their house. The roads had been plowed overnight and James was able to get the part he'd needed to fix the heater.

Julia paused again in her reading as she tried to think back to that snowstorm and sleepover. She couldn't remember if anything unusual had happened that night. It seemed odd to her Denny would have used that night as any sort of inspiration for his book when she had barely thought of it since it had happened. There had been nothing exceptional about it. The adults and children had all enjoyed each other's company, but they'd always had a good time together. Snowstorm or not.

She sneaked another glance at James and then went back to the book. It was written from Michael's point of view so the reader only knew his thoughts and heard his descriptions of what was happening. Michael described Lydia as not only giving in to his advances, but as becoming the one to initiate everything that happened after the initial kiss. Lydia's hands reached up to grab at Michael's collar to pull him in for a deeper, more sensual kiss. And then she'd let go of his collar only to take his hand and lead him up the stairs and into his bedroom.

Julia blushed as she read and pictured a vivid, erotic sex scene between the two characters, between her and Denny. Occasionally Lindsay would pop into her mind and she wondered if his detailed sex descriptions came from his experiences with her. But then the thought made her oddly jealous, so she put it out of her mind and focused only on the book as it was written - without Lindsay.

Midway through the book she started to get anxious. She needed to talk to Denny. Julia needed to know she wasn't crazy, and she needed confirmation straight from the author that the book was about her and Denny. At three thirty in the morning, she tentatively texted Denny.

So glad you all could make it for one last Halloween bash together.

She threw in a few pumpkin and smiley face emojis to keep the tone casual and then cringed at the juvenile text right after she sent it. Was it even possible to send a casual text message at that hour? Probably not, but she was going to give it a try. Besides, she had to make sure she could play it off later as a courtesy thank you from a host to her guest. To help convince herself she also texted a few of the other families who attended the party. Fingers crossed they'd sleep through it and would assume she was drunk texting when they noticed she'd sent it in the wee hours of the morning. The texts to the additional families were also a helpful distraction as her heart raced while she waited for a response from Denny. Just as she sent her final message to Maureen, Denny replied.

We had a great time, as usual. Thanks for hosting.

This was what Julia had wanted, to talk to Denny and to confront him about the book. And he was awake, too. Was he waiting to hear from her? She was almost certain it was true; he had expected her text.

Still, she couldn't respond with questions about his book

via text messages. It was all too impersonal and there was too high of a risk for miscommunication on a subject with which she needed complete clarity. Tentatively, she kept the conversation light while she built up her courage.

Sorry I woke you. I meant for you to get my text in the morning.

It's fine. I'm up reading.

Me, too

My book?

Yes

The three dots danced on her screen as she waited for his reply. She wondered how many drafts he was going through and wished she could see everything he had deleted. She knew from her own experience the deleted texts were always the most truthful. Everything afterwards was some watered-down and overly edited version of whatever she was truly feeling.

Do you want to talk about it? He finally texted back.

It was Denny's turn to see the dots and imagine the various drafts she was typing and deleting. Julia looked over at James and tried to figure out how he fit into everything. He was a good man and a good father. Too harsh and aggressive in his tone with her at times; too patriarchal in his belief that his word was final. And yet, judging from what she'd heard from her friends and family, and judging by what she'd witnessed in the neighborhood, they were likely at least as happy as anyone else was. She remembered when they had first started dating and how she couldn't get enough of him. Julia used to wake him up so they could have sex in the middle of the night after she'd had some erotic dream about him.

That was years ago. How can anyone keep up that kind of intensity for decades on end? How do couples endure years after years without their eyes occasionally wandering to something better across the way? The saying about the greener grass on the other side was a well-known adage for a reason. In Julia's case, it was the neighbor who was suddenly looking better with each passing hour.

She was sure he could deduce the many drafts she'd typed and deleted when he read her one-word response: *yes.*

13

DENNY, MAY 2014

D enny liked to write while Julia and Lindsay were at pinochle and the kids were next door under James's watchful eyes. He'd sometimes hang out in the kitchen with the women, sampling the food they were making and engaging in a bit of conversation before retreating back to his office with fresh ideas for his novels. If he was lucky, he was able to apply a few new details to whatever he was writing at the time. Usually, he would have to jot down a few lines on his legal pad to save for later. There his notes would sit for months, sometimes years, before he'd find the perfect story for them.

He had a good feeling when the two women returned from their game only somewhat drunk and a few hours earlier than they usually got home. That had him out of his office chair and opening his door a crack so he could eaves drop on their conversation.

He shamelessly stood directly at the door so he could hear better. It sounded as though Lindsay popped another bottle of wine and poured them each a glass. Though he couldn't see anything he pictured them in their usual spots:

Julia on the second bench from the deck sliding doors while Lindsay stood on the other side of the island. Lindsay wouldn't allow herself to indulge, so he was certain she would ignore the leftovers they'd brought back while longingly watching Julia pick at the food throughout their conversation.

This is stupid, he thought. He laughed slightly at his own misbehavior at the door and then went into the kitchen.

"Hey, hon. You guys are home early. Everything okay?" Not only had he abandoned hiding out in his office, but he also dropped any pretense of allowing the conversation to flow naturally since he laid out his curiosity as soon as he entered the room.

"Everything's fine. It was just a bust of a game. A few of the women have the flu that's going around, one had a funeral out of town, and another was out with her husband for their anniversary. It was only six of us tonight, so we didn't bother playing. We all ate, had a few glasses of wine while we talked, and then called it a night."

"That's too bad," Denny said. He wasn't sure what the right comment was since it seemed like they'd had a good time regardless. "Well, I'm writing in the back if you need anything."

"We're fine," Lindsay deadpanned.

"No, wait," Julia said. "I want to know if Denny's heard any of this."

"Not likely. Denny mostly keeps to himself. Aside from James, I don't think he has any neighborhood friends. Do you, hon?"

"That's right. I mostly keep to myself." Denny worked hard to keep the annoyance out of his comment. Did she always have to be so blunt about everything?

"See? But go ahead; ask him."

"Okay...Should I sit?" Denny asked. "Is this a loaded question?"

"It's pretty fucked up," Lindsay said as she gestured to the stool next to Julia.

Denny flinched slightly at Lindsay's language. She didn't swear much, and he liked that about her. The wine was going to her head; he could tell her level of sobriety by her language. With that one f-bomb it sounded like she was on her fourth glass of wine in about as many hours.

Julia had started the conversation and expressed interest in Denny's opinion, but Lindsay took over and steered from there. "Abby was telling us about the neighborhood myth that there used to be a bunco group years back the development was still being built. It disbanded and went to shit when the women started sleeping with each other's husbands and when two of the women started sleeping with each other."

"What's bunco?" Denny asked.

Lindsay sounded impatient when she answered. "It's a dice game but the layout is similar to what we do with pinochle. Different tables of four women playing games, the tables rotate so everyone socializes with everyone else. Drinks and food are involved. How is *that* your first question after what I just said?"

Julia chuckled at Lindsay's annoyance. "He already knew about it," Julia said more to Denny than to Lindsay. It unnerved him how well she could read him. Better than his wife could, that was for sure.

"I've heard rumors around the neighborhood about it," he confirmed. He couldn't deny it since Julia already correctly called him out, but he also couldn't tell them that Kari had mentioned it, in bed, a few weeks back.

"From whom?" Lindsay asked.

"I couldn't say, now. It was a while back," he said.

"And you never told me?" Lindsay asked. He did somewhat relish in the look of surprise and indignation on her face.

"It all happened forever ago. We weren't living here. And from what I've heard, everyone involved is gone. They've moved away. Moved on."

Lindsay turned back to Julia and began speaking as if Denny was no longer there. He didn't mind; it wasn't the first time, and it wouldn't be the last. It was late but Denny couldn't resist the dips the women left out. As he listened to their conversation, he ate a few generous scoops of taco dip. Eventually, Lindsay would remember he was there and would summarily dismiss him. He wanted to eat as much as he could before that happened.

"James doesn't know," Julia said with confidence. "He hangs out with a few of the guys on Evergreen for the occasional golf game, but he would have told me if he'd heard anything like that."

"Can you imagine our group turning into a bunch of swingers?" Lindsay asked.

"No," Julia said as she shook her head for added emphasis. "I'm still not convinced it actually happened. Maybe one affair; I could see that. But multiple women sleeping with multiple husbands? And then the two women leaving their husbands for each other? And all of it stemming from one bunco group? Nope. Sounds like a bad soap opera."

The two women continued to go back and forth about how it could have happened if it was indeed true. They theorized about if the women sneaked off in the middle of a game, or if someone slipped a note to the husband right under his wife's nose and in her own house. Denny didn't doubt any of it and nothing could surprise him anymore given his affair with Kari - one of the current pinochle members in Lindsay and Julia's group. Before the women got too involved in their conspiracy theories, he tried to change the subject with what he hoped was a safe question: "Whose house were you at tonight?"

Lindsay was mid sip so Julia responded, "We were at Stephanie's tonight."

With her attention back to Julia, Lindsay added, "You know she only insisted on hosting because she wanted to pitch her latest MLM side-hustle to us."

"What's that?" Denny asked.

"Multi-level marketing schemes. It's sales, but the bulk of someone's income comes from signing up people to join your business team." Lindsay put air quotes around business team to help drive home her disdain.

"It's not *that* bad," Julia said.

"It *is* that bad, Jules. I see this shit all the time at work with the cashiers and sales specialists and I have to shut it down before too much damage is done. One woman joins and start selling whatever - leggings, nail polish stickers, chalk paint, sex toys - whatever is popular and new and trendy at the time. But then she spends most of her energy not on selling her so-amazing-it-will-change-your-life products, but in recruiting others to do it too under her tutelage."

"Why shouldn't I join her? I like Stephanie and it sounds like a good opportunity. A way to earn extra cash and get discounts on products. I do *like* the makeup she sells."

"Jules, no. You're so much better than this."

Denny knew what was coming next because he'd heard similar speeches directed at him years back when she was still involved in his writing career. She was the one with the business background, never mind that he was a retail manager as well back in the day, and so only she truly understood how the sales world worked.

Even though he knew whatever Lindsay was going to say next was going to irritate him, he still preferred sitting at the island with them versus going back to the office. Probably because he enjoyed Julia's company, especially when it was without James.

"I'm better than what? It's an online startup where I'm in complete control over every aspect of the business. It's perfect for me."

"That's how Stephanie and all the rest sell it. In reality, you're a glorified salesperson who doesn't work in a store; you work from home. And you have to work harder because you don't make an hourly rate. You buy all of your own inventory that you may never sell, and the only way to make any real money off of it is to get a bunch of other women to join your team. I know you won't be able to do that part because Stephanie already has a handful of people in Scarlet Oaks selling as part of her team. She even has a few women from the surrounding developments, too." Lindsay paused to gauge Julia's response. To see if she needed to lay it on thicker or if Julia would concede. "Trust me, Jules. I have an MBA and I've worked in retail for most of my adult life. I know my shit when it comes to sales."

Julia reached for another chip. She scooped a generous portion of the cheese and beef mixture onto the chip before shoveling the gooey mess into her mouth. Denny couldn't tell if she was buying time or if it was Julia's way of avoiding officially agreeing or disagreeing with Lindsay. He pitied her. Lindsay would not allow Julia to question her business acumen without some sort of definitive outcome on who was right and who was wrong. Lindsay would not be avoided.

"Not to mention it's a pyramid scheme," Lindsay continued after the brief silence. "The more people you bring in, the more money you get. At some point people stop joining and the money stops, too. That's why I have to shut them down at work. Whole departments get involved and the drama of their side-hustle becomes Moyer's employee drama."

Julia finally acquiesced, "Yeah, I guess you're right."

"Listen," Lindsay said in a soothing and encouraging voice. "I don't want to hold you back, Jules. If you want to do it, you should."

Denny joined Julia in giving Lindsay a quizzical look in response. "I'm going to use the bathroom," Julia said as she pushed her stool back and made her way towards the hallway.

"Why would you say that?" Denny asked in a hush voice so Julia wouldn't hear him.

"Because she needs to hear the harsh truth. It could also ruin her friendship with Stephanie when it ultimately fails and she realizes what a heap of shit Stephanie sold Julia, as her friend, in order to try to make a profit off of her."

"You couldn't have waited until tomorrow to kindly encourage her to reconsider?"

"No, Denny, I couldn't." A few seconds passed before he was officially dismissed. "Don't you have a story to write?"

"Yeah, I do." He went back to his office but he didn't bother to close his door. While he did not want to be at the island with Lindsay anymore, he still wanted to hear if Lindsay would reconsider her stance and apologize or do something, anything, to make up for her heartless arrogance towards her best friend's potential business venture. Not that Denny thought it was a good idea. He agreed with Lindsay it was more likely to ruin friendships than to make Julia any real money. But there were better ways to go about having that sort of conversation with Julia.

He heard Julia and Lindsay's voices. From the office they were soft and too muffled for him to make out what they were saying. Then he heard what must have been Julia's footsteps at the front door since Lindsay's voice was still coming from the kitchen. Lindsay called out, "I have to work tomorrow, but we'll go shopping on Sunday. We'll get new makeup from MAC and do lunch."

The olive-branch of shopping and lunch was Lindsay's attempt to atone for her harsh criticism. As she always did, Julia agreed. "Sounds great. See ya." The front door shut, and Denny heard a few shuffling and clanging sounds as Lindsay, free from any feelings of guilt with Julia's enthusiastic response to their lunch and shopping plans, cleaned up the kitchen. She tossed out any remaining leftovers - lest she get tempted by them the next day - and she started the dishwasher which filled the ground floor with a soft hum as it washed away the filth from their snow-white dishes.

Denny went back to his novel and began toying with the idea of having Monica, his newest leading lady, get involved in some sort of semi-shady business venture that would cause conflict between herself and her romantic interest, Dom. Monica was a teacher and she struggled to get by over summer breaks and on a teacher's salary in general. Her desperation led to some poor financial choices and she refused to accept any help from Dom.

It wasn't perfect, but Denny could start to see how work and money could get in the way of two people who were trying to build a life together.

14

JULIA, OCTOBER 2019

Denny and Julia were going to discuss his romance novel outside, in the middle of the night. She changed out of her dingy workout shorts and stretched-out tank top and put on jeans and a sweater instead. Julia could justify the wardrobe change since it was cold outside and she needed something warmer to wear. What she would not be able to justify as easily was why she brushed her teeth, adjusted her hair as much as she could without the use of her hair dryer, and checked her reflection in the mirror multiple times before heading outside.

He'd suggested they meet out front to talk. The mere fact that they couldn't meet inside either one of their houses should have been a clear sign showing whatever they were doing, they shouldn't be doing it. Miraculously, neither warning flags nor alarms went off in their minds when they both agreed they couldn't simply stand outside and talk. If they were caught standing outside talking, the neighbors would talk as well.

What were the odds that one of their nosey neighbors would wake up and look outside to see them? Larger than one might expect. The Scarlet Oaks Knoll Facebook group page was often covered with posts about a suspicious car at some crazy hour in the morning, or about some dubious looking person they saw on their Ring cam.

Instead of standing, they decided to take a walk. If anyone asked, which Julia really hoped was unlikely to happen, they would say they couldn't sleep and had decided to try to walk off the booze and get a bit of fresh air to help them get to sleep. They were both still intoxicated when they came up with their plan, so the explanation sounded a lot more convincing to them than it should have.

"So," Denny began as they made their way around the first turn on the road away from their houses.

"So," Julia repeated. She found she couldn't even look at Denny. After spending the past two hours reading his book and picturing herself and Denny in various romantic and sexual situations, she felt awkward around him. As if those things had actually happened in the past two hours and she no longer knew how to act naturally in his presence.

"Would you like me to identify the elephant, or would you like do the honors?"

She smiled with relief at Denny's offer to lead the conversation she dared not have with him. "I'll leave it up to you." She wondered if he had a destination in mind as they were walking. Was it possible Denny had orchestrated the whole thing when he'd given her the book? Could he have predicted the outcome which had played out before him? A few days prior she would have said Denny didn't know her very well even though the families were close. That was a few days ago. Her opinion changed after she read his accurate portrayal of her as Lydia. She was keenly aware how observant he was and how it was possible he knew her better than Lindsay ever did.

"The book is about you," Denny said. Julia had known this

without a doubt, and yet she inhaled sharply at how blunt and definite it sounded coming straight from the author himself. "I'm assuming you read a bit tonight and that's why you texted me, still drunk, in the middle of the night. You read chapter ten, didn't you?"

"I am a little drunk, still. That's a fair assessment." She couldn't remember the specifics for each chapter. Once she realized what was happening, she started to speed through the pages in an effort to confirm her suspicions. She couldn't take it in fast enough. Regardless of her speed reading and skimming over some sections she'd refer to as fluff, she was sure she had indeed read chapter ten. Denny was referring to the first of many racy scenes between Lydia and Michael. But she wasn't ready to discuss that part with him yet.

"Everything I said is a fair assessment, or just your level of intoxication?"

Julia didn't want to answer, and Denny didn't force it. They walked in silence for a bit as Denny gave Julia time to figure out where she wanted to go with the conversation. He'd started it, but the reigns were passed to her now. The development was a large circle with four streets running north to south throughout the middle. A total of seventy-nine houses, all with similar layouts and all with exteriors that matched a preplanned color scheme determined by the builders who had long since moved on from Scarlet Oaks Knoll. Since they were cutting through the middle of the development and they would not go a complete lap, she had around ten to fifteen minutes before they would wind up back at their houses and would part ways for the night.

"You're right about everything," she said. They continued to walk. "I was reading, and within a few chapters it was glaringly obvious you'd written the story about me. About a version of me."

"Yes, it's just a version. And from an outside perspective."

"My kids aren't nearly as bratty as you made them out to be. Alexis would be pretty upset if she knew how you portrayed her."

"I didn't model the kids off of any of ours. That's inspired from other families and kids I've observed throughout my lifetime."

Julia nodded and they walked in silence some more. The two were forced to walk closely together since the neighborhood had painfully thin sidewalks. She wasn't sure if the countless times his knuckles softly brushed hers had been accidents or not. On her part, it was not accidental.

As they rounded another bend, she could see their houses in the distance. She glanced around the neighborhood for the umpteenth time that night looking at windows to see if anyone was up. No one was, as far as she could tell. Nothing but blacked out windows and sad-looking Halloween blowups that had been deflated hours ago.

Although their late-night meet up would go unnoticed by anyone else in the neighborhood, including their spouses, as long as they ended their walk and went back to their houses, Julia wasn't sure she was ready to end the night just yet. Her whole purpose in texting Denny was to confront him about the book and about Lydia and Michael's steamy relationship. She hadn't even scratched that surface. She hadn't done anything at all aside from middle-school level flirting with the brushing of her hand against his every few steps. Denny had offered up the information and even guided her to the start of the conversation, but she had detoured with the comment about how the kids were depicted, and then she'd gone silent and wasted a portion of their precious time looking at neighbors' windows and checking behind them to see if anyone was witnessing their potential indiscretion.

"We're almost back to the house," Denny said when they

were two houses down from Julia's house. "Is there anything else you want to ask me? About the book?"

"No," Julia said after just the slightest pause. As soon as the words left her mouth her brain started in with the inner monologue about what a coward she was and how she would look back at this moment and have so many unanswered questions and regrets. Simultaneously another voice in her head praised her for ending whatever it was that had pulled both Julia and Denny from the beds they shared with their spouses to take a secret walk around the neighborhood.

"Okay. Thanks for the walk, Julia. Maybe I'll see you tomorrow." Denny said as they approached Julia's driveway. There were small sconces on each of their garages between the doors. The lights illuminated a portion of the driveway. Julia and Denny were out of their reach as they were walking along the sidewalk.

Julia stopped at her driveway while Denny kept walking after he bid her goodnight. Instead of saying goodnight, or goodbye, or any other option that would be polite and socially acceptable in the situation, Julia's mind went back to the kiss between Michael and Lydia. She'd replayed it in her mind at least a half dozen times since she'd read it earlier that night. There was an entire paragraph devoted to detailing out the sensual touch of their lips as they finally let go of their inhibitions and allowed their base, animalistic instincts to kick in.

Could she really let him move away without feeling his lips on her own? She saw herself in the future, years in the future, rereading *Love Thy Neighbor* and wondering what would have happened if she'd done something, anything differently, the night of the Halloween party.

Julia turned off every voice in her head as she walked briskly through the soft light covering her driveway, and then back into the darkness again where she caught up to

Denny in the grassy strip which separated their two driveways. He had sensed her coming, had likely heard her footsteps on the driveway, and turned to her just as she'd approached him in the darkness.

There was no time to figure out the right words to say. She knew she should have finished the book and then played out a million different scenarios and conversations in her mind before settling on the right way to approach Denny about it. But then this was what he wanted, wasn't it? Why else would he have given her that book? Surely he has other books that do not star Denny as the main character and her as the love interest. No, he wanted this and so did she. That's why they were outside together in the middle of the night.

Part of her wanted to kiss him with as much intensity as she was feeling, but an even greater part of her wanted to recreate the sensual kiss between the characters. Without a care about where they were or whether or not anyone else was around, Julia took one step closer to Denny and put her arms around his neck as if they were going to dance. Denny placed his hand on her hips and moved them down and back just slightly until his fingers were resting firmly below her lower back and pulled her closer.

Mercifully, Denny took over just as Michael had. One of his hands went up to her face; his thumb gently stroked her cheek as his fingers went behind her ear and massaged her scalp with a gentle circular motion of his fingertips through her hair. His other hand, still resting on her lower back, pulled her even closer until their midsections were pressed up against each other and their noses were practically touching. Julia closed her eyes and gave in to the moment. Whatever was going to happen, she accepted it and even welcomed it. They hadn't actually kissed yet, but boundaries had been crossed. They might as well experience it all since they were going to live with the consequences regardless.

She sighed slightly from how sensual it felt to have Denny's hands caressing her face and gently squeezing her ass with a sense of urgency. Denny closed the space between them and they were kissing. It was different from the book. There was no aftertaste of wine from Denny's mouth. Instead, it had a minty taste to it from his toothpaste. The kiss was not as spontaneous as the one in the book. Julia even thought she could smell a slight scent of cologne or men's body wash on him. Was that left over from the party or did he somehow shower before he saw her?

Either way, she was certain he had wanted her for a long time and had set up the entire night, maybe even weekend, to lead them to that one moment in their front yards. She could analyze the implications of it all later, but at the moment all she could think of was how sexy it was that Denny had been watching her from afar for years. He had visualized, even put it into words and on paper, what would happen to them if they'd had the opportunity to be together. She'd started to feel it the day of their trip to the coffee shop and bookstore. She had her own pent up sexual tension just from seeing him throughout the party and not being able to do much more than have a brief conversation with him. From having his hand on her back without any hope for anything more.

She parted her lips, and without hesitation Denny followed her lead to deepen their previously chaste kiss. Her fingers found their way into his frosted-tipped hair and she lightly raked her fingertips through his thick tresses. Denny reached up and grabbed her hands in his as he pulled away. Julia was prepared to say she agreed, it was a mistake, and they needed to stop. They must both agree to never mention it to anyone. But before she could fully open her eyes and come back down from the high of their kiss, Denny was pulling her hands, pulling her, towards the side of the garage. He leaned back against his side garage door, the door he and Lindsay had painted years earlier while the Moores were on babysitting duty and had taken all the kids to get ice creams, and Denny pulled Julia against him.

Their lips found each other again, but this time the kiss was more urgent and showed less restraint from Julia. In the split-second Denny had pulled away, she'd been sure that was the end of it all. She'd been sure there would be no more intimate moments with Denny as panic surged through her and took her by surprise. There was a hard deadline with Denny, and she feared if she didn't act that night, she would miss her chance.

One of Denny's legs was bent as he propped himself up against the garage door. She straddled his leg and slowly rubbed up and down against his knee in a desperate attempt to relieve the buildup of longing which ached between her legs. He responded with an animalistic growl into her neck. Denny's strong hands found their way under her shirt and he raked them down against her back, his calloused fingertips roughly moving across her soft skin. Denny was relatively handy and was in decent shape, but Julia hadn't realized how strong he was.

Lindsay would sometimes give details of her raciest bedroom romps with Denny, but Julia often thought they were exaggerated if not a flat out lie. James, for lack of a better term, was the passionate one of the two. James would open ogle her in public. He'd also grab her ass or deeply kiss her in public as well. Denny had always been the gentleman of the two. Much too reserved to do anything so intimate around other people. She couldn't imagine Denny ravishing anyone in general because he was so level-headed and in control. He wasn't one to let his emotions or desires overtake him regardless of the situation. Looking back on it, Julia could see her assessment of Denny had been horribly wrong.

Denny further proved her wrong by moving his hands to

her breasts as he continued his exploration of her body outside, in his yard. She in turn reached down and began to unbutton his pants. Julia was so focused on undoing his pants, she didn't notice she'd started to fall forward towards him as he backed away.

Then they were inside his dark garage where even the light from the moon had vanished. The Moores had a three-car garage. The first two spots closest to the house were occupied with their vehicles. The third spot, the one right behind Denny and Julia, was covered in blankets. Moving blankets. They were moving.

Through deep, passionate kisses, Denny managed to say, "I don't want you to do anything you'll regret."

"No regrets," was all Julia could manage as she was finally able to undo the stubborn button on Denny's pants.

She took off her sweater and shimmied out of her jeans before somewhat blindly feeling around on the blankets for a good place to lay back. Before she could even situate herself, Denny was on top of her, and her hands were on his chest. She already knew it by sight thanks to the countless weekends they'd spent together at the local pool and on beach vacations, but she had no idea how muscular he was under the thin layer of pudge that covered his chest and stomach. Or how strong his biceps would feel as they strained to hold up his upper body while he continued to kiss her lips, neck, and breasts.

Lindsay popped into her head as Denny worked her nipples just as Lindsay had described it hours before. Julia felt both jealous that Lindsay had experienced this with Denny hundreds of times before, and stabbing guilt at the betrayal they were both committing. To help assuage her jealousy and guilt, she brought Denny's face back up to hers and reminded herself of the deep connection that had formed between them. This was not a one-night stand between two strangers.

"Do you want me to stop?" Denny asked. His breathing was heavy, and she could feel his hard length pressed up against her. Clearly, he wanted nothing else but to continue down their adulterous path. Julia wondered if, even in the blackness that surrounded them in the garage, he had sensed she was feeling conflicted about what they were doing.

Was he already so in-tuned with her and her body? Was it even possible? She thought back to the way he'd described her in his novel and thought, *Yes, he does know me that well*. She wondered what would happen if they did stop. Would they carry around the guilt of it all regardless of the fact they had stopped before taking it too far. As if it were possible to convince anyone, especially Lindsay and James, they hadn't already taken it too far. Hadn't already risked broken hearts and risked divorce if anyone found out about them.

It was too late to stop any of it. Denny had put the whole thing into motion when he placed the book into her red hands. The romance novel about Michael and Lydia, a version of Denny and Julia as lovers in an alternate universe where James was dead, and Lindsay and Denny were already divorced. He'd painted the image of them in the throes of passion and Julia couldn't unsee it. She couldn't stop thinking about how she needed to be with Denny. Needed to feel him crush her with the weight of his body; needed to feel his mouth on her chest; needed to feel him fill the inside of her with as much urgency and desire as Michael had had for Lydia.

"Don't stop," she begged.

Michael and Lydia had moved from the living room over to the bedroom. The only reason they'd done so was to keep their relationship temporarily hidden from the children. Michael and Lydia had been able to lay in each other's arms and bask in the relaxed and satiated feeling resulting from their epic romp in the sack.

Julia and Denny's experiences were again very different from their novel counterparts. Their time was limited. Though they were able to sleep a bit tangled up together in the pile of blankets in the garage, the sun would be coming up soon and they both needed to get back inside before their family members started to stir. There were no concerns about Lindsay. She wouldn't be up and moving until at least eight o'clock since she'd been up so late the night before drinking. James, however, was an avid runner who wouldn't allow a Halloween party to get in the way of his daily five-mile run around the community.

Still, Julia couldn't force herself to rise when she woke up. There was a fear deep in her stomach that the night had all been some sort of bucket-list item for Denny. Something he'd dreamt about for years but didn't necessarily want to pursue further once he'd attained his goal. She feared shifting the blankets underneath her or moving any part of Denny, who was still tangled up in her limbs and resting heavily over some parts of her body, would break the moment. She dreaded the daylight which threatened to seep into the garage windows at any moment as it would surely shine light on what a terrible mistake they had made.

"Good morning," Denny whispered in her ear as he nuzzled her softly.

Julia let out the breath she hadn't realized she was holding. She turned her head to sweetly kiss Denny, to experience at least once more what it was like to be with him and to kiss him whenever she wanted. Even if there was another tryst in their near future, at that moment they'd both need to leave the garage soon and go back to their real lives with Lindsay and James.

She sat up and Denny followed suit. Julia closed her eyes and breathed in Denny's scent as he leaned over and kissed her bare shoulder. His left hand covered her right one and she couldn't help but be hypersensitive to the feeling of his cold, hard wedding ring against her skin. And yet it all felt so right.

Julia thought she would crawl back into bed and toss and turn for an hour or so before she gave up and threw the covers back to begin her day. What did it say about her that sleep came easily for her? She didn't wake when James went out for his run, and she slept through the beginning of breakfast with the kids.

It was the smell of biscuits and gravy roused her from her sleep. As she showered, she tried to bring up the dreams she knew she'd had. They had been so vivid when she'd first opened her eyes, but then they were gone as soon as her feet hit the soft area rug under her bed. A scene or two would come to her as she showered. A fleeting image of Lindsay and Denny at a fancy dinner table. James, the only one still in his costume, was there, too, and all the kids were running around their kitchen table, but they were years younger. The whole thing was jumbled and nonsensical. She couldn't begin to guess what it all meant, so she put it out of her mind.

As she entered the kitchen James ran his eyes up and down her as if to assess something. Julia self-consciously ran a hand over her neck and wondered if she and Denny had been foolish enough to leave some sort of proof on each other's bodies. But no, she was just in the shower and hadn't noticed anything when she looked in the bathroom mirror. *I'm acting paranoid*, she thought as she dropped her necklace from her hand. That realization in itself increased her paranoia exponentially.

James must have noticed. He'd always said Julia was the worst liar he'd ever met in his life. The tell of the necklace was one thing, but in general she was unable to say something untruthful to someone without practically drowning in sweat and awkward glances around the room. She thought she might be sick, so she quickly sat down at the table next to Brice.

"Hon, can you come here for a minute. Please?" James's tone was slightly agitated, and Julia braced herself for the collapse of her entire world. How could she have been so stupid?

"Yeah. Sure," she called back as she gave Brice a quick kiss on his scruffy blonde hair. He had tried to duck out from under her, but Julia was too quick. She wouldn't be denied a quick sign of affection towards her baby.

James was still adding small bits of flour to the gravy to give it the thick, stick-to-your-ribs texture that made it a Herrick household favorite. Julia stood close to him, but still he lowered his voice to something just barely audible. His eyes were piercing, and Julia knew whatever he asked her, he would learn the truth. Even if she tried to lie, she would fail miserably. She thought about coming clean before he even had a chance to ask her. She braced herself for what was to come. She'd suffer through the initial explosion and then focus on picking up all the pieces again.

"I was talking to Denny last night." James paused for a minute and appeared to be assessing Julia's reaction to what he was saying. She merely nodded back with what she hoped was a combination of seriousness and nonchalance. Julia had trouble gauging the proper reaction and so she went with both, just in case.

"Are you okay?" James asked.

Ugh. She needed to get herself together and act natural. Just for once in her life she needed to keep a secret without tipping any of her hand. The idea was preposterous and an impossible feat for her, but she had no other choice than to try.

"Yeah, just a little hungover and sleepy. What did Denny say?"

James stared a few seconds longer before continuing, "Just promise me you're not going to get all crazy in front of the kids when I tell you this. You know how you get, and they don't need to see you getting all hysterical."

Julia knew a look of confusion and annoyance took over her face. She wasn't nearly as irrational as James liked to pretend she was. "I'm fine. Just tell me," Julia hissed back. Her head did hurt a bit and it made her crankier than she meant to be.

"Denny and Lindsay are telling the kids this morning. After breakfast he wants me to help him take down the fire pit."

Julia knew it was coming. She knew the Moores were leaving, but so far it all had just been words. Aside from the moving blankets in the garage, there hadn't been any proof of it actually happening. The dismantling of the communal fire pit was tangible. She should have realized their last fire, when Denny announced they were moving, would be their last fire. It only worked when your neighbors were like family. She wouldn't know her neighbors in a few weeks. How could they co-own and use a communal fire pit with complete strangers? Strangers who may want nothing to do with the Herricks.

Part of the problem was that she still hadn't given herself time to process any of it. The subject was off limits at the Halloween party and James didn't want to hear about any of it. Lindsay had asked Julia to keep it from the other neighbors until she told the kids in case someone got a little too tipsy and said something at the party. It was annoying and condescending, but Lindsay wasn't wrong about that. People's lips loosened with booze and laughter, why chance your daughter's surprise birthday party? It would get out soon enough. No need to rush to tell everyone the juicy gossip before it was absolutely necessary.

"You're not going to cry, are you?" James's question snapped Julia back to her kitchen and James's breakfast.

"No," she snapped back. Then she turned and walked back to the table before he could see the tears that formed in the corner of her eyes. She wiped them away and had them under control by the time she was seated at the table again, but James noticed. He always did.

The timer went off on the biscuits and James brought everything over to the table. For a moment, all seemed right with the world as Julia's beautiful family shared a warm, homemade breakfast on a brisk Sunday morning. The biscuits, Pillsbury Buttermilk much to the chagrin of James who wanted everything made from scratch, were delightfully flakey and light. The gravy was perfectly seasoned with pepper, sausage, garlic powder, and a pinch of red pepper flakes for an added kick. It probably wasn't up to the standards of anyone from the south, but it was just the way her family liked it.

Alexis regaled them all with stories of what the children got into down in the basement the night before. There was a karaoke contest, a few verbal fights at the photo station outside, and a hilarious incident involving a costume malfunction where three of the kids' costumes got tangled up and they tried to continue with the party as usual even though they were stuck together at the hips and knees.

"Also, Brice is totally in love with Liv. He followed her around like a puppy all night. It was pathetic."

"Did not," Brice demanded. Unfortunately, he inherited his poker face from his mother and the whole family could see it was probably true. James gave an irritated look to Julia which questioned how long they would allow the charade to go on before they told the kids what was really happening.

Alexis continued, "Then Hailey was mad because Brice barely paid any attention to her even though she wore something super sexy to impress Brice."

Julia almost spit out her coffee. She racked her brain for a bit but couldn't remember what Hailey had dressed up as. It was a Netflix character she couldn't put a name to. There had been some heavy coats of makeup and a little bit more skin than she'd been used to seeing on Hailey, but at the time Julia hadn't thought much of it. She'd been distracted the night before, that was for sure. James cleared his throat and ignored the comment about the ten-year-old next door trying to look sexy for his son. "Your mother has something she wants to tell you."

Daggers leapt from her eyes and impaled James a few dozen times along his forehead. He looked back at her expectantly, as he frequently did when something difficult was brought to the table. Let the mother handle it even though he often thought her an emotional wreck who was unable to control her tempestuous moods.

Julia had to accept that her eyes could not actually shoot daggers or harm her husband in any way. She looked over at her children instead and consoled herself with the idea that sooner was better than later anyway.

"The Moores are moving away, guys. Down to South Carolina. I'm so sorry. I know it won't be the same as them living next door, but we can go visit them and I'm sure they'll be back here to visit us."

"When are they moving?" Alexis demanded with the authority and indignity that only a fourteen-year-old girl can so eloquently achieve. "Why?" she followed up. Julia again saw her traits in her children, this time with Alexis and her strong emotional reactions.

"By the end of the week, I think. It's for Miss Lindsay's work. They don't want to move either, sweetie."

Alexis pushed back from the table with more aggression than needed and announced, "I'm calling Liv."

Julia reached across the table for Alexis's hand even though they were way too far apart. Alexis regarded her outstretched hand as if it were contaminated. "Sweetie," Julia said. "I need you to wait until she calls you, please. We know they're telling the kids this morning, but we don't know when yet. You need to let them hear it from their parents."

Alexis stood and shook her head in disbelief. "I can't even call? Why did you even tell me?" When it was clear no one had any answers to her questions, she stormed out of the kitchen. The family listened as Alexis's heavy steps ventured down the hallway, up the stairs, and into her bedroom. The final act was the predictable door slam. Still, both James and Julia flinched when they heard it.

Julia turned her attention back to Brice who was miserably pushing around his biscuits and gravy. Throughout her years as a mother, Julia had tried to prepare herself for her kids' first crushes and how they would likely crush their little hearts. She hadn't expected it to be so soon with Brice. And she hadn't expected to be the one to drop the hammer on him like that. She reached out to rub his shoulder, but he slid out of the chair and out of her reach. Without a word and as noiseless as a ninja, Brice made his way upstairs. They assumed he went into his room as well, but they never heard his steps or even the light click of his door gently closing. She told herself she would check on them later. At the moment they both needed some alone time to process everything.

"You couldn't have warned me a little?" Julia accused.

"I told you I was helping Denny dismantle the fire pit today, and the kids are moving away in a few days. You got your warning Friday night when Denny told you. You knew you'd have to tell the kids soon. I'm surprised you weren't ready for this." James had finished his own bowl and so he reached across for his son's. It was tainted with broken hearts and misery, but James devoured it as if he hadn't eaten in weeks. Julia knew it wasn't actually James's fault. None of it was. It wasn't his fault they were moving, and it wasn't his fault she was a wreck because she just cheated on James the night before. It wasn't even his fault he was so hungry; that was probably due to his five-mile run and not to his cold, black heart which was what Julia had pictured in his chest when he slid Brice's bowl across the table for a second helping.

Julia pushed her bowl towards the center of the table, no longer able to handle the thick gravy when her mouth and throat didn't work, and her stomach churned from anxiety. She waited for James to chastise her for being so emotional that she couldn't eat, but he was distracted by something over her shoulder.

"There's Denny. I should get out there and help him." He wiped his mouth with a napkin then dropped the napkin on the table and stood up. James walked over and gave Julia a quick peck on the lips then added, "I hated sharing a fire pit anyway."

Rage boiled inside Julia and she used everything in her power to hold her emotions in check as James walked away from the breakfast table and out the back door behind her. It was a sliding door that led out to their deck which had stairs leading down to the fire pit. She listened to his heavy steps, so similar to Alexis's, as he made his way down to Denny.

While he was out there living out his life goal of extricating himself from the neighbors, Julia was seething at the table. She stared down at the mess James had left. Over at the oven she knew there'd be droppings on the stovetop and likely caked-on gravy since James could never be bothered to rinse a pan. Her lips burned where he had just kissed her. It had been a perfunctory kiss which held no passion or purpose beyond fulfilling their customary kiss when greeting and when parting. She desperately wiped at her lips with her hands in an effort to scramble the nerve endings and to confuse them so they no longer distinguished between her aggressive smearing and his kiss. But it was no use. James's lips were too deeply imprinted into her brain so the feeling of them haunted her even when they had long gone.

Julia had to get out of the house. She needed some major distance between herself and her husband before she did anything crazy. Was she crazy? Was James right about her emotions? No, she wouldn't believe it. What she felt was the aftermath of their broken partnership where every fight or disagreement had been buried under a rug. At least on her end it'd been buried under a rug. She was pretty sure James had no problem yelling at her considering how often he'd done it throughout their relationship. And yet she was so set on making everything work she'd allowed it all the while keeping a smile planted on her face.

They should have talked about the car accident beyond James screaming at her. They should have talked about sending the kids to public or private school, beyond James's insistence on public and her allowing it to keep the peace. They should have talked about having a third child, which she'd desperately wanted, instead of James getting a vasectomy without even conferring with her prior. Fuck. It all came flooding back to her. Years and years of pent-up anger threatened to unleash all at once.

She even hated the way he overly adored her in public

and in front of their friends and family. Putting on a show of how much he loved and respected her through affectionate touches and grand gestures: the list she got on her birthday each year, his deference to her on any minor decision around the house, and his willingness to put in hours and hours of manual labor just to change the basement stairs so they had a landing in the middle because Julia had mentioned once she'd preferred it that way.

She'd dared to complain about James a few times during their pinochle games, and the group of women she'd been talking to shut her down. They'd said James was the best husband in Scarlet Oaks Knoll and she just couldn't see it. They claimed Julia didn't realize how lucky she was and that she'd better stop finding little faults in such an amazing man or he'd leave. "That's what happened with Stan," Kari had said.

Memories popped into her head like a poorly directed movie montage of the best of times and the worst of times. Julia's eyes pooled with tears as the hopeless situation of her life smothered her and threatened to weigh her down with such force that she could never hope to get up again. And yet, with all the anger and frustration she felt, only a single tear rolled down her check and dangled annoyingly from her chin. She clawed at it and cursed how everything in her life threatened to upend her sanity. A single tear refused to fall from her chin and it had her on the edge. Had James and Denny not been within earshot of her, and the kids, too, she supposed, she would have smashed at least two or three plates on the ground from the anger she felt at that single tear (and why not a million more tears if she was so upset?) which wouldn't fall.

She needed a cigarette. No, she hadn't had one since she got pregnant with Alexis and it would only make her more anxious. She remembered that about smoking. Sometimes it helped, and sometimes it threw her even farther over the edge.

Without any regard to the kids or James seeing her, Julia dropped to the ground and extended her arms and legs like a small child about to make a snow angel. She spread her fingers apart at what seemed like an equal distance and lightly pressed each finger and thumb pad to the ground with equal force. Up on the ceiling she noticed a small outline of a sticky toy one of the kids had thrown up to the ceiling years ago. It had long since come down but the coating that made it sticky reacted with their ceiling paint and left a subtle, but permanent, mark. She stared at the mark and breathed slowly and deeply until her panic attack finally subsided and she was able to stand up again.

She needed a friend. She needed Lindsay, but that was impossible. Lindsay was probably inside consoling her poor children about their impending move. A pang of guilt washed over her as she acknowledged she should be consoling her own children, but she was not in the right frame of mind to do it. If she'd gone upstairs and talked to them, their commiserating conversation would quickly turn to anger and agitation. It would end with things broken, perhaps even a riot upstairs with Julia leading the charge. It would give James ammunition to hold over her head forever as the prime example of Julia being overly emotional about life's little set-backs.

Lindsay had been Julia's go-to for the past decade. She would have to settle for Maureen or Abigail instead. It probably would have been an easier choice if Julia knew what she would say to them. Was she going to spill everything? The Moore's upcoming move? The affair? James's shitty behavior that he carefully hid from everyone else? The book? No, it would be insane to willingly let out all of that information into the gossip mill of the development. She could see it in her mind, within minutes of her meeting with one of the women she would be walking back to her house while behind the curtains and doors of her neighbors they would all be furiously texting back and forth with shocked-face emojis and gifs of people losing their minds. Some would say things like, "I knew it." She considered all of it even though Julia herself still felt in the dark. It was unlikely any neighbors could have predicted what had taken her by surprise.

In the end, Abigail and Maureen chose for her. Abigail was busy with a local charity which was revving up for the holiday season. She had to take a raincheck. Maureen, however, was free all day and was eager to sit and hang out with her. Julia took a deep breath before she reached for the dirty dishes on the table. She needed to clean the house before she left, but she also needed to keep her shit together while she was doing it. Smashing plates or screaming at that moment was not an option. What she needed was a giant abyss nearby she could drive to. She could scream her lungs out into the great nothingness and let everything negative in her life go. The image of her yelling into a giant, black pit soothed Julia enough that she was able to clean the kitchen without incident before she headed over to Maureen's house.

"Jules," Maureen greeted with a smile. Maureen looked fabulous, as if she hadn't been up until midnight drinking the night before. "I'm so excited you texted me."

Julia stiffened at the comment and wondered if it was a good idea to unload all of her issues and problems on this carefree, unsuspecting neighbor. Instead of bolting, which would have been seen as rude and uncharacteristic of Julia, she forced her legs forward and into the immaculate, child-free house. "Yeah, well we never get to talk just you and me. Kids, husbands, or friends are always around."

"Ugh, yes. Josh is always here. *Always*." Maureen groaned as they made their way to the giant island which stood as the focal point of the kitchen. "Ironically, he's not here now. He and Tim went to the driving range for a bit."

Julia admired the kitchen. The entire floor plan was open and almost every area of the first floor could be seen from the kitchen. Julia sat at the white marble island with the countertop which waterfalled down to the floor on each side. There were enough stools for five people, so Julia randomly chose the one in the middle while Maureen busied herself getting drinks together.

Her comment about Josh changed the entire tone of the visit and Julia relaxed a little at the idea of a bitch fest between her and Maureen. She was also encouraged to see Maureen setting up an array of spices and wet bar items on the island.

"You don't need to go to any trouble for me…" Julia began.

Maureen waved her off. "I was going to make these today anyway to try out this new recipe: Drunken Pumpkin Lattes. Look, I've already got the water boiling. You can be my taste tester today. It was meant to be."

"That does sound delicious," Julia agreed. She hadn't intended on drinking anything at Maureen's since it was before noon on a Sunday and she'd had so much the night before. But she had a difficult week ahead of her, and it seemed, as the hours went by, like it would be the type of week where anything went. An odd week where the unexpected was going to happen daily and she just needed to roll with it. A little extra booze would be an immense help.

"So," Maureen began as she started sprinkling spices and sugar on a dish before she rimmed two giant mugs with lemon juice and the spice concoction. "What's going on? I don't mean to be rude, but you look a little haggard. Like life has you bent over with no hint of letting up anytime soon."

Julia laughed slightly and put her finger on the tip of her nose to indicate that Maureen's assessment was dead on. "But let me get some drunken latte in me before I start letting it all out."

"This drink will loosen your lips alright. Alexa, play Young the Giant station." Maureen double-checked her old-school recipe card before dumping boiling water into a bowl with yet another mixture of spices. To top it off she added generous amounts of vodka and Rumchata. Julia's spirits lifted higher by the minute with the soothing music and the smell of pumpkin espresso which permeated the room. "Cheers," Maureen said as she slid a brimming-to-the-top mug over to Julia.

Maureen dove right in with a giant, intrepid gulp. It reminded Julia of her college years when she'd made Hot Pockets at two am and bit into them immediately after taking them out of the microwave and without bothering to remove the cardboard pouch. Boiling cheese had singed every part of her mouth and yet she'd repeated the whole chain of events multiple times throughout her tenure at college. As a sober adult she approached the hot drink slowly. She carefully tested it to see how hot it was. The chilled Rumchata must have cooled it a bit because it was hot, but not painful, as it flowed down her throat. The warmth of the fluid combined with the warmth of the booze and it lit up every nerve ending in her body with an almost orgasmic release of endorphins.

"Holy shit, Maureen. This is fabulous. Absolutely fabulous. Thank you."

"I'm glad you like it." Maureen's eyes were glowing with excitement and Julia wondered how much Maureen drank on a daily basis and what had led *Maureen* to an adult beverage before lunch on a Sunday. "Now that you've had a bit of a stiff drink, I'll confess I didn't randomly decide to test out my fall libation creations so early in the morning. I was going to test them out tonight with Josh, along with a new dinner recipe I found online. I changed my plans when you called. I knew you needed something strong and someone to talk to."

Julia cocked an eyebrow at Maureen; unsure of where she was heading with her comments.

"Because I look so haggard?"

"I saw you last night. With Denny."

15

DENNY, MAY 2014

The two families were at the local ice-skating rink to support Alexis and Liv's latest obsession, figure skating. Thanks to the Sochi Winter Olympic games, the girls were infatuated with figure skating in general, and in particular they were intrigued by the Russian figure skater, Yulia Lipnitskaya. At fifteen, Yulia was the youngest female skater to compete at the Olympics that year. Watching the young skater's graceful jumps and spins on the ice convinced the girls they both could be the next Yulia in a few short years.

What followed was relentless requests from both girls to both sets of parents for a Saturday night out at the ice-skating rink. Saturday evenings were penned on both family calendars as Family Friends night. On these nights, once a week, the Herricks and the Moores would get together for dinner and some sort of activity. The Saturday before it had been *How to Train Your Dragon* at the cheap theater since Brice and Hailey still had trouble sitting for too long and the parents didn't want to ruin anyone else's expensive movie experience. They didn't feel as bad about it when the movie had already been out for months and the tickets were a mere five dollars a pop. The Saturday before that had been bowling at Julia's request.

Denny wasn't sure if ice skating was an upgrade to the past few Saturdays or not. He himself was not an avid skater and didn't bother spending money to rent skates he wouldn't and couldn't use. Instead, Denny found a nice spot on the bleachers to watch the others.

James handled Brice and Hailey with ease since the rink had special walkers available for use by its smaller skaters. The kids clung to their walkers while they shuffled their tiny skates back and forth over the ice. They didn't seem to mind the glacial pace despite the monumental effort required to achieve the small amount of movement. Denny found himself considering James as he worked with the children. Frankly, he often found James to be an arrogant jerk to just about everyone. And yet he couldn't deny James had his moments, too. He always treated Hailey and Liv like his own children which made it a bit hard for Denny to completely hate him.

Lindsay and Julia were finding a tad more success with Liv and Alexis. Both moms had grown up going to skating rinks each weekend and it showed. Each was working with her own daughter and attempting to demonstrate basic moves like how to skate backwards or quickly stop themselves. Liv and Alexis did well given they'd never been ice skating before and only occasionally went roller skating in their driveways and around the neighborhood on walks.

Lindsay was in good spirits and the two of them had had a good week together. They were either in a temporary cease fire for the sake of the kids and their marriage, or things had finally started to turn around and they were starting to find their way back to each other. Either way, it still wasn't enough to keep him focused on his own wife instead of James's.

Julia was stunning. Whereas Lindsay was guarded on the ice and determined not to make mistakes, Julia was a free spirit. She took chances and fell on her ass a few times as a result. From the looks of her reaction her ego remained intact though he was sure her tailbone must have been bruised. Alone on the bleachers, he truly felt like an observer and allowed himself to focus on Julia, guilt-free.

It didn't last long. His phone began to vibrate in his pocket. He knew it was Kari without looking at it. It was always Kari even though he begged her not to call or text him so much. They'd been sleeping with each other for months; she knew his schedule and knew he was out with his family and the Moores' family for their weekly night out, just like every other Saturday night.

Things were getting out of control and he needed to end it. He wanted to end it, had almost pulled the trigger a few times even. What stopped him? Fear. Denny was in too deep and there was too much at stake. She'd already disregarded his pleas to not call and text so much. Imagine what she would do if he broke things off in a way that made her feel slighted, betrayed, or used.

At first, he'd merely been looking for someone warm to be with him and keep him company. Not just a warm body, though that was nice since his physical contact with Lindsay back then had grown more limited by the day, but also a warm personality. Denny wasn't exactly sure what it meant to have a warm personality or demeanor, but he did know Lindsay was cold to him and he couldn't keep existing with nothing but cold in his life.

Initially, Kari's laughter and physical touch had been like a spring awakening for him. Like standing in front of a blazing fire and feeling the heat spread throughout every inch of his body and soul. It caused the cold which once seeped through his whole body to finally relent and recede.

Quite literally, she was his warmth through the winter. Things changed around the time the actual spring weather rolled around and Kari was no longer satisfied having secret meetings with her secret lover. She wanted and demanded more from him. A trip out to another county where they could have a proper dinner in a restaurant. Denny had thought they were both on the same page with what had been happening between them: friends with benefits for a lack of a better term. He'd never said the words aloud to her nor could he ever say those words aloud to any woman. It sounded immensely insulting even to him. He should have realized she would eventually want an actual a relationship. He knew she wanted a future husband. Denny was failing at the one marriage he did have. He was in no way equipped or ready to start another, especially under such sinful circumstances. Not to mention the minor detail that he didn't love Kari. He barely even tolerated her at that point.

As Yeats once said, the poem's name alluding him as he sat on the freezing metal bleachers, "Things fall apart; the centre cannot hold." He felt a deep connection with the line as he mentally went through each of his options and found every scenario to have the same ending: his life falling apart.

The night before, he had dreamed he was on a beach with everyone he knew and cared about. Even his childhood yellow lab, Mackey, and his tabby cat, Tabitha, made a welcomed appearance in his subconscious. It had been a pleasant trip to the beach until everyone started to walk or even run away from him, going off into different directions. Some, including his small children, were running out towards the raging waves of the Atlantic Ocean.

A thick fog rolled in blocking his ability to see beyond a few inches in front of him. The sweet smell of the salty air turned mildewy as it thickened and filled his throat.

He was about to run towards his kids and the ocean when

he saw he was holding dozens of ropes in his hands. He somehow knew, the way people know things in their dreams, the ropes were connected to the people he so desperately wanted to keep close to him and safe. He held them tightly and felt a slight relief with the modicum of control it allowed. But the ropes started to cross. They pulled against and away from him with the taut material ready to snap if they were given any additional pressure or strain. There were knots where they crossed, and he could no longer tell which ropes in his hands belonged to whom. The center could not hold, and neither could he. All the ropes were yanked from his grasp leaving a burning sensation in his palms. In desperation, he ran into the frigid ocean and thrust his hands under the surf to blindly grope for his lost, possibly drowned, children.

He'd woken up drenched in sweat and freezing cold. He did not make a habit of putting much thought into what his dreams meant. Afterall, in one of his recurring dreams he arrives at his old grocery store job with his face covered in clown make-up. When he gets out of his clown car, he finds he's wearing only garishly colored large shoes and a squirty flower taped to his bare chest. Aside from those two accessories, he's wearing nothing else. What the hell could that mean?

But the beach dream had been too visceral to brush off to the side. Even as he sat on the frigid metal bench, he could easily recall the smell of the ocean and the feel of the thick, salty air clogging his throat. That particular dream felt ominous and had only added to his anxiety about the Kari situation.

Before he could figure out his next move with Kari, the women and older children emerged from the rink in need of refreshments from the tiny café area.

"Come sit with us, Daddy," Liv requested. Surprisingly,

Denny saw Lindsay's smiling, agreeable face just behind Liv. Typical. He was having an off day while Lindsay's mood was uncharacteristically upbeat. She even held his hand as they walked over to the table. Her hand was freezing cold from being out on the ice, and it took a beat for them to find a comfortable grip again since it had been so long. Regardless, when so many of their days recently were filled with nothingness and apathy, their tiny touches and smiles felt like significant steps in what he hoped was the right direction.

Once everyone was situated with hot chocolates and soft pretzels, the two women began to talk. Julia spoke about how much she missed work and struggled with being home all day every day. Denny rolled his eyes when Julia mentioned she couldn't go back to work until Brice was in first grade since that was the agreement she'd made with James before they were married. Lindsay wasn't unkind to Julia but she did lack empathy as Lindsay stood firm with her insistence Julia go back to work anyway regardless of whatever agreement she'd made with James years ago.

Denny tried to push his way into the girls' conversation about costumes and song picks for their upcoming Olympic debuts. He felt extremely uncomfortable hearing the women openly talk about, and sometimes bash, their marriages. He could only imagine what was said about him when he wasn't around.

"Sweetie," Julia warned, "blow on that and let it cool a bit before you drink it." Alexis nodded that she'd understood, and everyone went back to their conversations while Denny listened in on both. He was dismayed to find he'd missed the end result of Lindsay and Julia's discussion and that the women had moved on to gossiping about the other marriages in their neighborhood.

"Josh, Mike, and even Stan when he was around," Lindsay said. "They're all door hangs." Door hang was Lindsay's way of saying douche bag while around the children. "They don't do anything around the house, they make significantly less than their wives do – not that's a huge deal on its own," she said to Denny as if she could possibly sew his balls back on after she'd torn them off right there at the table, "but combined with their other bad behaviors...I just don't understand why they stay with them. Or, in Kari's case, even want them back. They're successful women, why are they with such jerks?"

"What did Mike do?" Julia asked.

"Opened up a few credit cards under both of their names and ran up their dept."

"What? When?"

"I don't remember. I think it came up at pinochle the weekend you guys were out of town visiting James's family."

Julia was about to respond when Alexis unloaded a mouthful of hot chocolate all over the table. Liv continued her conversation as if nothing had happened while Alexis hovered over the spill with her mouth still open, likely in an attempt to air it out and ease the burning of her tongue and mouth.

"Aw, Lexi, are you okay?" Lindsay asked.

Julia looked dumbfounded. "I told you it was too hot, Alexis. Why did you drink such a giant mouthful?" In an odd reversal of character traits, Julia looked utterly exhausted by her children being children while Lindsay took on the role of patient caretaker.

"We're okay," Lindsay said to the table in general as she and Denny helped Julia wipe up the spill.

Embarrassed by her lack of compassion for her daughter, Julia said, "Thanks. I guess I'm having a bit of a rough week." She gave a meek smile to Lindsay and then turned to Alexis. "Are you okay?" Alexis gave a nervous nod back as she tried to assess her mother's mood. "Good. Let's take it easy on the hot chocolate for a bit. Okay?" Another nervous nod from Alexis.

The women went back to their discussion about how their friends' husbands were deadbeats and unworthy of their wives. While the adults were engrossed in the conversation, they heard another *bleh* from the girls and looked to find yet another pool of hot chocolate beneath Alexis's gaping mouth.

"Are you kidding me right now?" Julia snapped.

"It's hot…" Alexis began to explain.

"Jules, why don't you get a few more napkins. I don't know if I'll have enough here," Lindsay said. She was mopping up the second spill while Denny took in the rare sight of a frazzled Julia.

Minutes later the table was cleaned up again and Lindsay was trying to pull Julia back into their gossiping conversation about the neighborhood husbands. Then Alexis and Liv started in about ice skating and spins.

"Mom," Alexis said, "Liv says Yulia started skating when she was four years old. I'm eight. We're doing this all too late. You should have signed me up when I was four," she demanded with her little finger pointed at Julia.

"That's younger than Brice. You wouldn't have been ready then," Julia said.

"Yes, I would. You ruined my chances at the Olympics."

"You really did, Miss Julia," Liv helpfully added.

It was hard to say how long the argument would have continued since it was abruptly cut off and forgotten about after Alexis's arm knocked her hot chocolate over sending steaming hot dark-brown liquid all over the table and the floor. Luckily everyone's laps were spared.

Denny leapt to action and created hot chocolate barriers with the napkin reserves Julia had gotten from the stand. While he prevented the streams from continuing to run off the table and into their laps, everyone else looked on with their jaws hanging open. Lindsay tried to stifle a laugh, but Liv caught it and let out a guffaw. Alexis was somewhere between laughing and crying while Julia gripped the table and clenched her mouth closed.

"Step away," Lindsay told Julia. "We'll take care of it."

Julia's white knuckles regained their color when she released the table and walked back towards the skating rink.

Denny kept working at the spill while Lindsay took care of the girls. She told them to head back over to the stand and get something else to drink, maybe a Gatorade or anything else that wasn't hot. When the girls were out of range, Denny whispered to Lindsay, "What was that all about?"

"I don't know," Lindsay said.

"I've never seen Julia get so mad at the kids before."

"Me either. I guess she's under a lot of stress."

"You think there's something going on with James?"

"With James? Like what?"

"I don't know. Maybe they're fighting or not getting along."

"No, he's the same jerk he's always been. I think she misses work and adult company." They both finished cleaning the rest in silence. Denny kept running the idea through his mind that Julia's unhappiness with James may run deeper than Lindsay realized. He was convinced their ideal marriage wasn't as ideal as it seemed to be.

Eventually Julia returned and looked a little more like her usual self. "I'm sorry, guys. I think I'm going stir-crazy being home with the kids all the time. I need to get back to work and interact with adults a bit more."

Lindsay rubbed Julia's upper arm and said, "It's okay. We've all snapped at the kids before. You were due." She gave a sweet smile to Julia and Denny couldn't help but feel a little spark of warmth at the Lindsay he'd fallen in love with.

The two girls returned with their drinks and Denny and Lindsay braced themselves for a meltdown when they noticed Alexis had gotten another giant hot chocolate.

Julia put her head down and pinched the bridge of her nose. Then she looked up at Alexis and calmly asked, "Can we agree that you don't actually like hot chocolate? You don't like anything hotter than room temperature."

"Yes," Alexis agreed.

Julia gave a slight nod of her head in agreement. "Good. So why do you have another hot chocolate?" It wasn't mean, or sarcastic, or even said with a raised tone. Julia sounded genuinely intrigued at how the entire situation had restarted and was about to play out again with the exact same ending as the first round.

"We told the man what happened, and he insisted I have another one."

Julia sighed. "Okay, Sweetie. Let me have it."

Alexis gladly handed Julia the hot drink. "He said to be really careful because it's extra hot. He just made it."

"I know, Sweetie. I know. Let's go back out on the ice before our two hours are up."

While Julia fought to keep her anger and annoyance in check, Lindsay and Denny smirked off to the side. At one point, Lindsay even buried her face into Denny's shoulder to stifle a laugh. Not at Julia, of course. Had it been any other day Julia would have found the whole incident hysterical herself.

Lindsay drove that night while Denny was texting in the passenger seat. Their evening out had been the sliver of hope he'd needed to end things with Kari. He got a glimpse of his former life, with the love of his life, and he wanted it back. It was time.

He texted a brief message to Kari kindly saying he'd enjoyed their time together, but he needed to think about his family and he needed to end their relationship. She did not take it well. She insisted they talk in person before ending what they had. Lindsay seemed distracted by his texting, so he sent back a quick, *fine*, and then started up a conversation with the kids in the back about their favorite part of their Saturday night.

That night he and Lindsay found each other once again, but this time it was in bed. In the middle of the night, actually. The kids were all wound up from ice skating and from the ice cream sundaes they'd had when they got home. It had taken Denny almost an hour to finally get them to sleep. By then Lindsay was softly dozing on her side of the bed. Denny was a little disappointed since they'd had such a good night together, but he understood. Lindsay was working so hard with her career and everything else in her life. She needed and deserved a deep, long sleep.

Sometime in the early hours of the morning, before the sun was up, Denny woke up to Lindsay straddling him.

"Lindsay?" he asked. She gently rocked over his growing length. Her head was back a bit, but he could see her eyes were closed.

Instinctively he began to slowly rub against her as well. "Lindsay," he tried again. This time she opened her eyes and looked around a little confused.

She laughed softly and asked, "Was I humping you in my sleep?" She started to roll off of him and he gently held her in place.

"Wait," he said. "We've already started…"

16

JULIA, NOVEMBER 2019

I f Julia had had a mouthful of Drunken Pumpkin Latte in her mouth, she surely would have defiled Maureen's virgin white countertops as the dark liquid spewed from her mouth. Luckily, her drink was on the counter and her mouth was empty when Maureen announced she'd seen Julia and Denny together. But how was it possible? They had been so careful. No, they hadn't been careful at all. It had felt cautious at the time, but walking the streets of Scarlet Oaks Knoll with someone else's husband at a time which couldn't even be clearly defined as late at night or early in the morning had been reckless and stupid.

Julia once again relied on her non-existent poker face to see if she could get Maureen to spill what she knew before Julia tipped her hand any further. She'd already revealed it wasn't an innocent encounter with the devastated look which covered her face. A gulp of her drink calmed her enough to get a slightly better hold over her facial expressions.

"Saw us what?" Julia asked.

"I saw you against the garage door with Denny," Maureen

said matter-of-factly as she pointed out her back balcony doors. There was a clear view of both the Moore's and the Herrick's backyards. They could see, at that moment, Denny and James taking apart the firepit and patio. Piece by piece her husband and lover were erasing any promise of future s'mores nights. Julia blushed as the two women briefly watched the men.

"Not me. It must have been Lindsay," Julia bumbled. She was in deep shit, but she was still having trouble taking her eyes off of Denny who had shed his sweatshirt as the cold morning transformed into an unseasonably warm day with a cloudless sky. James was wearing a tight-fitting T-shirt and was obviously the more muscular and toned of the two. But it was Denny who kept catching her eye.

"You would think he'd be out there with his wife," Maureen conceded, "but this woman had short brown hair. At least that's what I thought I saw."

The two sat in silence as they sipped their drinks. Julia noticed a mug out on the deck next to the chair which overlooked Maureen's backyard and ultimately the Moore's and Herrick's as well. Denny's side garage door was in plain view. Had Maureen wandered out the night before and not only witnessed it but heard them as well? Saw them disappear into the garage for what must have been at least an hour? She imagined Maureen sitting in the chair, a decaf coffee helping to keep away the chill as she saw the steamy tryst playing out just beyond her own backyard. She turned back to Maureen before lowering her head slightly and taking a few more generous sips of her drink. She hadn't eaten anything yet so they went straight to her head. With the help of the booze she relaxed rather than panicked at the idea of someone else carrying her burdens and her secrets alongside her.

"I'd understand if it *was* you," Maureen said in an effort to coax Julia's head back up.

"You'd understand? Have you cheated on her husband with Denny, too?" Julia half joked.

"Yes," Maureen said before taking the last swig of her drink. The recipe card was left discarded and unneeded as Maureen went into autopilot making the second round of drinks for them. Julia reminded herself that Maureen was a professional drinker, and it wouldn't be wise for her to try to match her drink for drink. But maybe she'd have just one more, because suddenly jealousy and anger were bubbling up again as visions of Denny and Maureen flooded her mind.

"Well, sort of. I don't know what you'd call it. It was just a slip a few years back." Maureen threw more spices into a bowl and coated the rims of new mugs. Maureen didn't bother asking Julia if she even wanted another heavy pour of spirits that morning. Nor did she bother getting the mug back from Julia. She had a whole cabinet full of giant mugs and Julia was mildly nervous as to how many drinks Maureen could make that morning. Given her love of alcohol she was sure Maureen's house was well-stocked with bottles of booze strategically placed throughout the house. It was possible any room of the house could conveniently be turned into a makeshift bar.

Maureen continued her story after Julia tried, and failed, to articulate some sort of response. "We made out one night then immediately agreed it was a drunken mistake. Something we'd never speak of again or let happen again. Not that the second part was that difficult. We aren't actually interested in each other. Never have been. We were both two lonely people looking for comfort and something to fill the void we were feeling."

As Maureen stood leaning against the island, Julia noticed she looked a lot older than her thirty-eight years. She wondered if the excessive drinking, occasional smoking, and job as an anesthesiologist were adding years to her face in

the form of emerging wrinkles and age spots. Not that
Maureen wasn't attractive. Even though she looked older
than Julia and their friends, she was, undoubtedly, the
natural beauty of the neighborhood. Maureen had her long
auburn hair pulled back loosely in a messy bun which looked
anything but messy. Her eyes had just enough makeup to
make them stand out without looking overbearing. She was
wearing a brown sweater which hung nicely around her hips
and skinny jeans which showed off her stunning legs. Fall
was her season. And though she had been lonely that night
with Denny, surely she was living her best life there in the
kitchen with Julia. She was practically glowing with happiness from the booze and gossip.

"I don't remember this at all. When? How did no one find
out?" Julia's brain fogged up again slightly from the drinks
which didn't help her memory. Regardless, she took the new
drink Maureen proffered and took another warm gulp of
what could only described as fall in a cup.

"You wouldn't remember or know. You weren't there.
Josh invited Denny over after tennis for a few drinks. You
and James were hosting a sleepover with the kids. I'm pretty
sure Lindsay was with you that night."

Unfortunately, the information wasn't much to go off of.
Julia and Lindsay were constantly having each other's kids
over for sleepovers since the moms often took the opportunity to have their own mom-date, too.

Julia's brow remained furrowed as she tried to pin-point
the date, but Maureen didn't care. It wasn't essential to the
story and she literally brushed the insignificance of the exact
date with a wave of her hand in the air. "Anyway, it was Josh,
Denny, and me one night having drinks and dinner. I don't
remember why James wasn't there since the moms had the
sleepover under control."

Julia almost commented how James wasn't big on

hanging out in general. Though they likely invited him, James likely supplied some excuse as to why he couldn't go out and be social sans Julia.

"Josh got sloppy drunk. I'm not sure how since he has the tolerance of a frat boy, but he did. Denny had to help me get him upstairs and into bed. When we came back down it was still early in the night. I told him he should stay and keep me company." Maureen had been looking out back again, but at this her eyes darted back to Julia. "Not in a sexual way. There was no premeditated intention for what happened later."

"And Denny said he was lonely? Who made the first move?" Julia asked. She wanted to know everything, and she was certain that every iota of information she could squeeze from Maureen would lead her that much closer to under-standing what happened between herself and Denny.

"We were drinking and discussing whatever random topics popped into our heads. Then he brought up work and I mentioned that I had just been laid off after the merger with Med Health. You remember that?"

Julia nodded her head. She vaguely remembered a bright sunny day a few years back when Maureen had joined her and the kids on a walk around the neighborhood. While the kids had been in good spirits and the weather had been pris-tine, her conversation with Maureen had been bleak. Both were commiserating about work. Julia had wondered if she would ever get back to her job as a dental assistant and Maureen had lamented about how she based her entire self-worth on her job. It had been devastating to her to be laid off.

"It was a dark time for me." Maureen took another sip and then looked outside at Denny and James as they continued to make quick work of the once lovely and inviting fire pit area. "Denny had just finished his last *Time and Again* book. But he was struggling with some heavy stuff, too. This is just between us. Right?"

"Of course."

Maureen gave a quick laugh. "I probably should have confirmed that sooner. But you know how this neighborhood loves to gossip." Maureen then detailed out the night for the Julia. Denny was lost and lonely. Lindsay was working more and more hours and seemed to still be at work mentally even when she was at home. Her excuse was that she needed to be the successful one since Denny was suffering from major writer's block and couldn't come up with another hit series in the science fiction genre. He'd hoped he could still write and be as successful with fiction in general, but his agent hadn't liked any of his new work.

Maureen and Denny were home all day and no longer working jobs they loved. Their spouses were less sympathetic than Maureen and Denny had hoped. Lindsay, who had once been Denny's biggest supporter, had started to hint about going back into management at the grocery store. Josh didn't see what the big deal was about being laid off. It wasn't because Maureen wasn't good at her job, it was because the hospital was going in a different direction and outsourcing anesthetists in order to save money. How, Josh had wanted to know, had that hurt Maureen's pride? She just needed to get over it and get back out there at a new hospital. Or she needed to go back to school to do something else. Either way, moping around the house was inexcusable.

"By the time we had gotten through all of our baggage, it was late. Denny had even commented how late it was, but he said he wasn't ready to go back home yet. He expected to find Lindsay, in bed with her computer doing work. He'd said just the sight of her on her computer was going to piss him off. On top of that, she'd probably tell him about another job opening she'd seen that day, or maybe there'd be a printout of a job opening she'd found on Monster.com."

Julia cut in, "I had no idea Lindsay had been doing that. I mean, she'd tell me in passing sometimes how Denny was considering going back into the workforce. I had just assumed it was Denny's idea. Not hers." Her heart hurt a little for Denny. *This is why they didn't talk about work together*, Julia thought. It wasn't a lack of interest or the need to put work stress behind them. It *was* the stress. It was literally coming between them in the bedroom in the form of a laptop on Lindsay's lap or an unwanted now-hiring printout on Denny's pillow.

"Right. He was quick to point out Lindsay wasn't always like that and they were just going through a phase. I had a similar phase with Josh. Just hit a sort of rough patch in the marriage where you wonder if you still love him enough to stay, or if it's faded so much that it's time to cut your losses and try again with someone new."

"That's how I've been feeling with James lately," Julia said. She still loved him, but some days she wasn't sure if it was enough. It wasn't the relationship it had been before kids. Building a life with James, rather than just dating him, had already put a tiny strain on their relationship. Things changed after they got married. It was subtle and hard to put a finger on, but it was there. Raising kids with James had changed everything. The love was there, but there was also an extra layer of exhaustion, fear, and tension at all times.

"Josh and I always thought it funny when people said marriage is hard. And we're asking, it's hard to live with the person you love and adore? How can that be? We were so naive in our early twenties. Practically kids still, though we felt like adults at the time."

Julia could have gone down a rabbit hole with Maureen about marriage and making it work, but she was still dying to get to the meaty details of Maureen and Denny. Just putting the two names together in her mind felt strange and she wasn't sure if it was a good idea to hear the details or not. But like the book about Michael and Lydia, she needed to know regardless of the outcome. She remained quiet again and hoped that Maureen would proceed without Julia prodding too much.

"Anyway," Maureen said. "Denny was so sad about going home to Lindsay, that I walked over to him and hugged him."

As Julia sat in Maureen's kitchen, she pictured it all happening. In her mind she could see Denny, at the island a seat or two away from where she was, looking as sad as he had the night of the last fire pit. Then she saw Maureen, her drink still in one hand because she never walked around after five pm without one, walking over and sort of friendly hugging Denny as he was slumped over in his seat.

"We hugged for a minute or so, which sounds brief, but when your body is pressed against someone else's, it's a long time. And then as we pulled away from the hug, we both naturally transitioned to a quick, comforting kiss. Just a peck. And then another. And another one that was a little more than a peck."

"Who stopped it first?" Julia couldn't believe how nosey she sounded or how insensitive. It wasn't a trashy day-time television show for her amusement; her neighbor was baring her soul and letting out a secret she'd harbored for years. "I'm sorry…"

"No, it's fine. It feels good to finally talk about it with someone. We both did. Neither of us wanted to take anything further. We just wanted…something. Once we kissed, we both realized kissing or taking it further wasn't going to make either of us happier. No hurt feelings. In fact, we both laughed afterwards and agreed that that was really, really weird and not something we would ever do again."

Maureen shrugged her shoulders like she was putting it all behind her once and for all. "I felt like shit about the whole thing for a few days, then I let it go. I focused on getting another job, which I found a week or two later, and on mending the giant sinkhole that had slowly opened up between me and Josh over the years."

Julia took a moment to let all the new information sink in through the light boozy fuzziness which had settled comfortably throughout her brain. When Maureen went to make another round, Julia was quick to hold up a hand and turn down a third drink. She'd appreciated the slight buzz, but she needed to be able to think clearly. She didn't want to do anything rash she would later regret - like sleeping with the neighbor. Did she have regrets? Regret was a strong word. She wasn't sure if it was the right word for her situation even though morally she knew it should be.

Most people would have stopped drinking themselves as soon as their guest, and in this case the only other person in the house, stopped drinking. But Maureen was not most people. She poured herself a third generous helping and carried on.

"And no one ever found out?" Julia asked. She was both impressed by their ability to keep it under wraps and encouraged by the idea that maybe her indiscretion with Denny could remain buried as well.

"No one."

"Have you and Denny ever said anything about it to each other?"

"Never. It was like it never happened. Although Denny and I weren't close to begin with, so it's not like much changed afterwards. We just fell right back into being neighbors who see each other in the backyard or at social gatherings."

"I can't believe I never knew this," Julia said incredulously.

"There wasn't much to tell." Maureen said with a shrug of her shoulders. "I get the feeling your story is a bit more interesting than mine."

Julia looked back at Denny and James. They were taking a break and having a beer on the patio under the Moore's deck. "And why is that?" Julia asked.

"I read *Love Thy Neighbor*."

Julia's face turned scarlet at the mention of the book. Had Maureen heard Denny's voice as the narrator, and imagined him as Michael as well? Imagined her and Denny playing out the scenes as she had?

"He told you about the book?"

"Just hints. He told me how he was going to start writing romance novels and was already almost finished with his first one. He slipped and mentioned the title. I don't think he even remembers that part of the night. I got curious and kept an eye on Amazon for it. Eventually it showed up with a woman's name as the author. I wasn't sure it was even Denny's until a few chapters in when it all clicked that it was about you and him. I'd wanted to ask you about it ever since, but I never got up the courage. Too afraid it might circle back to my own brief slip-up with Denny. For a while I watched you both at parties and gatherings or any time I saw you all out back for dinners or at the fire pit."

"I had no idea," was all Julia could manage. Denny's book had come out years ago. Had Maureen been waiting all that time for the garage scene she had witnessed the night before? It was unsettling to think of all the instances they had been outside, for whatever reason, while Maureen had been inside at her sink, looking out the back window at them. Or maybe she had been at the island with one of her many drinks taking in the scene in the backyard and desperately searching for a forbidden smile or innocent touch that lasted too long. Had Julia really thought the night before that they were invisible in the semi-darkness as they strode around the development in the dead of night?

"Not in a creepy stalker way," Maureen quickly added. Julia's face must have tipped her off to how inappropriate she found Maureen's confession. "I just meant that I've been curious since I read the book to know if it was based on any sort of reality."

"It's not," Julia said more aggressively than she'd intended. Not that it mattered. Maureen had just confirmed her biggest fear: the development would find out what was happening between the families and her neighbors would use the Herrick and Moore's messed-up lives for their own amusement.

"Oh," Maureen responded in either agreement or disagreement. It was hard to say, and Julia struggled to care either way. She needed to get control of the situation before any real damage was done.

"How come they're taking down the fire pit? I assumed maybe it was because your secret came out and the two houses were formally divorcing. But then James and Denny wouldn't be getting along so well if James knew. Would they?" Maureen's conscience must have been scrubbed clean from her confession to Julia. She assumed it was because Maureen saw Julia do much more with Denny than just a few quick kisses. Maureen was mildly drunk, and from Julia's perspective, Maureen was enjoying her interrogation a bit too much for Julia's comfort.

"Lindsay and Denny are moving to South Carolina at the end of the week," Julia said. Everyone would know by the end of the day anyway, and she couldn't keep that key detail to herself any longer.

It was Maureen's turn to be shocked. "In a week? How long have they been planning that?"

Julia shrugged her shoulders and finished the last of her

drink. "As far as I know it's all very sudden. Lindsay was unexpectedly transferred to a store down there. Right outside of Hilton Head."

"Shit. Are you okay? You guys have been inseparable since they moved in."

"I should go," Julia said as she set her mug back down on the island. She wasn't close with Maureen. Why did she think it was a good idea to spill her secrets to this woman she barely knew beyond the superficial basics such as work and drink preferences? "Thanks. For the drinks."

"Yeah, sure. Listen, if you ever want to talk, I'm here." Maureen walked her down the hallway and opened the door for her.

"Thanks," Julia managed. As soon as the door closed behind her she wondered if Maureen was already on her phone texting Abby all the juicy details of their visit. She doubted Maureen would say anything about Denny since she would risk being outed by Julia as well. But definitely the gossip about Lindsay's transfer and her sudden move. She knew the women would come up with all sorts of reasons as to why Lindsay would be transferred out of state with such short notice. Julia had come up with some interesting ideas herself over the past few days.

Rather than walk around the long way by taking the street, Julia cut through the yards, dipped down and back up out of the swale, and found herself face to face with James and Denny.

"Almost done," James boasted much in the same way they had when they were first building it. James's excitement about Lindsay and Denny's move was really starting to grate on her nerves. Couldn't he just pretend for one week to be sad to see them go?

Julia, with the help of her liquid courage, stole a glance at Denny while James's back was turned. Denny gave her a smile and a wink, and her knees almost gave way. The move, the affair, and the betrayal all hit so much harder in the light of day. She felt like she was going to be sick. "Looks good, guys," she said before she hustled up the deck stairs and into the house.

Once inside, Julia noticed she'd left her phone on the island. She picked it up and wasn't at all surprised to see a slew of text messages from Lindsay.

Thanks for Livs surprise bday party

Are you home?

Where are you?

Just got called into work. Pls check on Liv and Hailey. v upset. Denny is useless.

Come visit on my break so we can talk. fine swine at 2

Some were back-to-back and some had an hour or two between them. It was useless to try to avoid Lindsay for an entire week. She'd likely want to spend as much time as possible with Julia since she was leaving soon. In the past, during sloppy drunk conversations late at night around the fire pit or at one of their islands, Lindsay would lament how she had trouble finding good friends who were female. Those moments of vulnerability with Lindsay were few and far between. When Julia looked back on it, it seemed they had happened less and less as the years went on. Julia wondered if it was because Lindsay had made more female friends, or if it was because her steel armor had become stronger and had closed any remaining gaps which previously left her vulnerable to pain and emotions.

Julia looked at her watch and saw it was a little after noon. She decided to take a quick nap until one and then she'd run over to see how Hailey and Liv were holding up. It hurt her heart just thinking how this would be one of the last times she'd console them. Julia laid down in bed for a few minutes, but she was restless. She didn't allow herself to overthink it when she grabbed Denny's book again and started to read about the time one of the kids got their heads stuck in the staircase railing and Denny, or rather Michael, had to carefully extract him.

It no longer felt appropriate to walk into the Moore's residence without knocking. The kids were having a tough time and things were weird between her and Denny. She knocked loudly a few times and then failed to resist the urge to let herself in.

"Liv? Hailey? You guys here?" she called from the foyer.

The kids ignored her, but Denny called out, "In the kitchen."

Julia made her way down the short hallway which led into the Moores' kitchen. They lived in a development where all the houses were based around the same basic layouts. They would often go into a neighbor's house and find it was the same floorplan as their own, only with different paint, furniture, and countertops. That's how the main floor of Denny and Lindsay's house was, a mirror image of Julia and James's. It was both comforting and unsettling at times.

Though not nearly as unsettling as seeing Denny at the island chugging a glass of water. He wiped his mouth with the back of his hand and said, "Probably shouldn't have had quite so much to drink last night, or the beer with James today. I'm sure I smell like a brewery after the workout he just gave me."

"Yeah, I was a little rough earlier today, too. Did you guys finish?" She looked out into the backyard for herself before Denny could answer.

"Close enough. I asked James to help me take it down so

we could show the house better at the end of the week. I was going to do most of the work since I, or rather we, were the ones rushing it. But after we took down most of the heavy brickwork James dismissed me. Said he'd finish if I had packing and things I needed to get to."

"Sounds like James," Julia agreed. And it did. He liked to be in charge and do things his way. If Denny was working too slowly or doing anything that deviated from how James believed things should be done, James would view Denny as a hindrance rather than an advantage. Dismissal, once the heavy lifting was out of the way, was imminent.

"I've been getting the feeling he's glad to have it down. Maybe even glad to see us go."

As much as it annoyed her that James was sometimes a complete prick, she didn't want everyone else to know he was like that. Julia also feared it would hurt Denny's feelings to hear the way James talked about his family. Nice guy Denny getting shat on once again.

"I came over to check on Liv and Hailey. Lindsay said she got called in and wanted to make sure they were okay while you were out working."

Denny laughed without any humor. "Lindsay to a T. She doesn't think I can handle it."

"Are they okay?"

"Hard to say. They just went over to your house about a half-hour ago or so. You didn't see them?"

Julia had been so engrossed with the book she'd missed hearing them at her house. She laughed at her bad luck. They were with their friends; there was no way she could compete with friends. She'd have to catch them another time. If there was another time. It was Sunday and they would be gone on Saturday. Not to mention all of the packing which still needed to be done. How had they all not realized how lucky they were on those lazy summer nights out back where they had hours and hours to just hang out and enjoy each other's company?

Julia realized she was standing in Denny's kitchen with no real reason to stay. "I'm going to get lunch with Lindsay at two," Julia said partly to engage in some sort of relevant conversation and partly just because she was feeling awkward.

"She told me. I'm sure she's going to try to see you as much as she can before we leave. Lindsay doesn't make friends easily." It was sweet to see the tenderness in Denny's voice when he mentioned that.

"Yeah, she doesn't make it easy sometimes," Julia half joked.

"No, she doesn't." Denny set his glass in the sink and made his way around the island to Julia.

She was suddenly very aware how anyone looking into Denny's back sliding doors would be able to see them in the kitchen. Although James was taking a break as well, it seemed, he could be back at it again in any minute given his ridiculous work ethic. She also had to worry about Maureen out on her deck with her loaded drinks. If Maureen hadn't already passed out somewhere in her house, she could easily be on the deck watching it all.

Julia could either step back into the entrance hallway, which would still have her in view of the sliding door; to the right, which would put her in the formal dining room; or to the left, which would lead to a hallway off the family room which led back to their master bedroom. Her decision to take a few steps to the left may or may not have been the final nail in her coffin. Regardless, it would be something she'd dwell on for years to come when thought about how it all went down.

She moved a few steps to the left as Denny walked towards her. She was looking over his shoulder at the windows and sliding door to see if they were still in view of her husband or in view of Maureen. Denny likely took it as an invitation.

"I can't get last night out of my mind. Can't get you out of my mind," he said.

They were inches apart in a hallway adorned with family photos of the Moore family throughout the ages: wedding photos, pregnancy pictures with a giant baby bump in front of a sunflower field, babies, toddlers, kids. Everyone happily stared at Julia and Denny as they spoke about their infidelity the night before and contemplated continuing their journey into complete debauchery.

Julia closed her eyes tightly and gently shook her head as if to make everything go away and go back to normal again. But there was no denying any of it. And when she was honest with herself, it was a long time coming. Unfair as it was to James, she'd taken to comparing him to Denny every chance she got. Denny wouldn't have yelled about the car accident, he wouldn't have called her irrational or claimed she overreacted, and he certainly wouldn't have made any major decisions without her approval. She was certain of it given how often Lindsay clearly wore the pants in her marriage to Denny.

She wasn't ready to leave James or even consider the idea that maybe she didn't love him as much as she had on their wedding day, but she also wasn't ready to give up this alternate lover who offered so much more than what she had at that moment.

"I…" she opened her eyes again and was met with Denny's pleading eyes. He was begging her to confirm it was real - that his writer's mind hadn't imagined what had happened between them the night before. Maybe if she hadn't spent another hour that afternoon reading about the steamy romance between Michael and Lydia, or maybe if she hadn't stepped into the bedroom hallway and opened the door to the conversation they were having she could have lied and said it was all a mistake and she had felt nothing.

Mostly, and still terribly unfair to James, maybe if she'd been more honest with James about her unhappiness, the affair would have never started to begin with.

Maybe it didn't matter anyway since she was a horrible liar. "I don't know what to do," she finally managed.

Denny reached out and tucked some of her hair behind her ear. It wasn't particularly sexy, yet it was done with such tenderness. Julia saw it as an attempt for some sort of skin-to-skin contact without being too aggressive or coming on too strong since she had just admitted her confusion about their situation.

"I can't stop thinking about you either," Julia breathed. Denny took the slightest step closer after her promising confession. She inched back an equal amount which happened to be in the direction of his bedroom. Lindsay's bedroom where Julia had spent countless nights swapping outfits and trying out new make-up brands and application techniques.

"The kids..." Julia whispered. She didn't want them to catch their parents in such a position. Though they would hear if anyone came home and it wouldn't be a big deal for her to be there with Denny, especially now that so much had changed with the move happening in a few days.

"Won't be home till dinner. At the earliest," Denny finished. His hand reached for her hand and he massaged it as they moved at a snail's pace backwards towards the bedroom. It was different from the last time they were alone together. In the hallway she was mildly buzzed, but nothing compared to the night before, and Denny had only had one beer with James. It was daylight outside. People in the neighborhood were going about their business. Hell, Maureen may have even seen her walk over to Denny's..

Julia's back was about to hit the door, but Denny reached out and turned the handle behind her to open it. Julia had a million reasons to leave. And on any other day she would have listened to them. She never strayed. She hadn't even had an emotional connection with another man beyond a light friendship which would be described as an acquaintance at best. She'd been doing the right thing for so long it didn't seem so bad for her to stray. To make a mistake. Besides, as Lady Macbeth once said, "Things without all remedy should be without regard. What's done is done."

It was only for a few more days. Just until they moved and then she'd be good again and work on fixing her marriage with James.

It was that particular bit of logic which pushed Julia over the edge again. In one of the chapters of *Love Thy Neighbor*, Lydia had grabbed Michael by his collar when she initiated a kiss. Julia grabbed a handful of Denny's shirt collar and pulled his lips down her to hers. Their kiss, while still full of lust and desire, had already become comfortable. Their first time was awkward and on a cement floor with moving blankets haphazardly strewn under them. They had to figure out what worked for them and what they each liked in bed.

In the bedroom those things could be properly sorted and worked out. Denny and Julia weren't going to question if they would wake up the next morning full of regrets. Neither would wonder if the other person was truly into it or merely drunk and emotional. Neither would accidentally knock their head on the cement floor.

Chemistry in the bedroom had never been an issue with Julia and James. Sex had always been the glue which held them together for the past few years while everything else slowly went to shit. They had a bit of a routine down with go-to positions they would go through with slight variations from time to time based on the situation.

There was no routine with Denny. It was somewhat unnerving, but mostly it made the whole experience that much more exciting. Neither knew what was going to happen next. A small part of her wondered if he was going to pull out the nipple clamps. She hoped not. It was other people's thing, sure. But it wasn't hers and she didn't want to recreate anything he'd done with Lindsay.

Afterwards, she was sad they couldn't lay in bed together and enjoy each other's company. Denny had to start organizing and packing up the house, and Julia needed to go meet Denny's wife for lunch, so they both forced themselves to get up and get moving. Denny went to take a shower, but Julia didn't dare use any of Lindsay's shower things right before seeing her. Some women smelled another woman on their man and knew their husbands had been cheating. Similarly, Julia did not want Lindsay to smell herself on Julia. While Denny showered, Julia did what she could, washing up with just the bathroom sink and the basic bar of soap by the faucet.

She cleared her throat and walked over to the frosted glass shower door. "I'm heading out," she called over the hum of the shower. The door swung open, and a soaking wet Denny grabbed her jeans by the belt loops and pulled her to the shower opening. His face drenched hers as he gave her one last passionate kiss. When she finally pulled away, she found Denny's face was flushed from the heat of the shower and their kiss.

At that moment, Julia felt no guilt. Possibly because there were no illicit text messages or complex lies and manipulations with their spouses so they could secretly meet at a specific time or place. Their affair was complicated and deceitful, but it didn't feel that way yet.

Denny gave her one last sweet, chaste kiss on the lips, and then one on the cheek as if he couldn't resist not kissing her. Julia laughed and brought her hands up to block the water which was splashing off of him and out the shower door towards her. One of her hands went back down to his, which was still tightly hooked into her belt loop. "I can't be late," she said as she gently unhooked his fingers, gave his hand a quick squeeze, and then pulled away from his wet, slippery grip.

"Okay. Okay," he agreed. They held hands like newlyweds as Julia kept walking towards the door. Finally, she had gone too far, and their fingertips lingered slightly before parting for good. As she closed the bathroom door, she heard the shower door close, too. Out in the hallway everything looked exactly as it always had for the past few years. Nothing and everything had changed.

Julia went straight from Lindsay's bed to meeting Lindsay at Fine Swine. The name of the restaurant referred strictly to the food since there was nothing exceptionally fine about the location or decor. It was in a strip mall across the street from a cluster of big box stores, including Lindsay's.

As if to show everyone her time was more valuable than theirs, Lindsay was her usual late self. Or maybe that was too harsh. It was hard for Julia to tell anymore what she felt. James groaned every time they waited for Lindsay and he'd made snide comments about how successful Lindsay was at work when she could barely manage her simple, day-to-day activities such as going out to eat or picking up her kids on time.

In the past, Julia accepted the tardiness as part of who Lindsay was and she didn't take it personally. Those days were gone. It felt personal at Fine Swine and it put her on edge before Lindsay even arrived. Julia sighed as she entered the restaurant and quickly scanned the seating to confirm Lindsay had not yet arrived. Although she'd eaten practically nothing that day, she wasn't hungry. Julia found a booth in the back corner and started to read on her phone until Lindsay got around to remembering their lunch plans - the plans Lindsay had made for them.

When Julia went to cross her legs, she had trouble getting her foot off of the ground. After a few tugs she found her shoe was stuck to the ground with an impressive amount of chewing gum. "Ugh, gross," Julia muttered to no one in particular. She found an old pen at the bottom of her purse and leaned down towards the booth seat to work the gum out of the treads of her sneakers. She knew it looked like no one was sitting in the booth, and Julia mildly enjoyed the idea of Lindsay showing up and being annoyed at the thought that Julia was the one who was late.

As she was giving the business to the gum, she heard shuffling in the booth next to hers and voices. It sounded like two young men in their late teens or maybe early twenties.

"You *didn't* hear?" asked young man number one.

"No. I took Kallie out to the Poconos for the week. She wanted it to be all romantic so she got a remote cabin without any wi-fi," young man number two explained.

"Oh, man. That sounds terrible."

"It was okay. We did other stuff to pass the time."

Julia rolled her eyes as the other one laughed - probably at some obscene hand gesture from young man number two. She considered sitting up so they could see there was someone around, almost the age of their mother, who was heard them. But she still hadn't made any headway with the gum and she hated the idea of walking around with a sticky shoe.

"Nice. Speaking of other stuff. Moorehead's finally been caught sluttin' it around."

"No way! I knew it!"

"Shhhhh. It's still supposed to be low key."

"I hope they fire her ass."

"They won't. They don't want to lose their precious female manager. They're sending her off to another store."

"No, shit. That's awesome. We can finally relax. Maybe get a dude in here who isn't so intense. Someone who doesn't get a period and lose his damn mind one week a month."

"Exactly. Get someone in here who doesn't whore around and give special treatment to whoever they happen to be fucking that week. I heard we're getting a transfer from Henrietta, New York. Young guy in his mid-twenties."

"Let's hope Ronnie doesn't fuck him, too," number two laughed at his own joke. "Anything going to happen to Ronnie?"

"Nothing. He's staying. Didn't do anything wrong as far as management's concerned. She took advantage of him since she's his superior."

"No, shit," number two repeated. "When's she leaving? Who else knows?"

"End of the week. Most of the store knows but we're not supposed to. Hard to keep that sort of thing quiet."

"Shhhhh...Be cool. She just walked in."

"Jules?" she heard Lindsay call out. "Hey, guys. How are you?"

Number one and number two mumbled polite hellos as if they hadn't been talking immense shit behind Lindsay's back just seconds before.

Julia slowly lifted her head from the booth and sheepishly said, "Hey, Linds. Just scraping some gum off my shoe."

The two employees and Julia shared a knowing gaze before number one mumbled some reason they both had to leave. The two gathered their barely eaten meals and hauled ass out of the restaurant. There was a slight shadow over Lindsay's face as they breezed by her before she covered it up again with her classic fake smile and perky attitude.

Once she started to notice the barely perceptible details of Lindsay's demeanor, Julia could see she was frazzled down to her core. Lindsay's customary impeccable posture appeared to require every last ounce of her energy and threatened to break her in half. But she was not one to slouch, regardless of the situation, so Lindsay trudged on refusing to allow even the tiniest part of her routine to falter. Lindsay would never allow her appearance to mirror her harried social and work life.

"Did you order anything?" Lindsay asked. Her eyes were still glued to the door even though the two employees were long gone.

"No, not yet. I was waiting for you."

"To be honest, I'm not that hungry. But I'm sure you are. Please, get something."

Julia resisted the urge to read too much into Lindsay's comment about how Julia always wanted to eat. Julia wasn't obese, but she did have a nice soft cushion in comparison to Lindsay's toned, sleek figure. And on Lindsay's part it was a fair assumption given that Julia did indeed love all food.

"I'm not hungry either." Her stomach was ready to explode with the new stress from overhearing the men's conversation in the booth next to hers. Nothing was clear anymore and all of her thoughts were contradicting each other. She wanted to hold and comfort Lindsay, because she knew deep down Lindsay was her own worst critic and she likely never gave herself a break or took time to appreciate how far she'd gone in her professional life. She also wanted to scream at Lindsay for cheating on Denny with some coworker and then uprooting the lives of their families (certainly the lives of the Moores more so than the Herricks) because of her indiscretion.

She wanted to scream at herself for doing the same thing to James. The husbands were at home, blissfully unaware of their unfaithful wives. She knew James was in the dark, but maybe Denny knew or had suspicions. He was an observant person. He had written her perfectly based on his previous observations. But maybe it was different when it was *your* wife and *your* marriage. Maybe Denny overlooked some of the tell-tale signs, if there had been any to see.

"Jules?"

"What?" Julia asked.

"I asked what's wrong and you dazed out on me. What's going on? Is James being a dick again?"

"No," Julia said instinctively without actually thinking about it. "I mean, yes. A little. But just his typical sort of comments. Nothing terrible."

"So everything's okay?"

"No. My best friend is moving away and barely gave me any notice," Julia said.

"It's for work, Jules. There was no notice. I told you maybe a day or so after I knew myself."

Julia didn't respond. She wanted to give Lindsay ample time to elaborate or apologize.

Lindsay must have taken Julia's silence as a cue to move on to another topic. "How are the kids?" Lindsay asked. Her eyes pleaded with Julia to give her a bit of good news. To say that shockingly the kids were excited for a new life and new adventure down south.

Julia tried to swallow but her mouth and throat were too dry. "I didn't get a chance to see them yet. By the time I got your messages the kids were already at my house with Lex and Brice. They wouldn't have wanted to hear anything from me then." In an effort to ease Lindsay's mind and to take away from the fact that Julia had failed at the one thing Lindsay had asked her to do, she added, "Lex and Brice will help them through it. That's what friends are for."

"I need to be able to count on you," she said with a bit of condescension in her voice. She wondered how often Lindsay took that same tone with Denny when they discussed work, the kids, or anything else. Julia's cheeks heated with shame at having let Lindsay and the kids down, and also with anger at Lindsay for acting like a saint when all of their problems had actually been started with Lindsay's poor choices at work.

"I know; you can."

Lindsay kept speaking as if Julia hadn't responded. "I'm leaving tomorrow. All hell is breaking loose in Bluffton and they need me there as soon as possible. That's why I wanted to do lunch. To tell you in person."

Julia was amazed at how easy it was for Lindsay to lie to her face. She'd had her suspicions in the past. Times where she was sure Lindsay had lied but Julia couldn't prove it. After a bit of time passed, she'd even felt guilty about misjudging Lindsay and believing the worst in her instead of the best. And yet there was Lindsay effortlessly lying to her face. She could prove it this time and it made her question, once again, all of the instances in the past.

"Tomorrow? What's happening in Bluffton?" Julia probed. She was intrigued to see how far Lindsay would take the lie and how easily she could do it.

"Some inventory issues. Lots of missing products and suspicious circumstances. There's a handful of department heads who are likely involved. They need me out there now as someone who's biased and doesn't know anyone involved. I'll help with the investigations and then I'll have to help smooth over store morale if we have to fire a bunch of managers. Hopefully they have some sort of succession planning in place because I'll probably need to replace half a dozen or so managers if this plays out how they think it will."

"Sounds chaotic."

"Nothing I can't handle."

Julia began to question what she'd thought she heard before. She was so sure the two employees had been talking about Lindsay. Who else could they have been talking about? And yet, did she really want to put full trust in what two random people she'd never met? Put full trust in what sounded like work gossip?

"And you *have* to leave tomorrow? How can they possibly demand that of you?"

"It's not exactly a demand. They made the request and I agreed. I'm not going to be one of those female managers who puts her family first rather than doing what's best for the collective group. Guys do it all the time with the wife available to pick up the pieces behind him. Denny will do the same. Besides, knowing I'll jump when they ask means I'll have a better chance at whatever promotions come later."

Julia had seen a slow change in Lindsay's attitude towards her family and work over the decade they'd been friends. One year she'd left Thanksgiving dinner early to make last-minute changes for their Black Friday sale. As the years went on her weekly work hours went from forty, to fifty. Once she became store manager, they vacillated between sixty to seventy hours each week. If it was an inventory week or major holiday, she was more likely to work seventy hours. If it was any other week, she would be there for at least sixty hours each week.

"Right. Work first, family second." Julia surprised even herself with the attack. The idea of Lindsay leaving made her bolder in whatever she was going to say or do. It just didn't seem to matter as much anymore if Lindsay got mad at her not.

"Damn right," Lindsay said. "Because my work is what's putting food on the table and paying the mortgage. Denny's writing career is plummeting, possibly beyond repair, and he won't even consider trying anything else. He's too lazy to commit to a regular nine to five and too selfish to give up his dream job even though he's barely breaking twenty grand each year. Someone needs to step up and provide financial security for the family, and I don't mind being the one to do it."

Julia and Lindsay had had conversations similar to this before, but Lindsay had never been so candid about her disdain for Denny's work ethic and job. She tried to put herself in Lindsay's position and she wondered if she would feel the same way. It was such a stark contrast to their first dinner together when Lindsay had bragged about Denny's accomplishments.

"Don't act like this is an easy decision for me," Lindsay continued. "I know what people have said about me even before this transfer came up. I work too much. Don't see my kids enough. I'm not a volunteer mom at the school, ever. And then there's Denny. The perfect martyr. Poor Denny has to pick up all the slack with the kids all while being married to an aggressive bitch."

"Who said that?"

"Please. Before I quit pinochle I heard the other women whispering about me. And I hear it at work all the time. Employee gossip runs rampant around here and I can't help but overhear it. The two that were in here and rushed out as soon as I showed up? I bet they were talking about me, too."

Within minutes Lindsay had proven Julia was just as bad as everyone else when it came to strong women in the workplace. "They said you were sleeping with some guy named Ronnie." Julia had wanted to say something to Lindsay about it but she knew she didn't have the courage.

She was grateful Lindsay opened the door to the conversation.

Lindsay nodded and gave a slightly incredulous laugh that Julia couldn't read. Even though she'd just been schooled by Lindsay, Julia couldn't get the idea of Lindsay sleeping around out of her mind. The tirade against Denny confirmed that their marriage was rocky if not obliterated given her resentment of him.

"Typical," Lindsay said. "I've already been interviewed by human resources three times in the past year about so-called affairs and secret rendezvouses." She brushed some hair from her eyes and looked back at the doors to the restaurant.

"You've never told me," Julia said.

"Why would I? It's embarrassing. And even when it turns out to be a complete fabrication of someone's imagination, it still sticks in people's minds as having some sort of truth to it. People find out and they look at you differently.

"Two years ago, I had to do interviews with HR about sleeping with an eighteen-year-old cashier. Eighteen, Jules. One of the other cashiers anonymously claimed to have seen me having sex with him on my desk one night. Once I was given the date of the alleged incident I looked in my calendar and saw I had an orientation that night from six to ten. My office is right outside the training room where we have orientations. Unless that was part of the orientation, there was no way it happened. The store closed at nine and said cashier had punched out at 9:07. But I was guilty until proven innocent. And don't think HR isn't suspicious. After having three separate investigations, they're convinced at least one must be legit. If you're repeatedly accused, people will believe you're guilty whether you can clear your name or not."

Lindsay read Julia's reaction and narrowed her eyes at her. "You believed them, didn't you? Even just for a split second you believed that I, someone you've known for years, was having an affair you didn't know about, just because a couple of guys were talking about it as if it were fact."

"No, I would never think that about you." Julia had such conviction in her voice she almost convinced herself as well.

Lindsay dropped her head into her hands. "No, you're right. I'm sorry. It's been a hellish week for me." When her head rose again, her eyes were moist and threatened to betray her by releasing decades of pent-up tears.

"Are you okay?" Julia asked.

"I'm fine."

"I don't think you are."

"It doesn't matter. There's too much at stake right now. I'll worry about myself once we're settled in South Carolina."

"I'm worried about you."

"Don't be. Just keep an eye on Denny and the kids for me. I know I've said some shitty things about him, but I still love him. I'm hoping this move will be good for us. Let us hit a redo on our relationship."

"Yeah. I'll help them out. Of course."

"I'd better get back. I'm sorry. This wasn't a very good lunch date."

"It's fine. You have plenty to worry about. Just focus on whatever you need to do right now. If you want, James and I will have Denny and the kids over for dinner. You can join, too, if you have time."

"That'd be great. Thanks, Jules."

17

DENNY, MAY 2014

Denny was holed up in his office trying to figure out what obstacles could come between his two characters: Penelope and Mark. He was about halfway through the book and enjoyed writing every minute of it, but it was mostly the two coworkers who quickly fell in love and were living happily ever after with the sporadic high-heat love scene thrown in here and there to please his agent. Not that he minded writing the love scenes or spending hours poring over the details of what it would be like to be intimate with Julia. He didn't use anything from his experiences with Lindsay since it felt too intrusive to her and their marriage. He didn't actually have any sexual experiences with Julia, and so it felt only mildly wrong to picture their potential rendezvouses when trying to write his steamier scenes.

The real difficulty came in trying to come up with a problem for the characters. The old trope of Dom feeling guilty about falling in love again after his fiancé died along with the storyline about Monica's controlling ex-boyfriend causing problems had been more than played out in the romance genre. He'd already covered it himself a bit in *Love Thy Neighbor.*

Exes and dead spouses existed everywhere. But in reality, they rarely had the power to overcome true love or to get between two people who could be classified as soulmates. He needed something more.

His agent and editor hadn't liked his chapters about money problems and Monica getting involved in somewhat questionable business dealings. They both claimed it was too realistic and too depressing for the readers. His readers had work and money problems; they were reading his books to escape those problems.

Denny's office door was open and he heard the kids come in from outside. They spoke with Julia and Lindsay before they headed down to the basement to play. It was Saturday and Lindsay had off of work, so he didn't want to completely shut himself off from the family. But he also didn't feel guilty writing once Julia showed up with her kids. The kids would all entertain themselves and the women would get lost in conversation. He knew they wouldn't miss him when he made his way from the kitchen to the office as soon as the women were engrossed in the latest gossip on the newest neighbor down the street.

He was mid-sentence in a heated love scene between his characters when Lindsay called for him. As if he himself had been caught mid-act, he momentarily felt ashamed and stopped writing immediately. He knew he wouldn't be able to finish the scene once his mind returned to his office again with his wife and her best friend in the kitchen down the hallway.

"What's up?" he asked as he walked into the kitchen.

Julia and Lindsay stood at the sliding door to the deck. They were looking out at something in the backyard.

"The kids just came through and said Josh told them to go

inside for a bit while he sprays some chemicals on the trees out back." Lindsay told him.

"Huh," he replied. Denny walked over to the door and peered out with the women. Sure enough, Josh was out back with a few men in landscaping uniforms pointing out various things in the trees and garden which made up Josh and Maureen's backyard. At the time the trees were only a few years old and offered minimal shade or privacy, but Denny looked forward to the next decade or so when the oaks and willows would fill out and both neighbors would benefit from the shade and privacy they would provide.

"We'd better close up the windows just in case." Denny said. "There's a bit of a breeze coming this way and I'd hate for us or for the kids to be inhaling any of those chemicals."

"You're not going to say anything to them?" Lindsay asked.

"What can I say? It's their property and it's not illegal."

Lindsay turned back to the yard to keep watch over everything. For a while they all stared out the back doors and windows though nothing was happening yet.

"What are you ladies up to today?" Denny asked in the way of making polite conversation while they waited to see the chemical spray situation play out. He also wanted to gauge what the rest of his day would look like as well. He'd either get back to writing in an empty house, or he'd be dumped with entertaining all the kids while the women went out.

"We're definitely getting lunch somewhere, but we haven't decided where yet." Lindsay said.

"Julia, where do you want to go?" Denny asked.

Before Julia could open her mouth Lindsay answered for her, "Jules wants to go to the new burger place, Man Down, off of Lurren Road. They just put in a huge lounge area for the adults --"

"Complete with fire pits and giant comfy chairs. And they have a massive outside play area for the kids," Julia chimed in.

"But I don't want to go there because I know I'll end up with a giant burger and a huge pile of fries which I'll devour in record time. I want to go to Ikea where the only thing I like is a small salad and then the kids can hang out in the play area while we shop."

"You're taking the kids either way?" Denny asked. "You're a saint. I love you."

"Love you too, babe," Lindsay shot to Denny before turning back to Julies. "I really don't want burgers, Jules. We'll both feel so sluggish if we overdo it for lunch."

"But Ikea is all the way out in Philly. Man Down is right down the road."

"If we go out to Philly the kids will nap on the way and then everyone wins when our kids are well-rested and well-adjusted little people for the rest of the day."

Julia thought for a minute before she said, "Fine. The kids love the Ikea hotdogs anyway. Let me text James and let him know our plans for the day."

"What's James doing today?" Denny asked as Julia was typing. He knew he'd be busy with something. James always was. That's why he assumed he would be stuck with babysitting duty if the women wanted to take an afternoon off to themselves - something he would have supported if they'd suggested it.

"He's got it in his mind that he wants to run a marathon before he hits forty which is this October."

"In his mind?" Denny teased. "You don't think he can do it?"

"Oh, I know he can, and he will. I've never met anyone as stubborn as he is about this sort of thing. I say it like that because it will be all that's on his mind for the next five months. I'll feel like a single mother between now and then with how much he'll be running and training."

She stopped texting and looked up at Denny. "But he's excited about it, so I am, too," she said with a forced smile.

Lindsay was at the deck door again when she gasped. "Look at that cloud of chemicals. Can they really spray like that without any warnings to the neighbors? People have dogs and children out."

The three of them were at the door again watching as a man in a hazmat-like suit and a gas mask sprayed a fog of chemicals all over a cluster of trees in the back corner of Josh and Maureen's yard. Josh and Maureen were nowhere in sight.

No one answered Lindsay because no one knew. Denny had been a bit nonchalant about it before, but even he had to admit it was making him uncomfortable given the close proximity of their house to the Josh and Maureen's house. Surely if they hadn't closed the windows, they would have breathed in at least a small amount of whatever the landscaper sprayed into the air surrounding the cluster of trees.

Julia said, "Oh no, there's a little squirrel on that one. Do you guys see it?" She attempted to point out the door, but it only came out as a smooshed pointer finger pressed up against the glass giving no real direction to what she was trying to show them.

"I see him; he seems to be okay. Maybe it's not anything too harsh. Just something to keep the bugs off; not enough to kill an actual animal," Lindsay said more towards Julia than Denny.

But it wasn't a mild chemical. The three of them watched through the dim yellow fog as the small squirrel took a few more steps on the branch. His abdomen got closer to the bark with each step before it finally laid down and let its limbs fall and dangle lifeless beneath it. Right behind the smaller squirrel was a larger one. It took longer for it for to succumb to the deadly fog since it was somewhat bigger than the other. Possibly an older sibling or parent even.

Denny was the first to look away from what would surely be a slaughter. The landscaper wasn't through yet and spring was in full swing. Those trees had been teaming with life prior to the man's arrival. He noticed Lindsay taking in the scene with the same expression she wore while idly cleaning the house and emptying the dishwasher. A blank stare that held neither joy nor pain, but rather apathy and neutrality.

Beyond her he saw Julia carefully wiping aside a tear before her friend noticed. It wasn't his place to try to comfort Julia. Doing so would have made them all uncomfortable since he'd done such a good job keeping his distance for the past few years. But he kept the detail in his mind for later when he'd figure out a way to incorporate that part of her character into his current story, or maybe a story in the future. Because even after *Love Thy Neighbor* was finished, he still found himself using small details and character traits from Julia in all of his leading ladies.

"I'll gather the kids," Lindsay said as she turned away from the carnage. "We can all fit in the van, so I'll drive."

18

JULIA, NOVEMBER 2019

"I told Lindsay we'd have Denny and the kids over for dinner tonight. Lindsay, too, if she can make it. They're asking her to start in Bluffton tomorrow and she's drained by the whole thing. She almost cried at lunch today," Julia told James when she'd returned home from lunch. They were out back and James was stacking some of the bricks and stones from the old fire pit into neat piles under their deck and against the house.

The plan was to keep all the supplies and figure out a new location for the fire pit, though Julia couldn't imagine it anywhere else. She couldn't imagine sitting by the fire again and not reliving, even if just for a second, that awful conversation where Lindsay casually announced she was leaving them all.

"Really? Lindsay almost cried?" James asked.

"Yes, James. She is a person."

"So you say…"

"I already have a frozen lasagna ready to go, so I'm going to heat that up and make a side or two. Is that okay?"

"Yeah, that works." James said.

"Are Liv and Hailey still here?"

"All day long." James put another stone on the pile and then turned his attention to Julia. He took off his work gloves and grabbed her hands in his. "Hey, everything's going to be okay."

"I know." Julia said.

James pulled her into a sweaty embrace and roughly ran his hands up and down her back in an effort to sooth her. His affection was what always kept her coming back to James. Yes, he frequently overreacted and sometimes let out a fury of anger over what Julia thought was trivial or at the very least minor occurrences. But as much as he appeared to be a stereotypical, emotionally unaware guy, he let his sweet and softer emotions out, too. She got more hugs and sympathy from James than she ever got from Lindsay.

Julia pulled away first. "I'm going to run next door and let Denny know. See if he needs help with anything. Lindsay asked us to help out with Denny and the kids since she has to leave so quickly."

"Okay. Whatever they need."

Julia cocked an eyebrow up at him. "Because they're leaving soon anyway?"

"And it's the right thing to do. Geez, Julia, I'm not the heartless asshole you make me out to be."

Again, Julia was reminded despite his flaws (and she was also aware she certainly had many herself, too) she really did love James. She went to give him a quick kiss goodbye. He responded by pulling her in for a deeper, more intimate kiss. Her arms went naturally around his neck and relaxed against his strong shoulder and neck muscles as their sweet goodbye kiss increased in intensity. Julia also loved that part of James. The part which treated her like his newest girlfriend, someone he couldn't get enough of. So what the hell was she doing risking everything with Denny Moore?

James pulled away and said, "You are incredibly tempting right now, but I need to get this stuff stacked and clean up the yard. I can't leave this mess overnight."

"Okay. You're right. I need to go tell Denny about dinner anyway."

As soon as Denny answered the door, Julia realized what a bad idea it was for her to see him right after getting all worked up with James. She could have texted him about dinner. She could have sent his kids back to him with the message. She could have called. None of those options were appropriate though for the additional message she had: Whatever was happening between them was wrong and needed to stop immediately. That sort of conversation needed to be done in person regardless of how uncomfortable it would surely be.

"Julia," Denny said as a smile grew across his face. Denny's eyes darted up and down the street to see if anyone else was watching her at his door. "Come in," he said, likely unconvinced they were actually alone given how much the neighborhood saw behind seemingly closed curtains and doors.

Before anything could begin to happen again, Julia said, "We can't do this anymore, Denny."

Denny's head dropped a little as he shut the door behind them. He gave a defeated and hollow laugh. "Lindsay got to you."

"We're married, Denny. With kids - "

"So we don't deserve any happiness?" Denny countered. Julia faltered, unable to give a response or to adequately explain her feelings about how she still loved James and couldn't risk him or anyone else finding out. How she'd felt a rush of guilt over her anger towards Lindsay which was misplaced given the conversation she'd just had over the lunch they never ate.

"Let me guess," Denny said. "Lindsay said everyone is always after her at work. She's innocent but they keep coming after her for no reason. Or rather, because she's ambitious and all men hate ambitious women and will slander them in any way possible in order to keep them down in their proper place below the glass ceiling."

Kind of, Julia thought. Her already confusing situation was only getting worse. She wasn't sure what to think anymore.

Denny said, "Does it really make sense that different people over the past few years would make up some sort of story about her? Would lie about fucking her or about knowing other people who were fucking her?" No response from Julia. "How often does that happen in your workplace, Julia? How often are the women in your office accused of illicit behavior? What about James's office? He's a man in a position of power. How many women have accused him of improper advancements or of screwing in the back office after hours?"

"*You* said yesterday that I was being too hard on Lindsay. You begged me to take it easy on her because *she* was the victim," Julia said. Denny was like a whole new person with his sudden anger and resentment towards Lindsay. It unnerved Julia to see how much hatred lingered behind his eyes.

"I know. I've been Lindsay's biggest defender even though she hasn't done the same for me in recent years. And I know this sounds hypocritical. No, not just sounds. It *is* hypocritical given what's happened between us. But I don't care anymore."

Denny's eyes found hers again. They were still standing in the foyer and Julia considered making her way into the kitchen so they could sit down and talk. Maybe with her on one side of the island and Denny on the other.

He reached out to her, but he dropped his hand before it made contact with hers and said, "Lindsay *was* having an affair. Since she's only here or at work, it must be with a coworker. I think that's why we're moving. Moyer's gave her an ultimatum: termination or transfer stores. Work's her life so she chose to uproot everything rather than risk the career she's worked so hard for."

Julia couldn't begin to understand why it was so hard for her to believe Denny over Lindsay when she herself always thought Lindsay to be a liar. Regardless, she found herself beginning to ask, "How do you -"

"Liv accidentally threw out her retainer. I had to dig through the trash to find it. I found a crumpled-up note with Lindsay's name on it. I don't even know why it caught my eye or why I bothered to open it. But I did. It was a goodbye, clearly from someone she'd been with, intimately, signed with the letter *R*."

Julia's face or maybe even just her eyes flickered with recognition at the initial.

"I knew it," Denny said.

Julia attempted damage control even though every last piece of shit had already hit the fan. "I had no idea about any of this. Lindsay never told me about the accusations or the investigations." She raised her hand and took a step towards him, but he backed away. "I know as much as you do," Julia said. In the moment it felt true since she had no way of knowing if Ronnie was R. Besides, Denny didn't need to know the specific details of what Moyer's employees were saying about his wife. How they had nicknamed her Moorehead.

Denny didn't bother grilling Julia any further. He had all the information he needed. He was back to his hatred towards Lindsay. "We were equals when we first met. Both of us with college degrees and no actual job or career to show for it. Just working our way up through whatever retail jobs we could find. When we were on our way together, every-thing was good. Really good. But as soon as my writing career started to tank, while her career skyrocketed, I wasn't good enough for her.

"I always knew that was going to happen. I knew everyone would realize what a hack I was as a writer. Would see the real me and they'd be disappointed, to say the least. Disgusted is more like it with Lindsay."

Julia couldn't say anything. She kept searching in her memory for signs of what Denny was saying about his rela-tionship with Lindsay, and to her surprise it was all there. The little digs at Denny and his career which weren't playful jabs as Lindsay had tried to portray them and as Julia had once taken them. She could see the underlying truth in Lind-say's reactions and words throughout the past few years. Lindsay's real personality had been there all along and she'd chosen to ignore it.

Her anger returned as she thought about how Lindsay had accused her earlier that day of being like everyone else in believing the rumors and gossip about her. More lies from her best friend. No, not her best friend. Less than that. Just a neighbor really given how little Julia knew about her and her life outside of the bubble they'd created around themselves whenever they were together. James didn't seem surprised by Lindsay's actions lately, but Julia sure as hell was. The only reason she could come up with was that she never knew Lindsay at all - at least not in the areas where it had mattered: the bigger picture beyond favorite books, music, and food. Beyond having some drinks and a good laugh together. When it came down to it, she knew Lindsay about as well as she knew Maureen.

The realization dissolved her anger into sadness. She couldn't turn to James with it. He was supportive to an extent, but not with Lindsay. According to him he'd always seen the real Lindsay, and Julia was too in awe of her friend to believe him when he pointed it out to her. James would have little sympathy for Julia since he'd repeatedly begged her not to get so involved with the neighbors. Besides, he'd already comforted her earlier. Anything more would be seen from his point of view as Julia dragging it out and refusing to move on. James's support in such matters had limitations which she had already reached.

But Denny would comfort her, and she could comfort him. He was leaning against the front door, looking so sad and vulnerable. Julia told herself, *Just one more time*, as she walked towards him. In the past their kisses had been rushed and desperate. Both parties lost in the excitement of the unknown and forbidden. This kiss was slower and contained no excitement. Julia's hands went to his face and she was surprised to feel tears running down his cheeks.

From what Julia had seen, James had cried twice over the course of their entire marriage: when Alexis was born and when Brice was born. That was it. She assumed his next cry would be at her death, if she goes first, and even then she won't be there to see it. She wondered if maybe they were mismatched after all. Perhaps James and Lindsay, with their mutual lack of emotions, were a better fit for each other. No, that didn't make any sense either. Lindsay was mostly indifferent towards James, and James was downright hateful towards Lindsay. Not to her face, of course, but in conversation with Julia in the comfort of their own home.

None of it mattered at the moment though. Unlike with James in the backyard, they would not be breaking off their kiss to be continued later. There was no later and there was no going back. What difference would it make if Julia and

Denny slept together one more time? Tomorrow was the day to break things off for good. Their indiscretions began Friday night with Denny's book and her innocent text; might as well let it continue to play out throughout the weekend.

Julia hated the sneaking around part. She'd heard of some people having affairs partly for the thrill of the secret and the adrenaline which came with the possibility of getting caught. While there was an initial thrill in the beginning, the dirty feelings of betrayal and guilt had long since taken over.

She'd also heard some affairs have nothing to do with unhappiness with spouses and everything to do with unhappiness in life, or a desire to recreate or rekindle some lost happiness from their past. When Julia first heard this, not long after she'd gotten married, she'd scoffed at the article. Of course people would claim their affair wasn't about the other person, and the other person was probably happy to believe it. Why would someone cheat unless there was something going on with the spouse?

She considered the question as she hopped in the shower back at her house. Although she was sure she wouldn't be able to convince anyone else given the circumstances, she loved James. Her affair with Denny had little to do with James and everything to do with Lindsay. James sometimes joked how Lindsay was her second spouse since she spent all her free time with her and would consider her and her family in many of their major decisions. The Moore family was an intricate part of discussions about vacations and even vehicle purchases - the Moores already had a van so the Herricks didn't need to get one.

Although there was never anything sexual between Lindsay and Julia, Lindsay was like a secondary spouse to her, and Lindsay's abrupt departure felt as bad as she imagined she'd feel if James suddenly walked out on her and the kids.

Was embarrassment one of the stages of grief? Because that was there, too. Julia held much more stock in her relationship with Lindsay than Lindsay did. Always had. When they discussed family vacations, Lindsay had the last say in everything. At the time Julia told herself it was because Lindsay's job was more demanding, and because Julia and James were more laid back than Denny and Lindsay. It only made sense the Moores had more say in the decisions than she and James did.

The epiphanies came one by one as Julia let the hot water scald her skin. It was always leading up to this. While she took the move as an unexpected turn of events, Lindsay had seen it coming all along. Or maybe Lindsay hadn't seen the exact scenario play out this way, but she had known eventually opportunity would knock, and Lindsay would up and leave everything for it.

"Hon, are you okay?" James called from the door of the bathroom.

"I'm fine. Almost done."

She could hear the door open and close as James let himself into the bathroom. "You don't usually take a shower in the afternoon," he said.

Julia wished he'd just say whatever it was he wanted to say. "I was helping Denny move some stuff in the attic and I got some insulation on me. Just washing off really quick." She heard the lie and immediately thought of Lindsay's ability to cover her tracks with an improvised tall tale. Shame and hot water washed over and she wondered for the hundredth time how she ever let things get so out of hand.

"Okay. I need to shower, too, before dinner. Can I hop in with you?" Julia could already see James taking off his shirt and unbuckling his jeans through the frosted glass shower door.

Panic set in as she knew it was not an innocent request. At no point in their relationship had they been able to take a shower together without it turning intimate and sexual. Was any couple able to do that?

"Sorry, but I'm getting out now actually." Julia reluctantly turned off the water and threw a towel around her body before coming out of the shower.

"That's too bad. I have some unfinished business with you after you left me this afternoon."

He started to pull at her towel, but she gently pushed his hand away and walked past him towards their bedroom. "I have to preheat the oven and get ready for dinner."

James nodded that he understood even though she could read the feeling of rejection on his face.

"Later tonight. I promise."

"Okay. Later tonight," he agreed. James wouldn't read into it. He rarely read into anything. As far as he was concerned, they had a great marriage, great sex life, and an amazing family. What would he be worried about? Why would he ever be suspicious? Her hatred towards herself increased as Julia compared herself to James and again found him to be the better half of the couple. She didn't deserve him.

Lindsay was able to make it to dinner that night, and the two families had one final meal together before everything changed. According to Lindsay, nothing would really change except how often they saw each other. The Herricks would visit them in Bluffton a few times during the fall, and then the Moores would be back up to visit during the winter - as long as Lindsay's job allowed it.

Julia rolled her eyes as Lindsay went on about her transition to the new store and how even though it had a lower volume of sales, it was not doing well. She would be working her ass off getting it back to where it needed to be.

They're not coming back, Julia thought as Lindsay droned on about work commitments. She scanned the table taking in Lindsay, Denny, and the kids. Lindsay would still need to take time off to visit family. There was no way she would take additional time off to visit friends, too. Typical Lindsay with her assumption that the Herricks would drop everything to go down to see them while the Moores wouldn't do the same.

James didn't say much throughout the dinner. He neither committed to future plans nor outright rejected the possibility. Julia knew she would never convince him to take time off of work to go down to see their former neighbors in South Carolina. He'd only put on a good front during dinner, perhaps some would say a neutral front, for Julia's sake. And she was sure deep down he didn't hate Denny. They just didn't have as much in common with each other or get along as well as the women did. But that wouldn't be enough for him to go out of his way for the Moores any time soon. And Lindsay was earning zero points with James during dinner as she monopolized the conversation and lobbed passive aggressive, sometimes downright critical, comments toward all the adults at the table.

"Now that I'm not around as much, maybe this is a good time to look into dental school, Julia," Lindsay innocently suggested.

"I like assisting."

"I know. But it's so monotonous to do the same work every day. Wouldn't you like to try something new? Something more challenging?"

It was Denny's turn when the conversation moved on to books. As the table discussed what they'd been reading lately,

Lindsay managed to interject how one of the author's was a one-hit wonder who had never been able to recapture the success of their first best-seller published two decades earlier. Julia, and she suspected the rest of the table, didn't miss Lindsay's lingering stare at Denny as she spoke about the "washed-up has-been" of an author she'd been reading.

Making her way around the table, she questioned James, yet again, when he would be made partner. Unlike Denny, James fired back with a comment about how important family is and how he wasn't willing to sell out for more money at the expense of his family time. At that Lindsay backed down. Luckily, the children were spared Lindsay's candid comments that night.

But Julia had to admit Lindsay's lobbed verbal assaults were only a small part of what was a mostly pleasant evening. The majority of the night had been full of laughter and fond memories of the two families together throughout the years: at the lake, surviving the chicken pox, snow days, and so much more.

Julia supposed that was the reason why she still couldn't say no to Lindsay's request to have a few drinks out on the deck after dinner. One last time.

"I always liked your deck better than mine," Lindsay said as they settled in. She and Julia sat on two wicker chairs facing outward towards Maureen and Josh's house rather than towards the table in the middle of the deck. They each had a heavily poured gin and tonic in their hands. The women absently sipped as they spoke and looked out into the backyards below them.

Julia furrowed her brow a bit. She couldn't remember a time when Lindsay had envied something she had. "Why do you like my deck better?"

"You have a better view than I do. You can still see the

Drury's yard from my deck. But on yours it's blocked by the Warren's shrubs."

"Oh, yeah. I guess you're right. I never noticed."

They went silent again and sipped their drinks. "So, what's on your mind?" Julia asked.

"Nothing in particular. Just wanted to spend some quality time with my best friend." Lindsay gave a lazy smile towards Julia as she raised her glass in a mock toast before taking another sip.

"Really? It's your last night here...nothing?"

"You're not going to get all emotional on me, are you? Can't we enjoy my last night without turning it into some pathetic sob fest?"

Julia stared back at her, unable to settle on the best response out of the myriad of comebacks swirling around in her mind.

"We'll see each other again. We'll text, Facetime, visit."

"You're going to use vacation time to come up to Pennsylvania? To visit us?"

Lindsay didn't break eye contact with Julia, but there was something happening. A small flicker of her eye, or a brief twitch that was almost a blink but wasn't. "Sure. But I figured it would be easier for you guys to come down and see us first since work will be hectic for me in the fall with the transfer. And it's perfect for the summer since we're right outside of Hilton Head."

"I hate Hilton Head." A lie. If Lindsay was going to lie Julia might as well join her.

"You don't."

They both turned back to the darkened yards of their neighbors. It was late. Most of the houses were dark or had their curtains drawn. Everyone except Maureen. Maureen was back lit so they could clearly see her as she fixed what was likely at least her second martini while Josh sat in the living room and watched TV.

Lindsay broke the silence. "One thing I'm not going to miss? Having that ho as a neighbor," Lindsay said with a nod in Maureen's direction. Like a poorly written scene in a movie, Julia choked on her drink in response. As she coughed, Lindsay continued. "Did you know about that?"

Lindsay's eyes were back on Julia who did a silent prayer of thanks for the dark night which hid the scarlet coloring suddenly covering her face. "What?" was all Julia managed in response. As far as Julia could tell, Lindsay couldn't read her reaction.

They both turned back to Maureen. She was sitting at the island with a book and a dwindling drink even though she'd just poured it. Completely unaware of the verbal takedown happening in the yard behind her. Josh was just as oblivious to it all as he sipped his beer and made occasional hand gestures towards the football game he was watching.

"It was a while ago. She doesn't even know that I know," Lindsay said.

"Know what? What happened?" Julia had already heard Maureen's version of what happened, but she was dying to hear how it compared with Lindsay's account.

Lindsay narrowed her eyes at Julia to assess either Julia's actual knowledge of what happened, or whether she should confide in Julia. If there was ever a time Julia needed to keep it together, it was at that moment. She had no idea if Maureen would ever point a finger at Julia to deflect from herself. Ugh. Why couldn't Denny and Lindsay just move already and let everyone get on with their lives?

"I assumed Kari and Maureen would have gotten trashed some random night, highly likely given they're both func- tioning alcoholics, and it would have slipped out into the neighborhood gossip mill," Lindsay said.

"What would?" Julia needed to hear it from Lindsay. She refused to add anything to the conversation until she heard everything.

"Kari fucked Denny." Lindsay didn't take her eyes off of Maureen as she said it. No, not Maureen. From her angle and point of view, Julia hadn't realized Lindsay was actually looking beyond Maureen's house to Kari's house. It was across the street from Maureen's and slightly off to the right.

Julia thought she was going to be sick.

Lindsay paused to take another drink. Maureen did likewise as she turned a page of her novel. For some odd reason Julia expected Lindsay to cry or show some sort of emotion. Was she stoic due to the many years passed since it happened, or was Lindsay so far removed she wasn't capable of such emotions anymore?

"What? Are you sure? How'd you find out?" Julia was curious about how it all went down, but she was also nosey for her own selfish reasons. What misstep had Denny and Kari taken and how could Julia avoid it herself? And how many women in Scarlet Oaks Knoll has Denny slept with?

Lindsay took a deep breath and set her empty drink down with a loud clunk on the small table between them. "I'll get you another drink and you can tell me all about it." Julia offered. "Fuck, Lindsay. I had no idea." Even though Julia couldn't stand Lindsay lately, she also desperately wanted to loosen Lindsay's lips a little more to see what else would come out.

"I probably shouldn't."

"You barely had anything to drink with dinner. You'll be fine."

Lindsay looked back towards Maureen's and Kari's houses. "Yeah. Okay. One more," Lindsay said.

Minutes later Julia and Lindsay had fresh drinks and Julia waited patiently for the tonic to help relax Lindsay enough for her to divulge all her secretes. What little patience Julia had was gone, so she spoke first. It was natural for her. They'd always ruthlessly gossiped about neighbors without shame in their search for all the juicy, damning details.

"How'd you find out about Denny and Kari? God, it sounds so weird to say out loud," Julia said. And it did. Partially because he was Lindsay's husband, but also because she didn't even know Denny and Kari knew each other beyond acquaintance-like conversation at community events and parties.

What a twisted, *Desperate Housewives* vibe their development had. For a minute her mind wandered to the rest of the neighborhood and she considered who else was secretly having affairs or even swinging a few streets or houses away from them.

"Nothing original," Lindsay said. Julia was familiar with Lindsay's occasional disgust when she mentioned Denny sometimes, but it made more sense now that Julia knew about his indiscretion with Kari. Of course Lindsay was disgusted with him; it wasn't completely about work or the other little things Denny did that annoyed Lindsay. It was the betrayal. No one betrayed Lindsay and got away with it.

She turned her gaze back towards Julia. "A while back I had an important walk-through with district higher-ups. My first one as the store manager even though I'd already been in position for almost a year."

At this detail Julia could put a general time frame to the story. The kids had all been young when Lindsay was promoted to store manager. Elementary school for the older kids and kindergarten for the youngers. Just a few years after the Moores moved in. A lifetime ago.

"Everything had to be perfect since I was already under more pressure than any of the guys in the same position. The assumption being I would fail or at the very least wouldn't be able to run the store as efficiently as my male counterparts. Never mind the fact that my overall numbers destroyed the previous manager's.

"Before the boss men showed up, I was stopped by a customer in the plumbing department and our plumbing guy had called out sick that morning. The customer, a young guy, didn't think I could work the machine and I insisted on it just to prove him wrong. Stupid on my part and a losing battle I will never win. A mishap with the pipe threading machine doused my shirt and pants with oil. I went home to quickly change and there's Denny and Kari going at it on my bed. At nine in the fucking morning."

Another long pause as Julia attempted to put together all the pieces, and as Lindsay mentally recovered after reliving that horrid nightmare of a morning.

"I couldn't even storm out because I had to change clothes and clean up a little before I went back to work. Once I was back at work, I had to walk my district manager around the store as if I hadn't just caught my husband fucking some random neighbor. I'm talking not even just making it through the day, I had to be on top of my game regardless of my home life. They don't care about my shitty marriage; they care about the bottom line. They probably would have thought me weak as if their own wives aren't cheating on them, too."

"Why didn't you come over here? You could have borrowed clothes, cleaned up, talked, whatever you needed."

"We barely knew each other, and I had to get back to work. Besides, after I had some time to think about it, I decided I didn't tell anyone."

Julia stared back at Lindsay with one eyebrow slightly raised. Both drinks had been abandoned. "We'd been friends for years by then. Vacations, holidays, birthdays, funerals.

That was four or five years after you moved in. How did we barely know each other?"

Lindsay ignored Julia's most recent comments and carried on with what she'd said earlier. "I'm only telling you now because I'm leaving; it doesn't matter anymore."

Julia sensed the change in Lindsay as she transitioned from slightly buzzed to her nasty drunk persona. Or maybe it wasn't a different persona. Maybe it was the real Lindsay and it only came out when she wasn't lucid enough to hide it. Lindsay was right. Julia was once again reminded they didn't know each other as well as they thought they did.

The stare down was broken when James poked his head through the sliding glass door. "You're not staying up much longer, are you? It's a school night and we have work tomorrow."

Lindsay took a large swig of her drink and rolled her eyes as she turned back to the backyard and away from James.

"I'll be in soon," Julia answered. It was a vague answer that left James annoyed, she was sure of it, but she wasn't about to get into it with James in front of Lindsay. Lindsay already had enough ammunition against James; Julia tried not to add any more if she could help it. As if Lindsay should be giving anyone marital advice.

"You sure you can stay out here? He seems pretty pissed his wife isn't in bed by nine sharp. That you're having a few drinks. Admit it, he keeps track. If I asked him right now how much you had to drink at dinner and how much you've had out here with me, he'd be able to tell me exactly what you've had and how much of it you've had."

Down to the milliliter, probably. But she refused to allow Lindsay to change the subject from Lindsay's marriage to her own. "What happened with Denny when you walked in on him? What did he say? What did she say?"

"Kari started to say, 'This isn't -' but I cut her off before she could finish. Called her a slut and told her to get out of my house. Denny was speechless, and that was fine by me. I didn't want to hear whatever bullshit he was going to give me. I had to get back to work."

"I still can't believe I didn't know. Is that why you stopped going to pinochle?"

"I was reminded how much I hate most women. I had no interest in doing pinochle after that. I didn't want to be the next Scarlet Oaks Knoll swinging bunco rumor."

Julia was ashamed she hadn't figured it all out sooner. Lindsay told her she couldn't do pinochle anymore because work was too demanding. Lindsay also made a few comments about how vapid the other women were. The comment about the neighborhood ladies being vapid should have been a red flag, but it wasn't. "I didn't even notice a blip in your guys' relationship," Julia said. She couldn't get over how it all happened right next door without her knowing anything about it. She had so many questions; Julia didn't know where to start.

James popped his head out again and Lindsay snickered as she finished the last of her drink. "Jules, you coming in?"

"She is," Lindsay answered for her. "I'm leaving now, James. Thank you for your generous hospitality. I'll see myself out the back here."

"Yeah, sure. Bye, Lindsay," James said in a tone more suited for someone he would actually be seeing in the next day or so. "Jules, make sure you wash those out before you come to bed. Don't need the whole kitchen reeking of gin in the morning." Then he was gone again.

"Yeah, Denny and I are about as good as you and James, Kari and Stan, and all the other miserable marriages in Scarlet Oaks." Lindsay stood up made her way down the deck steps to the backyard.

Julia walked over to the deck railing and called down to Lindsay, "That's it?"

Without missing a step or looking back, Lindsay threw a quick wave over her shoulder before she slowly disappeared into the darkness of her own backyard towards her basement door.

Julia could have stayed on the deck all night contemplating what had just happened between them and everything she'd learned about Denny and Kari, but James was waiting for her inside. She washed out the glasses and headed into the bedroom where she expected James to be waiting to finish what they'd started earlier that day. Instead, she found James reading *Love Thy Neighbor*.

"What is this, Julia?" James was still dressed and sitting on a large rectangular ottoman located at the end of their bed to store extra pillows and blankets.

Instead of thinking out the best way to explain the book while giving the least amount of information as possible, she could only focus on chastising herself for leaving the damn book out on her nightstand. She'd covered it with a few others, but that hardly made it invisible. Why hadn't she thrown it in the nightstand drawer? It would have taken minimal energy and it would have saved everything.

"Julia?" James demanded with decreased patience.

"It's one of Denny's books. He lent it to me last night, at the party."

"It's one of his? He's writing romance?"

"Yes." Julia made her way to the bathroom under the guise of brushing her teeth and getting ready for bed. Really, she needed to get herself together and figure out how to salvage the situation without making James suspicious.

When she pulled her head back up from the sink, she saw James in the mirror reflection standing in the doorway still holding the book.

"It's you," he said.

"Not really - "

"And Denny. He wrote a romance about you two. Did you read it?"

"About half. I just got it last night. But it's not really us. Just made-up characters based on real ones." Julia turned to face James so they didn't have to continue the conversation through the mirror. She reached out to take the book but James pulled back and stepped away from her.

"Is it like the other book you brought home from your little outing with Denny? *Manly Defenders*?"

"That was a joke, James. And no, from what I can tell by what I've read, it's more like a somewhat racy Hallmark movie than book porn." It was a stretch and she knew it. Though it wasn't a reverse harem like *Manly Defenders*, it also wasn't going to make its way onto the Hallmark channel anytime soon either.

"Book porn. Nice, Julia. And laying out on your nightstand for everyone to see. For the kids to find."

Julia slipped into bed hoping James's comment was the last of the conversation. He'd had the final say about how Julia needed to be more careful, as usual, and they could move on with their lives. Except he didn't climb in beside her.

"You're not coming to bed? It's late." Although she didn't particularly want him in the bed with her, she did want him to put down the book.

"I'm going to stay up a bit and read. I'll go to the living room so I don't bother you." He turned off the lights and shut the door on his way out.

Julia was up for a few more hours thinking everything over. Once she felt on the verge of being caught, she had more regrets than she'd ever expected. How could she have risked everything with James for a few moments with

Denny? She didn't even know Denny. As far as she could tell, he had always been the perfect husband and father. The one she occasionally wished James was more like: even-tempered, laid back, creative, less abrasive with the kids.

How silly to think that was all there was to him. To not even consider there was more beneath the surface like his ability to cheat and lie. Maureen. Kari. And then her. She was just another name on Denny's list. And those were the ones she knew about. A few days ago she hadn't known any of it. In the next few days even more could come out from behind the shades and curtains of the McMansions scattered throughout Scarlet Oaks Knoll.

19

DENNY, MAY 2016

"Denny, the last time we met we devoted a lot of time and discussion to Lindsay's feelings about how your marriage has changed. Today I want to hear more from your perspective about which aspects of your marriage have flourished and which aspects have struggled."

He and Lindsay were seated at opposite ends of the clinical couch placed against one of the walls of the therapist's office. The coffee table between themselves and Dr. Morgan had a small vase of plastic flowers next to a box of tissues.

Denny adjusted himself slightly in preparation for his response. He could never tell if he should be directing his comments towards Lindsay or the doctor. It seemed strange to be sitting on the couch with Lindsay facing the doctor instead of sitting in some sort of circle so they could easily see and address one another throughout the session.

"Yes. I agree with some of the things Lindsay said before." Nothing about the counseling sessions felt natural to him. Aside from the awkward seating arrangement around the fake flowers and unused tissues, he couldn't figure out what to call his wife. He rarely used her actual name during their marriage and or even when they were dating. It had always been hon or babe. Sometimes they didn't even use names or nicknames because it was obvious they were talking to each other and didn't need such formalities. The name Lindsay, or even Linds, felt alien and foreign to his tongue.

Lindsay glanced at her phone, typed out a quick message, then placed it face down on the table. She did it every session even though she said she wouldn't look at her phone and would focus on the two of them. Within the first ten to fifteen minutes of the session she'd forget and reflexively answer something for work before setting the phone on the table for the rest of the session.

"But I don't think work was a big enough focus when Lindsay talked about the different factors that have come between us."

It took them a few months to stop interrupting each other, but those sessions paid off because Lindsay simply glared at some point over Dr. Morgan's head as Denny continued.

He turned from Dr. Morgan and directed everything to Lindsay, which was more comfortable for him anyway. He'd have had conversations with her in the privacy of their own house if she'd have allowed it. "You changed, Linds. Always so focused on your job and the next position up. And I admit that's one of the things I loved about you. I do still love that about you. You're a great role model for the girls. The best when it comes to demonstrating what real tenacity and drive looks like."

Dr. Morgan had told them to focus equally on the positives and negatives. He hoped he'd laid it on thick enough to move on to the negatives. "But at some point, your drive turned into an obsession. It's not financial security. We're fine. We have a huge house, two kids who want for nothing. We live comfortably enough. It's so much more than we had just a few years ago and I remember being pretty happy even way back when we had less."

Dr. Morgan jotted a few things on her notebook and nodded as she listened. "And what are some events or instances that led to this change in classification of Lindsay in relation to her career?"

"Last Thanksgiving, we were having dinner at my parents' house. We'd agreed no phones. But there's Lindsay, before we even got dessert onto the table, checking her email."

Lindsay continued to stare straight ahead. She'd crossed her legs when they first sat down. As Denny spoke, she crossed her arms as well.

"And I get that as the store manager she's always on call. Kind of like a doctor, dealing with life and death situations at all times."

Lindsay's mouth opened to defend herself, but Dr. Morgan had been waiting for it and she had her hand up to stop her before anything was actually said. It was enough though for Denny to check his sarcasm and stick to basics, just as Dr. Morgan had preached in sessions past.

"You left Thanksgiving dinner for work. You picked work over family. You pick work over family."

Lindsay took the pause as permission to chime in, "So you fucked one of our neighbors because *I* work too much?"

That was enough for Dr. Morgan to step in. "Lindsay, we're focusing on Denny's concern about work. Do you have a response to Denny's comments about work?"

"My district manager texted me on the work phone that I've been instructed to keep on me at all times. There was a last-minute change in our Black Friday roll out and my manager, and his boss, were stopping by the store first thing to see my implementation. They were going to visit every store in the district, over eighteen stores, starting with mine.

Since I was first in line and earliest in the day, the expectation is that mine would be flawless. I didn't have a choice. I did not *pick* work over my family."

"Denny?" Dr. Morgan prompted after the two sat wordlessly on the couch for what felt like an hour.

"How many of the store managers in your district are divorced?" Denny asked. "Your district manager, his boss. Are they still married?"

"Let's keep our conversation here focused on the two of you and your marriage."

Denny wouldn't be stopped. "I'm pretty sure most of the other people in her position, and higher up, are divorced. The job isn't sustainable. The long hours each day on top of the extra time put in for holidays, inventory, emergencies... When does it let up? When will it end?"

Lindsay didn't answer.

"You have this take-charge attitude that comes out at work. I know you have to to keep everything running smoothly. But then you started to bring it home. It turned our homelife into this employer-employee dynamic. Everything I was doing was wrong or wasn't good enough for you. The way I fixed dinner, corrected the kids, dressed myself. Never good enough." He took a deep breath before he continued. "That's why I slipped with Kari." Lindsay cringed slightly. "She didn't look at me like I was incompetent. She trusted me with everything. Trusted me to take care of everything in the house and she was overly appreciative. The antithesis of our relationship at the time."

"Then it's still my fault you cheated. No matter what I say about this, it always comes down to me being too shitty of a wife for you to honor your vows and keep your dick in your pants."

Denny was ready to pounce with a few choice words and phrases, but the doctor beat him to it. "I'm going to stop you both there. We've had these conversations, or versions of these same conversations, over and over again. I've told you this before, but I'll say it again in the hopes that it may one day stick with you: You're both acting like martyrs carrying around bundles of pain on your backs every minute of every day. It will break you and it will break your marriage.

"I can't promise forgiveness will save your marriage. But I can guarantee that it is the only way to find any sort of happiness, with or without each other."

"Honestly, that's not a possibility for me." Lindsay, still not looking at Denny, addressed the doctor alone as if he was no longer there. "He brought a neighbor into our bed."

"I keep hearing you mention the fact that it was a neighbor. You said the two of you weren't very close. You and Kari didn't talk or go out together aside from a monthly gathering of women in your neighborhood."

"She cares the other neighbors may have seen. It's all about her image," Denny answered for Lindsay.

"Wouldn't you care if all the men in the neighborhood knew I was screwing James behind your back?"

"Yes," he heard himself admit. In the past he'd refused to take blame or apologize for what had happened between him and Kari. The day Lindsay caught them, she'd unleashed a string of invectives as she changed into new work clothes and then she was out the door and back to work. Impressively robotic in her ability to shut down her emotions and to focus on whatever she felt needed to be done.

And she stayed that way, like a robotic roommate when it was just the two of them. She shut him out, and in his mind, it somewhat justified his affair. Her apathy and indifference to him only filled Denny with his own resentment.

But Dr. Morgan was right. It was a miserable existence for both of them. If it was just the two of them, if they hadn't had kids, they would have separated before it ever got bad enough for him to cheat. But they did have kids. And as the kids got older, they would only pick up on tensions and unhappiness in the house even more. What sense was it to stay married for the kids if even the kids knew it was a charade?

Lindsay looked at him but said nothing.

"I'm going to be honest here. I see no improvement from when we started. Denny's singular, 'yes,' is the closest I've seen to anything resembling empathy from either of you. I'm going to leave you two this final thought and then I'm going to schedule you both to come back in a month rather than next week. In a sense, your marriage is over. When it ended is hard to say, but at this point I feel confident in saying the relationship you had when you first got married, is gone. You have the opportunity to start over now with a new marriage. It's not nearly as exciting or full of lust as the beginning of your first marriage, but it can be as full of love as it once was.

"To get there, you both need to acknowledge what happened that led you to stray. Lindsay, according to Denny you strayed from the marriage and found solace and feelings of importance from work; and Denny strayed physically in the form of an affair. You need to process the pain it caused, you need to forgive the betrayal that haunts you both, and then you need to decide if it's worth it to do the work involved in creating your new marriage where the past still exists, but no longer burdens you."

The car ride home was quiet. Lindsay drove and Denny blankly looked out the window while running through memories of his marriage through his mind. Only the good stuff. He didn't allow any of the bad to creep in. "I'm sorry," he said into the window. He hadn't meant to say anything which was why he was still facing away from Lindsay when he'd said it. But the apology was there regardless, before he could second-guess it again. He'd wanted to apologize from the beginning, but a combination of pride, anger, and a few other complex emotions and feelings he couldn't put a finger on had stood in the way.

He turned to look at her and found her attention still focused on the road. "I'm sorry," he repeated.

"I heard you." Her hands moved deftly over the steering wheel as she merged from the exit back into the sluggish traffic of their community. "You haven't said that to me before. Not about this."

"I should have," Denny acquiesced. He offered his olive branch and waited the rest of the drive home for her to offer one as well. It didn't come. They picked the kids up from Julia and James's house while maintaining the farce they'd been out on their weekly date night. At their house they went through the usual school night routines of making sure homework was completed and bags were packed and ready for school the next day.

Just when Denny was ready to write off any and all positive steps forward from that day, Lindsay reached for him under the cover of darkness in their bedroom. She put an arm across his chest and nuzzled into his neck. He could hear her taking in his scent and feel her relaxing into his body as if it brought her feelings of safety and security.

Denny kissed her on the top of the head and brushed her hair away from her face. Her eyes were closed as if she wasn't ready yet to fully experience with all her senses what was happening between them. For a few seconds he thought about giving up complete control to Lindsay and letting her guide whatever was going to happen between them. Except he didn't trust Lindsay's pride to step down long enough for them to reconnect the way they so desperately needed to.

He slid one of his legs over Lindsay's and gently rolled

himself on top of her. In typical Lindsay fashion, she allowed Denny only a brief moment to lead. With surprising strength, she rolled on top of him and reclaimed control of the situation. He didn't care. They needed to be lovers in the bedroom again, regardless of how it happened.

20

DENNY, NOVEMBER 2019

M onday morning, after Lindsay left for South Carolina and the kids were loaded up in their carpool for school, Denny got a text from James.

Hey

I know you're busy with the move, but can you come over and help me with something in the garage?

Everything about the text was out of character for James. He never took off work for anything less than doctor's appointments and unavoidable circumstances such as severe illnesses and deaths in the family. James also never acknowledged Denny might be busy with anything. Much like everyone else in Denny's life, the assumption was that he wrote for an hour or so each day and then idled through the remaining hours doing whatever he pleased.

Lindsay had been acting weird the night before. While she didn't outright cringe at his touch, she had done everything she could to avoid him while hastily packing some last-minute items. At the time he assumed it was because she was about to move a few states away to begin the next chapter of her career in a location where she knew no one. But then that sort of thing wasn't daunting for Lindsay. She thrived in circumstance such as that. Something had happened the night before while she was on the deck with Julia. He could feel it.

He could try to avoid James for the next week until they were officially gone, but that idea didn't set right with him. It felt cowardly. And to some extent, even though their friendship was superficial and out of convenience, he felt like he owed it to James to go over. It was the least he could do for all the damage he had done the past weekend.

Sure. What time? Denny texted back.

A few hours later he felt like the lamb to the slaughter on his way over to James's garage. The doors were open, as they usually were, and James was sitting on a workbench in the garage bay that housed all his tools.

James stood up and took a few steps towards Denny. Any pretense of moving a few heavy objects dropped as James got right to the point. "I never liked you or Lindsay," he said.

Denny merely nodded his head in response. James was not a subtle man and Denny had already surmised James's feelings towards him and his wife within their first few meetings. Still, he took a deep breath and braced himself for the unknown. He had no idea what James was capable of when he was mad or how much he even knew he should be mad about. Regardless, whatever was coming, Denny knew he deserved it. In a way, he embraced and anticipated it. Willed it to come and finally be over with.

"And now that I found out you wrote a book about banging my wife -"

Denny's hands went up at the verbal attack on his work. "I use real people as a starting point, but it's just stories."

"Don't insult me with your bullshit explanations, Denny. The cover is a picture of you and Julia, as neighbors. Actual events that happened between our families fill most of the pages. But what's really disturbing are the sections of the book which can only be described as graphic, erotic fantasies involving you and my wife. Is that what's been going through your head for the last decade? Every time we're enjoying family time, you're turning it into some low budget porno in your mind to include in your next trashy book?"

James was in striking distance now though Denny didn't think violence was his style. He was a family lawyer, and he knew how much trouble could accompany an assault charge. Not that Denny would ever press charges or dare to mention whatever went down between him and James beyond their encounter in the garage.

"The sex stuff is me writing to the market. Women love it." James's eyes flared at the comment as if Denny had specifically called Julia a sex fiend or some other unsavory name, so he clarified with, "Women in general. My target audience. That's why I add it in there. And it's not about Julia. We did go camping together for vacation and that did make it into the book. But aside from describing the white-water accident where Julia went overboard, nothing else about that trip happened. All I did was take the bare minimum details of a real-life event to use as the skeleton of my book. I invented all the meat I put on top of it."

"You're such a fucking hack," James muttered. The hatred in his eyes was intimidatingly intense and Denny wondered how many times Julia had been in a similar situation with James. He understood a little more why she would have found comfort with him.

"I know I am," Denny conceded. He didn't need James to tell him. Lindsay, his editor, his agent, his readers – they'd all hinted or out-right said something similar to him in recent years.

Unsatisfied with their conversation, James cocked back and rocked Denny's left eye and cheekbone with his fist.

Denny wasn't sure it would even classify as a sucker punch because he'd half expected some sort of physical scuffle with James from the moment he got the text message. But what did surprise him was the timing. James hit him after he'd agreed he was a shit writer. Wasn't he already down?

"Are we done here?" Denny asked as he straightened back up again. He couldn't hit James back. He had, after all, been sleeping with the guy's wife for the past few days. And James had been right about everything. He never should have written a book about his neighbor's wife, never should have used a picture for the cover that looked just like her, and he never should have included explicit sex scenes regardless of what his agent said his target audience wanted.

"Stay the fuck away from my wife and my family," James sneered. Denny waited for another hit, but it never came. James turned and went into his house.

Once he was alone, Denny allowed his hand to touch the tender, swollen section of his face to feel for any blood or significant damage. As he turned to head home, he noticed Mary Jane, Laura, and Mandy at the end of the driveway shamelessly peering into the garage.

Laura, the leader of the speed walking crew of work-from-home moms who took to the streets for a power walk each day during their lunch break, called out to him. "Are you okay, Denny? We stopped when we heard the scuffle between you and James. Do you need us to call the police?"

Denny could sense the sheer pleasure radiating from the three of them as they took it all in. Laura was poised with her phone and ready to increase the drama with a few taps of her finger since surely the number for the local police was already located at the top of her extensive list of contacts.

"No, thank you. Everything's fine." Denny went off towards his house without glancing back.

"Are you sure?" Laura persisted as Denny quickly

increased the space between him and the women. "Okay. Well, we're here if you need anything. As your HOA board members or just as friends."

As Denny closed his front door and looked out the peephole. He saw they were off again but with a little extra pep in their steps and a whole lot of gossip to overanalyze and spread.

At the island Denny held a baggie of ice to his face in an effort to decrease the swelling. He wasn't sure what he would tell the kids. They never noticed his haircuts or the time he'd shaved the mustache he'd had for over three years, but he was sure they would notice this. That's just how it worked with kids. Their senses had superpowers allowing them to taste hidden vegetables in food, overhear secret whispers while remaining blissfully unaware of a parent's screams, and the ability to notice anything a parent tried to hide though they were unable to find a pair of shoes sitting by themselves in the middle of a clean floor.

As he sat, he imagined how the rest of the week would go. There would be rumors about everything: the move, the fight with James, maybe about him and Julia if anyone had seen them. The weekend had already dragged on for an eternity, and the week ahead of him felt impossibly longer than even that.

There was no way he could see Julia. He didn't even want to attempt to contact her. What if James had her cell phone? It didn't seem completely out of the question given his temper, and in his sometimes erratic and overbearing behavior towards her. He also couldn't risk permanent damage to Julia's relationship with James. In another universe, maybe the universe of *Love Thy Neighbor*, he still imagined a world where he and Julia somehow end up together.

He loved her. He didn't dare do anything else to jeopardize her happiness. Even if Julia found her happiness with her asshole of a husband, Denny needed to accept it and move on - just as he had done for the past decade.

He picked up his phone and began searching online for a moving company. Moyer's had offered to supply a complimentary moving company for them since Lindsay and Denny were moving at the company's request, but Denny had been the one to turn it down. Too many strangers rooting around through their things.

He didn't want to bother Lindsay with changing his mind and asking Moyer's to pay for and to arrange the moving company after all. He would arrange it all himself and then surprise Lindsay that night in South Carolina.

There was nothing keeping them in Scarlet Oaks Knoll anymore. It was probably painful for the kids to stay the rest of the week. Best to conduct the move like a bandage and rip it off all at once. Start over immediately rather than stay in limbo waiting for one life to end and for the new one to begin.

21

JULIA, DECEMBER 2019

S carlet Oaks Knoll's school district is number one in the tri-county area and there's easy access to major highways. Homeowners in the development who put their house up for sale have received full asking-price offers, if not more, on their houses within days, sometimes hours, of their houses being listed.

Lindsay and Denny's house was no exception. A retired couple claiming to be downsizing bought the enormous house using cash from the sale of their previous house in a Philadelphia suburb. The various tedious steps involved in the buying and selling of houses all went smoothly and the new owners were settled in time to celebrate Christmas in their new home.

Julia came home from work one Friday to find an array of what she would call garish Christmas decorations spewed all over the front lawn of her new neighbors. The Herricks and the Moores both liked consistency and basic themes for their holiday decorations. One year they had a Disney theme with a few select characters and props, another year it was all white lights carefully and evenly displayed around windows and along their rooftops.

She wasn't even sure how she would describe what she saw in the neighbor's yard. There was no overarching theme. The decorations appeared to be a collection started a few decades prior where the owner added a few new choice items each year without ever discarding the older items regardless of how worn they'd become. Plastic reindeer of different sizes and styles were scattered throughout the yard. One giant Santa was at the chimney, another was hanging from the roof with his body permanently dangling above of one of the garage doors, and yet another smaller Santa was in the front yard, standing on the back of a firetruck and pivoting back and forth as he waved at the people who passed by. There were lights of all colors and all sizes covering every bush and tree. They even draped lights over the basketball hoop they'd set up for their grandkids on the curb next to their driveway.

Without any concerns about being discreet, she took out her cell phone and snapped a few pictures to send off to Lindsay. As expected, an hour later or so Lindsay sent back a few emojis showing anger, disgust, and laughter. They both said they missed each other, and then that was that.

It was typical of their conversations since Lindsay moved away. The Moores had spent a few weeks in a hotel while they toured South Carolina real estate and put in offers on various houses. The market was just as tight there as it had been in Scarlet Oaks Knoll, so it took some time for them to find a house that was just right.

When they did get pictures of the tentative new house (their offer had been accepted but it was weeks away from closing) Julia heard the death knell with each ding her phone gave alerting her to a new message and photo. One was a picture of the neighborhood pool party pulled from the development Facebook page. Families, about the same age as them, filled the page along with tables of food, a volleyball tournament, and multiple waterslide blow-ups for the kids.

Lindsay's soon-to-be neighbor was the president of the PTO and asked her to join. To everyone's surprise, she did join as part of her vow to get more involved with her kids' schools. Her work had slowed down for the winter and she could devote more time to Denny and the kids.

Julia had initially pictured Lindsay as being miserable down south with no friends and missing the perfect life she'd left behind in Scarlet Oaks Knoll. How naive Julia had been. James had called her that innumerous times throughout the years they'd known each other. Sometimes she embraced the title as she felt it showed her optimism and her determination to believe the absolute best in everyone until they proved otherwise. As she'd grown older, she'd become ashamed of her rose-colored glasses. She wasn't seeing life how it should be or even could be, only how she wished it was. And James had been right when he told her she'd get burned more often than not by her misguided optimism.

Julia never saw her copy of *Love Thy Neighbor* again, and she and James never discussed it after the night he'd read it out in the living room. But she did bring up their argument about the car crash after everything settled with their insurance company. She'd felt emboldened when the insurance companies agreed she was not at fault. The woman she'd collided with, Shaina, had told her insurance company exactly what she'd told Julia: She always cut in line and the other cars were supposed to yield to her.

The conversation with James was only possible after a glass of wine and a particularly good date night followed by passionate sex. She'd almost drifted away to sleep allowing the problem to stay hidden, for the time being, rather than ruin the night by bringing it up. But Lindsay's comments about her marriage to James in comparison to Lindsay's marriage to Denny had haunted her. Julia couldn't shake the feeling that Lindsay was right, and she couldn't bear the thought of their marriages being comparable.

James hadn't blown up as she thought he would. He listened without interrupted as she spoke. Her head was on his chest and they were both looking at a black tv on the wall across from their bed. Then he'd agreed she was right. He knew he had a bad temper and needed to get it under control. He knew there were days when he was on the verge of losing her and that was why he worked so hard to make it up to her, and the kids, with his over-the-top gestures.

The conversation didn't end with any actual resolution. James's temper continued, and they didn't discuss it again. But the shouting happened a little less, there was an occasional apology afterwards, and her anger started to move towards a sort of annoyance and understanding. It was a slight change which she expected to increase to a more substantial change as time passed. Her optimism again? She thought not, though it was difficult to know for sure.

Alexis found a new best friend at school. Kids were resilient. They grieved and then they moved on. Madison played on the field hockey team and each weekend she and Alexis would practice in their backyard. Alexis confided in Julia one evening during dinner that she would like to try out for the field hockey team next fall. She'd always wanted to play, but Liv said it was sexist since the players all had to wear skirts.

Hailey and Brice sometimes Facetimed on their parents' cell phones. The first week it was almost daily. The second week they still spoke daily, but only for ten or twenty minutes before they ran out of things to talk about or had to run off to some activity happening outside of the virtual world.

Julia moved on as well. What choice did she have? The first few weeks they'd Facetimed a bit when Lindsay's schedule allowed it. It wasn't always a good time for Julia to talk. Dinners and bedtime routines were interrupted by Lindsay's calls and by Julia's willingness to put her life on pause to answer. She'd so desperately missed her former life with Lindsay she was willing to do anything to hold on to the last remaining threads.

It stopped when James put an end to it. She'd reached for her phone during dinner one day and he glared at her. Dared her to pick her friend over her family. Julia knew he was right. She was embarrassed he'd even needed to call her out on it. Two of Lindsay's calls went unanswered before she stopped calling altogether. Lindsay was not one to be ignored. Julia's calls to Lindsay were fifty-fifty if Lindsay would answer, so eventually those stopped, too.

Early December Stephanie posted in the Scarlet Oaks Knoll Facebook group about a book club she was starting. Wine, appetizers, and book discussions every third Friday of the month. Julia always liked Stephanie and she jumped at the chance. Since she'd quit pinochle after hearing about Maureen and Kari, she'd needed something else to help her connect to women in the neighborhood. She needed friends in general and something to look forward to each month.

James scoffed and claimed it was a somewhat more sophisticated version of her pinocle group. She agreed. Pinocle, bunco, book clubs, sex toy parties – women enjoyed eating and drinking with some sort of theme or activity thrown in as well. What was wrong with that? Just as long as everyone kept their hands to themselves.

BEFORE YOU GO...

My biggest thanks to you for taking a chance on an unknown, indie author (that's me, in case I'm being too vague). And since you've gotten through to the end, and then some with this little blurb as well, I'm hoping I can ask one more huge favor. Please consider leaving a review at whatever fine establishment you purchased this from and on GoodReads, BookBub, or any other bookish social media outlet you peruse in your spare time. Rave about how much you loved it, or tear it down and release whatever pent-up anger and emotions you've suppressed for the past decade or so—I'm grateful either way.

HAPPY READING,

Leigh Donnelly

WANT MORE? OF COURSE YOU DO!

Scan the QR code or go to leighdonnellyauthor.com for behind the scenes material, bonus chapters, links to my social media accounts, and info on all of my books.